PRAISE FOR *THE ALLIANCE*
and other novels by Jolina Petersheim

The Alliance

"Petersheim has written a novel of hope forged in unlikely circumstances and a romance sparked in the cold of despair. Readers of faith who have questioned their place in the world, who wonder what they might become if society's bounds no longer held them, will be enthralled."

BOOKLIST

"This unusual dystopian work mixes hope and faith with fear and cynicism . . . [in an] astute meditation on the intersection between belief systems and the politics of aggression."

PUBLISHERS WEEKLY

"[With its] intriguing plot, riveting storytelling, character depth, [and] twists and turns, this . . . drama will leave readers eager for the sequel."

CBA RETAILERS + RESOURCES

"A riveting and thoroughly entertaining read from beginning to end, *The Alliance* is unreservedly recommended and certain to be an enduringly popular addition to community library general fiction collections."

MIDWEST BOOK REVIEW

"Finally, an apocalyptic novel ablaze with hope—just the kind of story I champion. A must-read."

SARAH MCCOY, *New York Times* bestselling author of *The Mapmaker's Children* and *The Baker's Daughter*

"*The Alliance* is a gripping story that shows how cultural differences drop away in the face of life-altering circumstance and only the most deeply held truths survive. I raced to the end and wanted more. Can't wait for the conclusion of this series!"

FRANCINE RIVERS, *New York Times* bestselling author of *Redeeming Love* and *A Voice in the Wind*

"Through her authentic, sympathetic characters, Jolina Petersheim conveys hope and redemption in impossible situations. Readers will not want to leave the world portrayed in *The Alliance*, even as it falls apart around them."

ERIKA ROBUCK, author of *The House of Hawthorne*

"An absorbing and thought-provoking 'what if?' drama that takes a compassionate look at what divides and ultimately unites us."

MARYANNE O'HARA, author of *Cascade*

"Beautifully written and unique, *The Alliance* examines the conflict between our humanity and our need to protect that which we hold dear. A book that begs to be savored on many levels."

LISA WINGATE, national bestselling author of *The Sea Keeper's Daughters*

"I've just discovered rising star Jolina Petersheim, and I'm hooked! *The Alliance* was a mesmerizing peek at what might happen if everything we thought we believed was suddenly tested. I can't wait for the next installment!"

COLLEEN COBLE, author of *Mermaid Moon* and the Hope Beach series

"Captivating. Intriguing. A story that takes us beyond what we believe. This well-written tale marks Jolina Petersheim as a poignant storyteller."

"*The Alliance* is a cut above. Lovely prose and a fascinating concept make this unique novel a sure winner. Petersheim just gets better and better."

The Midwife

"This powerful story of redemption, forgiveness, and the power of Christ over sin challenges readers to consider modern attitudes in light of eternal truths."

"Petersheim is an amazing new author. . . . [*The Midwife* is] a tale that explores what happens when you have a second chance at making things right, even if it opens old wounds."

"An emotional work that is sure to draw in parents and non-parents alike with an extraordinary story full of troubled characters."

The Outcast

"Petersheim makes an outstanding debut with this fresh and inspirational retelling of Nathaniel Hawthorne's *The Scarlet*

Letter. Well-drawn characters and good, old-fashioned storytelling combine in an excellent choice for Nancy Mehl's readers."

"Petersheim's emotional story leaves readers intrigued by the purity of Rachel's strong will, resilience, and loyalty."

"Like Hawthorne, Petersheim clearly dramatizes the weight of sin, but she deviates from the original by leaving room for repentance."

"From its opening lines, *The Outcast* wowed me in every way. Quickly paced, beautifully written, flawlessly executed—I could not put this book down."

"A powerful and poignant story that transcends genre stereotypes and is not easily forgotten. The caliber of Jolina's prose defies her debut author status, and I'm eager to read more."

"You are going to love this book. Be ready to enter an amazing new world, but make sure you have a box of Kleenex for this journey."

THE
DIVIDE

JOLINA PETERSHEIM

a novel

Tyndale House Publishers, Inc.
Carol Stream, Illinois

Visit Tyndale online at www.tyndale.com.

Visit Jolina Petersheim online at jolinapetersheim.com.

TYNDALE and Tyndale's quill logo are registered trademarks of Tyndale House Publishers, Inc.

The Divide

Designed by Ron Kaufmann

Edited by Kathryn S. Olson

Published in association with Ambassador Literary Agency, Nashville, TN.

Some Scripture quotations are taken from the *Holy Bible*, New Living Translation, copyright © 1996, 2004, 2015 by Tyndale House Foundation. Used by permission of Tyndale House Publishers, Inc., Carol Stream, Illinois 60188. All rights reserved.

Some Scripture quotations are taken from the *Holy Bible*, King James Version.

The Divide is a work of fiction. Where real people, events, establishments, organizations, or locales appear, they are used fictitiously. All other elements of the novel are drawn from the author's imagination.

For information about special discounts for bulk purchases, please contact Tyndale House Publishers at csresponse@tyndale.com or call 800-323-9400.

Library of Congress Cataloging-in-Publication Data
Names: Petersheim, Jolina, author.
Title: The divide / Jolina Petersheim.
Description: Carol Stream, Illinois : Tyndale House Publishers, Inc., [2017]
Identifiers: LCCN 2016057081 | ISBN 9781496421449 (hardcover)
  | ISBN 9781496402226 (softcover)
Subjects: LCSH: Mennonites—Fiction. | Interpersonal relations—Fiction.
  | GSAFD: Christian fiction.
Classification: LCC PS3616.E84264 D59 2017 | DDC 813/.6—dc23 LC record available
  at https://lccn.loc.gov/2016057081

Printed in the United States of America

23 22 21 20 19 18 17
7   6   5   4   3   2   1

To my parents, Merle and Beverly Miller, who always thought outside the box enough to encourage my writing dream

ACKNOWLEDGMENTS

Well, here you have it, friends: my fourth novel. There were times during *The Divide*'s creation that I wasn't sure I would ever reach this stage of the process, and now—because of an indomitable group of supporters—I have.

First off, I want to thank my wonderful publishing team at Tyndale House, who were equally determined to make this story the best it could possibly be.

A special, heartfelt thank-you to Karen Watson, Stephanie Broene, and Kathy Olson for your unending patience. You all are a joy to work with.

Thank you, Wes Yoder, for your good humor and kindness.

A huge thank-you to my family members, who are so essential to the juggling act of parenting and writing. Betty and Rich Petersheim, Jen Weaver, Joanne Petersheim, Beverly and Merle Miller, Josh and Caleb Miller: Each of you has helped me pursue this dream in one way or another (but mostly by babysitting). I am deeply grateful.

To my best friend, Misty: Thank you for your wisdom concerning these characters and for being honest when I asked where you wanted this story to go. Your input helped shape so much.

To Joel and Marissa Kendhammer: Your testimony was key to helping me learn to overcome fear with faith. Thank you for letting God use you.

To my daughters, Miss A and Miss M: Oh, how I love you! Thank you for helping me keep life in perspective, even when I'm on deadline. Being your mama is my favorite job in the world. You are each so special and precious to me.

To my husband: You are the one who sees me on the good writing days and the bad, and you love me regardless. Thank you for being my constant supporter, editor, and friend. Moses's voice would sound like a girl's if not for you. I love you so much.

Thank you, Lord God, for being patient with me and loving me unconditionally as I journey through this life. You are a good, good Father.

CHAPTER

1

Moses

YOU NEVER KNOW how hard something's going to be until it's too late to change your mind. As I watch Leora ride away on the back of Jabil's horse—her loose, dark hair snapping like a pennant—I have to fight the urge to go after her. But I know, for her sake and for the sake of her Mennonite community, I have to remain.

It's a good thing I do. About ten minutes later, part of the perimeter collapses with a movement as graceful and altering as an ice cliff sliding into the sea. Hot coals shower the ground. Smoke rises. I crouch behind the scaffolding, preparing to defend the property as long as I can so the families have enough time to escape into the mountains.

The first man steps through, his figure a blur in the choking haze. I adjust my rifle, trying to find the man in the scope. I'm not fast enough. Another man runs in, and another. The fourth one pauses for only a second, but that second costs him his life. I shoot a few more times, and then I stop to reload, pressing rounds into the chamber one by one, but my fingers are shaking. I look up to see a man leveling a gun at me. My body braces for impact, which is ludicrous. You can't brace yourself for something like that. I take a shot in the stomach and fall to my knees. I try to get to my feet but stumble until I'm sitting back in the dirt. I support my upper body by bracing my left arm on the ground and using my right arm to hold my abdomen.

There's so much adrenaline coursing through me that I don't feel pain. Instead, staring down at the wound, I feel only disappointment. The community's lives are resting in my hands because their pacifist ideals won't allow them to fight back against the gang, even to protect their families, and now I am not sure what will become of them. This thought brings with it the first wave of debilitating pain and nausea. I should be grateful Leora left with Jabil, for even without raising a weapon, he could probably do a better job of protecting her than I. But I can't help wishing I could relive these past hard weeks, starting when I crashed in her meadow to the moment—just an hour ago—when we kissed in front of the burning perimeter, the community's last line of defense, which somehow helped put Leora's and my own defenses into place.

I hope Jabil makes her happy. I hope he loves her the way I would, if our world weren't so messed up. But it is. I let the pain sweep me under. Oblivion is easier than reality.

Sal

Believing Moses good as dead, the gang rushes past him.

I have been hiding in the shadows of Field to Table, waiting on the off chance that Moses might need me. And now he does. I study him a moment, aware that he will die out there if I don't help him, and yet aware I might die if I do. I think of my son, Colton, on his way up the mountain, and realize there's no point keeping myself safe for him if I never use my life to do any good. Taking a breath, I duck low and dart past Field to Table, the lane, and the blanket of coals where the fallen perimeter once stood. Moses is lying on the ground, the front of his shirt soaked with blood. My first thought is that he *is* actually dead, and then I see movement as his body involuntarily strains for air.

The gang seems so intent on finding things of value, and being the first to wreck the next house, they do not notice us behind them. I understand they are going to pillage and probably burn the rest of the community to the ground, and I suppose I should care. But I don't. I don't care about anything but getting Moses out of here alive. I drag him by his boots under the scaffolding and press the side of my face to his mouth. His ragged breath fills the curl of my ear. He opens his eyes. Though he appears disoriented, I can tell he comprehends what's happening. I lift Moses up as gently as possible and feel behind his back. There's a wet spot about the size of my hand. I don't know as much about healing as I claimed when I got that deacon to let me stay at Mt. Hebron, but I *do* know it's good the bullet appears to have gone straight through.

I shrug off my parka and my warm shirt. Shivering in my tank top, I use the shirt to stanch the blood. The gang works their way closer. Only seconds before they see us. I grab Moses again by the boots, and it takes every ounce of my strength to drag him over to the store and get him inside. His head bumps against the separation where the double doors lock into place, but I figure he won't mind a headache as much as he would mind whatever the gang will do to him if they discover he's alive after picking off some of their men.

I take a break, breathing hard, and check Moses's wound. He is bleeding out, but I have no other choice: he can't stay in the entrance. Hooking my hands behind his armpits, I continue dragging him past the store's emptied cooler section to the narrow hall. There are two doors, positioned side by side. The first leads to a unisex bathroom with no mirror above the pedestal sink; the second leads to the mechanical room. I push this door wider and drag Moses into it. Inside, I notice a large furnace along the back wall. Behind it is just enough space. I move him there and hurriedly back up to make sure he can't be seen from any side. Dust furs the vents of the furnace, and dead moths appear like bits of shiny paper on the floor. Though my eyes take in these details, I don't really see anything. I slip in behind Moses and hold him like an overgrown child. I try to keep the life in his body, even though blood drips warm down my hand.

An hour seems to pass, but I have no idea how long it's actually been. Spasms jerk the muscles of my back, and my tailbone feels bruised from my position between Moses and the wall. He drifts in and out of consciousness. His breathing is steady, but so's the blood flow from the gunshot wound. We have to get out of here, but there's nowhere to go. Why don't they come?

The answer arrives soon enough, with the sound of glass shattering at the front of the building. My heart in my throat, I visualize the gang's movements—trashing their way from the cash registers, to the café, to us . . . down the hall. The overlap of footsteps and voices. Light from a torch passing by the crack beneath the door. The bathroom door opens next to us. I hold Moses tighter, his body now limp against me, and hope against hope that he won't make a sound.

The door to the mechanical room opens, the rubber seal scraping along the uneven cement. Shadows cast by the torch loom across the wall as a man steps inside. I tremble as he yanks open an old metal cabinet that hangs near the entrance. After a minute of searching, he slams the cabinet doors shut. The torchlight grows brighter, and the sound of the crackling pine louder than before. Not even daring to breathe, I remain frozen as I clench Moses against me. Suddenly, as if satisfied there's nothing of use to him in this room, the man turns and leaves.

The entire store building grows quiet. Slowly, I try to change position and listen. Moses stirs. I hold him for a little longer and then whisper, "I think they're gone." Tears of relief and sadness burn my eyes. My first words since I gave my son away.

❖

Moses can no longer stand, he is so weak from the blood he lost while walking ten miles from the burned community to town. His spine is curled forward, his folded arms braced on his knees. I look back through the warehouse's right window and almost jump out of my skin. A pair of dark eyes are staring at me, the facial features appearing distorted through the fractured glass. The eyes narrow. Shuffled steps precede the clatter of rotating bolts and locks. The right door opens. A sun-battered head sticks out, draped with a tangled mane of silver hair. I turn and point at Moses, as if *I* am the one who refuses to speak and not my grandmother, Papina, who uses silence to communicate her grief. She raises an eyebrow and twists her lips, the combination creating a fault line of wrinkles.

"It was dark," I explain. "Moses was in the wrong place at the wrong time."

Papina turns her eyes from me and looks at the man in question. She taps her bare foot, and then she waves a rangy arm—jangling with bracelets—toward the warehouse.

I nod my thanks and walk back to Moses. "My grandmother will look at you."

He doesn't respond. I go down a step and gently tilt back his head. The skin of his face, not covered by his beard, is ruddy, and the V of his T-shirt outlined with sweat. I crouch and put an arm around his shoulders, forcing him to his feet. He wobbles upward, like a drunk. The trip to Liberty obviously battered him further, but if I had left him at Field to Table, he would've died. He could *still* die. But at least he has a chance now that he's here.

Papina, standing at the top of the steps, shakes her head

and descends when she sees Moses can no longer walk on his own. I turn his body, and she tries to support him by wrapping her arm around his hip. Together, we work our way up the crumbling flight. Once we reach the landing, my grandmother goes inside. I stay close behind Moses in case he collapses. He hauls his feet over the threshold and leans against the wall.

Needless to say, the old T-shirt factory's locks can't keep people out. Even before the EMP, the factory was a playground for teenagers wanting to cut their teeth on petty crime. Refugees—scrawny and interchangeable in their androgynous wardrobes of grime—are now sprawled on mats scattered here and there across the concrete floor. Papina brings over one of these mats, plops it on the tile, and motions for Moses to sit. He can't see her because his face is lifted to the ceiling, the cords of his neck shimmering and taut. I step over the mat and take his elbow. He jolts and glances at me, fever in his eyes. I grab another mat. Placing them side by side, I take off my parka, drape it over the pallet, and help him sit down.

He stays still for an instant, and then draws up his legs. My grandmother comes out of the room to the right and sits beside Moses, her layers of skirts sweeping up the dust. She peels his arms from around his shins and puts a hand on his chest, forcing his torso down until he is lying on his back. She lifts his T-shirt and examines the skin around the stitches I made, using the needle and thread from a cheap sewing kit I found under a shelf at Field to Table.

Less than a day has passed since I sewed him up, and yet I can already see how the stitches are cinched and oozing, that thin tributaries of red are spreading from the unruly, spider-black stripe. I wonder if I killed him with infection in my botched attempt to heal. Cursing, I move from behind my grandmother and walk to the other side. She passes me a flask from one of the bottomless pockets of her skirts. I take it and look at her, awaiting my orders. Papina points to Moses's stomach and mimes pouring liquor over the wound. I don't know why she doesn't do it herself, but I unscrew the cap and obey her instruction. Moses slurps his breath in through his teeth, and then peeks at what I am pouring over the stitches. He reaches for the flask. I attempt to pass it, but Papina frowns and intercepts me. Screwing on the cap, she slips it into her pocket. Apparently her generosity has limits.

Moses gives my grandmother a sidelong glance. She pulls his shirt up higher and palpates the area around his wound. Pulling the shirt down, she shrugs.

I explain, "Looks like the wound's infected. I shouldn't have sewed you up."

Moses tries propping himself on his elbows. He grimaces and lies back down. Somewhere in the warehouse, a refugee hollers, and then abruptly goes silent, like a radio switching off. We all three turn toward the sound. Papina rises to check it out.

I turn back to Moses. It feels awkward, being just the two of us again, which is strange, considering that—for hours— I put pressure on his bullet wound to keep him alive.

I ask, "You remember anything?"

He swallows before speaking. "I remember the perimeter falling and the gang coming in." A pause as he gathers his thoughts. "And I remember getting shot, but I don't remember much after that. I have no idea if the community made it up the mountain in time."

"I'm sure they're okay." I touch his arm. "I'm sure Leora's okay too. You did a brave thing, Moses." He doesn't respond, just keeps his eyes closed, so it's easy for me to say, "I know how you're feeling right now, being separated from someone you love. I gave my son, Colton, to Leora because I knew he'd have a better life with her than he would here, with me."

Moses finally opens his eyes and looks over, the blue of his irises swimming with either fever or fatigue. "I never said I loved her."

I think to myself, *You don't have to.*

❖

The refugees are nightly drawn from foraging in the streets back to the warehouse, like chickens returning to their coop. Papina holds out her hands as each files through and accepts whatever pilfered item she deems valuable enough to cover room and board: canned food, jewelry, bullets, toiletry items. I scoot across the floor, closer to Moses, which is laughable. He can offer me no protection as he thrashes in his sleep, his cheeks stained with fever. I would feed him ice, but ice is now such an impossible concept, it seems more like a dream.

Most of these refugees tramp upstairs, where the worst of the lot stay. A few others remain on the main floor, with Moses and me. I can tell they are new to the warehouse and its occupants by the worry flaring in their eyes as they squint toward the candlelit corners of the room, perhaps searching for a recognizable face. I, in fact, recognize two of the five refugees. The first is a twentysomething woman with straw-blonde hair who used to work at Burt's Grocery. The second was a lifeguard at Liberty's public pool.

Neither of them seem to recognize me, even though the guy—Travis, I think—dropped out of high school the same year I did. Despite my long dark hair and distinct Kutenai features, for years I've perfected the ability to blend in with any crowd, since becoming a hodgepodge of everyone around me is far less painful than getting picked on for standing out.

My cousin Alex files through next. My grandmother grins and embraces him, making no attempt to hide the fact he's her favorite grandchild, just as Uncle Mike is Papina's favorite son. I get to my feet. Alex glances up as I stride toward him.

"Hey, hey, Sal," he croons. "Where've you been hiding?"

"None of your business." My tone is flat. I've never cared for Alex's overblown display of charm and affection, especially when I know he likes me as much—or as little—as I like him.

"Ah." He raises his eyebrows. "But it soon *will* be my business."

"What're you talking about?"

Alex and I move to the side as more refugees come streaming in.

"Dad got me a job," he says.

"Really?" I can't fake any excitement.

"Yeah, the government's hiring some people to take a census of the ones who're left."

I roll my eyes. "There *is* no government."

"That's what you think."

My cousin has this driving need to one-up me, so I take every word that comes out of his mouth with a grain of salt. "Then give me some kinda proof."

Alex reaches into the back pocket of his jeans for a battered leather wallet. In the credit card section, he thumbs out an identification card and passes it to me. Laminated with contact paper, the card appears very similar to a license, except the numbers and words have all been written out by hand. Even the picture of him—an uncanny likeness—is just a sketch. I look up at him and am annoyed by the smug look on his face.

"So what?" I say. "You could've paid to have this made."

"Well, I didn't," he snaps. "I'm getting a uniform, gun, and everything. I even get paid a percentage for every person I turn in."

"What are they going to pay you in?" I sneer. "Dollars?"

Alex's dark eyes flare. "You'd better show me some respect."

"Or what, you're going to count me in your 'census'?"

"You have *no* idea what this is all about, do you?"

I cross my arms. "Obviously not."

Alex leans close. I can smell his black-market cigarette breath. "They're doing the census so they can figure out where to place the camps."

"What camps?"

My cousin smiles, satisfied by my interest. "Work camps." He pauses for effect. "Refugees are going to be used to clear land, plow, and plant in exchange for some of the food they grow. And they'll do it, too, since everybody who's left is starving."

"I still don't believe you. There's no way any government's organized enough to set something like that up. If they were, they would've already done it."

Shrugging, Alex slips his identification card back into his wallet. "You'll find out."

The tall, middle-aged man ducks under the doorway. He doesn't look around the candlelit warehouse like the others, just shambles across the room with his back still stooped, as if the ceiling is the same height as the door. As he approaches my grandmother, she nods and accepts the pieces of silver he's holding out. I despise her in that moment—healer, poisoner, thief—almost as much as I despise the man: Leora's dad, Luke, who has the same shameless scruples as she. Luke has no business being here, where nothing good takes place. Especially not when his orphaned family—and my son— are trying to survive in the mountains.

For the second time in one night, I rise from my pallet beside Moses, where my parka, bearing his bloodstains, serves as my pillow. Luke turns toward me as I draw close. He appears startled, his gaze widening as I search his face, trying to see if there's still life in his eyes or if addiction has snuffed it out, like it snuffed out my dad's.

"I'm Sal," I say. "I saw you a few times when you were working for my uncle."

He nods cautiously, as if trying to anticipate what I want.

"I know your family," I continue. "They took me in."

Luke glances over at my grandmother, who's returned to her room to deposit his coins. He rams his fist into his pocket to hide his trembling hand. "How are they?" he says.

I raise my eyebrow. "I was about to ask you the same thing."

"Look." He spreads his hands. "Leora told me I can't come home until I get better."

"Don't think you got much chance at getting better by being here."

"I'm here because I have something for your uncle."

"What?"

"Me." He sighs. "Figure if I turn myself in, they'll leave my family alone."

"So you're going back to drug running?"

"Just until I can pay off my debt."

"What if you get addicted again? You know you won't be able to handle it."

He shrugs. "I got no other options. Gotta take the risk."

I don't have any other options for him either, so I go and

lie down in the corner on my pallet as Moses mumbles in his sleep. The thick plaster walls are bloated with mildew. A starling swoops in and out of the holes in the ceiling's ragged trellis, searching for an opening only to hit another wall. I try to ignore this bird, which reminds me a little too much of myself. I instead focus on the alternating mix of shadow and light as, upstairs, the refugees get settled in.

Lying here, I try to picture Colton, his cheeks flushed with the warmth of the fire I imagine him sleeping next to, since it makes it easier for me to be in a place that is dry and warm if he is dry and warm too. I try to picture Leora singing softly in the background. One of those incoherent community hymns, I'm sure.

Most of all, I try not to feel guilty—knowing Colton might be sleeping near a fire, but there is surely no roof over his head, if the community made it to the mountains like they planned. But I had to give him up if he was to survive, and for the first time, I understand that maybe my own mom didn't leave me and my dad at that apartment because she didn't want us. Maybe she left us because—like Luke, like me—she also felt she didn't have another choice.

CHAPTER

2

Leora

I HEAR THEM OFF in the distance before I can see them, and my grip tightens around the handle of the ax. With my gloved hand, I wipe splinters of wood from my face and hair, and try peering through the thinned trees. I pray it is our men returning, and not drifters coming to see what they can take from us. Wrenching the ax blade free, I take one more hit, cracking the stubborn spruce in two. I set the halved piece on top of the pile and look over my shoulder, shivering with cold and with dread as I wait to see the source of the incoming footsteps.

Wind blows through the forest, causing snow to sift down through the pines, speckling my head wrap and sending a cardinal into flight, his red brilliant against the contrast of evergreens. I steady my breathing and bite the inside of my cheek. My lungs strain against the urgency to retreat, yet I find myself crouching even lower beside the stack of firewood. Jabil Snyder is the one who breaks into view first, carrying a stringer weighted with trout, their mottled backs glistening in the winter sun.

The exposed portion of his face reveals the stubble that has grown in the three days he's been gone, chopping holes in the ice-covered lake across the valley. The men have made an effort to provide sustenance for our Mennonite community, which—over the past months—has become reliant on whatever we can hunt and gather from the woodlands.

Jabil does not see me hiding behind the woodpile, and I do not slip out from behind it. Instead, I rise and let the ax fall from my hand, the blade piercing through the snow crust until all but the smooth, timeworn handle disappears. My adrenaline subsides.

We haven't seen anyone over these past three days, and Charlie remained behind to provide us with protection in case our compound should come under attack. But this whole time I've been on high alert, unable to convince myself a single armed *Englischer* and the smattering of mostly elderly Mennonite men—who would *not* arm themselves and defend the compound if the need were to arise—could hold back even the smallest gang intent on harming us.

Would I defend my siblings and my grandmother, regardless of whether that required me to go against everything I've been taught to be right?

While I ponder this, Jabil's men talk and laugh as they make their way up the old logging trail toward the new compound. More than their telltale stringers of fish, this reveals that they had a worthwhile journey. My younger brother, Seth, and Jabil's youngest brother, David, bring up the rear of the group. They talk, their toboggan-capped heads bowed in collusion, their rucksacks jangling with stringers free of trout. I am grateful Jabil took them with him, though supervising two teenage boys, overeager to become men, was surely not an easy task.

Seth snickers and looks around, as if making sure no one can eavesdrop on their conversation, which lets me know they must not be talking about anything good. He spots me against the tree and halts. We stare at each other in silence. I raise my hand and smile. He doesn't wave back, just turns toward David and continues walking. His slight stings, and yet I deserve it. For too long I have treated him like a son rather than a brother—endlessly reprimanding him without maintaining a bond of friendship—so he is pulling away from me in the natural course of adolescence, without granting me the same respect he would give *Mamm*.

"Leora?"

I startle. So focused on my sibling failure, I didn't hear Jabil approach.

He walks up and places his mackinaw around my shoulders. The fabric wafts of fish, sweat, and snow. "You shouldn't be out in this," he says. "It's too cold."

"I come out here all the time."

Without touching me, he draws the lapels of his coat over my sodden wool coat beneath it. "I know."

The acceptance in his voice makes me restless. I bend to pick up the ax, but he moves faster than I, slipping it into the rucksack on his back—the stringer of fish trapped in his other hand. Keen for a reprieve from the elements, the rest of the men do not wait for us; they continue hiking together up the trail, their boots marring the runner of snow.

Jabil extends his hand before him as if to say, "Shall we walk?" It's a gallant gesture, which seems inconsistent with his rugged appearance. However, my own appearance shows how very kind Jabil's gesture is. The tide of post-EMP destruction feels to have swept away my femininity, like every other woman's.

He asks as we begin copying the anglers' steps, "See anyone while we were gone?"

"No. You?"

"Two guys trapping." He pauses. "Making their way to Kalispell."

"What's in Kalispell?"

"The airport."

I look over at him. "They think they can fly from there?"

"No. They want to join the militia."

My heart pounds. I sense Jabil studying me, as if attempting to pinpoint the reason I chose this day—a harsh, bitter day—to split firewood for the community when he made sure we had a plentiful supply before he left. I don't tell him why, for there's no need.

As the perimeter's gate opens to admit us, and Jabil pulls it open further to let me slip past him, I know—and *he* knows—that the person I was waiting for today, and every day, was Moses Hughes. The former soldier whose plane crashed in our field the same day the EMP turned my life upside down. Moses is the one I cannot forget. The one who—despite his absence and my own better judgment—I am waiting for. The one I cannot leave behind.

❖

The men work fast in the gathering dim. They scrape off the trouts' glittering scales and expertly fillet the flesh from the delicate ladder of bones. Myron Beiler lights a wick sticking like a flag out of a small tin container of lard and sets a cracked globe over it before moving the tin to the center of the rock table, so it's easier for the men to see. The fillets will be evenly distributed among the community, regardless of the amount each man caught. The bones and heads will all be boiled down in one large kettle to make broth. Nothing is wasted. Not anymore.

Jabil, beside me, sees me studying the men. "What are you thinking about?" he asks.

"That my brother didn't get any fish."

"You won't go hungry."

I don't look at him. "We're *all* hungry."

"That we are." Sighing, he takes off his woolen hat to scrub a hand through his hair.

We continue walking across the compound—hearing the clang of cast iron inside cabins, smelling the rendered lard sizzling in skillets, or seeing the narrow gaps between logs, highlighted by the fires glowing in the hearths. Our destination, the smokehouse, is lengthwise to the perimeter. A simple construction—as time and materials required of all our buildings—the smokehouse is a narrow shed with holes slatted along the top to vent out smoke that often curls around the structures of the community, like fog.

Jabil walks over to the latch and jerks it sideways to pull open the door, letting me step inside first. The smokehouse doesn't have a lock, although Bishop Lowell considered adding one when he and the deacons were trying to map out the community. But he concluded that if we are willing to steal food from each other's families, none of our families deserve to survive.

I am taller than the majority of my female peers, but I do not have to stoop as I slide beneath Jabil's arm. The movement makes his coat—which I forgot to return and, of course, he did not collect—sway heavily around my knees. He moves in behind me, keeping the door propped with a log to protect my honor, which is almost comical considering so many of our moral tenets have now become invalid. Poles line the room from one end to the other, strung with various slivers of meat. It is mostly fish, but there is also some prized venison, and even some elk that Malachi was fortunate to harvest on the ridge opposite us. It is a nice supply, nearly impressive, but it's obvious there isn't enough to hold us over winter.

Even before we fled the valley, we foresaw the annihilation of our storehouse, and the men started hunting with every available means, so they could restock our meat. At first, before ammo became scarce and there were no shooting restrictions, it looked like we might be all right. However, almost five months later, not only is our ammunition supply dwindling, but so is the amount of game available to be hunted. The men have been forced to go to extreme lengths to procure a portion of what was once a cornucopia of abundance.

From his rucksack, Jabil extracts the trout fillets and drapes all but three of them over one of the empty poles. He holds the remaining three out to me. We look at each other in the darkness. Smoke wafts up from the trench, filled with water-soaked hickory chips.

I say, "What about our agreement to share food?"

"I *am* sharing food. I'm just sharing it with you."

Holding his eyes, I take the trout, shrug out of the damp mackinaw, and hand it back to him. He accepts his coat and crouches, placing another handful of wood chips onto the fire. He steps outside and then turns and looks back at the entrance of the smokehouse, where I'm standing, holding his pilfered gift. I stare at Jabil, trying to understand why someone who would never raise arms to defend me would steal from the community for my sake.

"I'm not going to allow you to compromise your conscience, Jabil, just to keep us fed."

"I'm not compromising anything," he says, then turns and walks up the path to his family's cabin, his shoulders slanted with the weight of the lie.

I tighten the sling, securing Colton against me, as our family files from our dwelling into the early-morning darkness. The remaining community trickles out of their cabins and pools at the epicenter of the compound. The moon illumines their expressions that are as careworn as their clothes. The rigorous circulation of people has trodden away whatever grass was left after construction, transforming the pathway into slimy mud when it is warmer, and something akin to very rough concrete when it's frozen, like today.

The twenty individual one-room cabins have peaked roofs covered with hand-hewn wooden shakes—a monotonous project tackled by Jabil and his brother Malachi, who worked together before the EMP and are an indispensable team. These cabins are placed closely together on the ten-acre patch, and five outhouses were constructed, one for each group of four cabins. Needless to say, the rudimentary lavatories emit an unpleasant odor that will only be exacerbated come spring, when the bitter cold of winter will no longer hold back the concentrated reek.

The community all shares one water source: a freshwater spring that the men dug out and made larger, which was our incentive for choosing this plot of land and is the focal point for our entire circular compound. In between the Risser and Beiler cabins, pants, shirts, and dresses are morphed into sheets of ice, as the fabric hardens the instant it's hung wet on the line. Most of the women, myself included, have given up freeze-drying clothes and instead just hang them inside on twine strung from wall to wall above the fire. Although the strung clothes do make the already-tiny cabins feel even smaller, I am grateful that my fingertips are no longer freezing as I hang the clothes on the outside line.

My siblings, *Grossmammi* Eunice, and I pause on the

edge of the gathering, a position that seems to reflect our place in the community's hierarchy. I hear the members murmuring among themselves in Pennsylvania Dutch. I glance around, trying to figure out why this familiar, lilting language is rife with confusion, and discover that Bishop Lowell is not waiting to address the group from the wooden platform where he usually stands to conduct our meetings; and so everyone is wondering who struck the triangle that called us from our beds.

I turn and scan the assembly, looking for the bishop's white hair and chest-length beard, the combination making him easy to spot despite his short stature. I have just noticed him cutting through the crowd when Charlie, the *Englischer*, assumes the bishop's position on the platform.

This platform was built to give the community members a dry place to stand while drawing their water, because the area in front of the spring was turning into a swamp due to a combination of water and foot traffic. Since then, the small platform has become Bishop Lowell's stage, regardless of the fact that the wood is caked in strata of dried and frozen mud.

But now, this is where Charlie stands, his eyes roaming over the people. Though Anna, in front of me, is almost as tall as I am, she leans back, unintentionally pinning Colton between our bodies, who just giggles in delight and tugs her hair. Charlie evokes in Anna the same level of intimidation he evokes in me, and being overprotective, I dislike him for it.

Charlie tilts his head to the side and folds his arms across his chest, as if unsure what to do with them. "This every-body?" he asks.

Jabil responds from in front. "Yes, Charlie."

"Good." He nods. "I want everybody to hear what I got to say. I'm sick and tired of spending hours hunting down meat and bringing in food, and then having those among us who never do much of anything round here getting the same cut as me." He pauses. "Whatever happened to 'don't work, don't eat' like we said in the beginning?"

I knew this conversation was inevitable. Regardless, I am not prepared for it and find my heart clenching with fear. Charlie is directing his anger toward a handful of people, and my brother, Seth, is certainly at the top of that list. Our *vadder* left when Seth was eleven, right at the age when he started to need him most. Therefore, Seth had no one to take him hunting, trapping, or fishing. No one to teach him a good work ethic, and no one to help guide him through that difficult transition from boy to man. My brother is man enough by age that he should be doing much more to help out around the community and not only pulling his own weight, but helping to pull the weight of our fam-ily. Instead it seems I am the only one left to do our part. I hate knowing we are more of a hindrance than a help to the people of Mt. Hebron, but it is a truth I've had to live with for quite some time.

Bishop Lowell finishes pushing his way through the crowd. His walking stick digs for traction as his predawn shadow moves across old snow. He doesn't step onto the platform but peers up at Charlie, his body language as relaxed as Charlie's is combative.

Bishop Lowell says, "You woke us for this?"

Charlie rears back. "What are you talking about? I was planning to walk my trap lines this morning but hardly had enough energy to get out of bed!"

My sister's left hand goes to her mouth, a new coping tactic whenever she's nervous. I glance at her flaking nails, revealing her nutritional deficit. Reaching around her, I take that hand and gently squeeze her fingers three times, signifying, *I. Love. You.* She squeezes four times, signifying, *I. Love. You. Too.* My eyes sting, for this simple communication, which a toddler could probably learn, has only been acquired in the past few days.

Without raising my gaze, I say aloud, "'Don't work, don't eat.' Are you suggesting the ones who cannot work, such as children and elderly, should not receive as much as you?"

"Not specifically children and elderly," Charlie replies. "More along the lines of anybody who's able to do more for the community but isn't. That includes—" he pauses, eyes drifting to Seth—"teenage boys who don't act like men."

Anger and shame contour Seth's cheekbones. Colton's weight sags the sling as I release him to touch Seth's shoulder. But my brother jerks away. Seth stares at Charlie and then pivots on the hard ground, his lanky form swallowed by the gloom. I am torn between wanting to run after him and wanting to stay to see how the rest of the meeting plays out.

Myron settles my indecision by stepping forward. He

takes off his hat, dragging a hand through his floss-thin hair. "I didn't say anything," he begins, "'cause everybody else seemed fine, but I was so weak on our fishing trip, I almost passed out. I know none of us wants to talk about taking food out of the mouths of anyone here, but I also know that what Charlie says is true: I can't keep going out after food unless I'm getting a little something more to eat."

Discarding his cane, Bishop Lowell climbs onto the platform. Charlie shows him no deference but remains where he is, so that the elderly bishop has to stand on the outer rim. The bishop glances at Charlie and then out at the crowd. "Charlie's been our main scout since the EMP and knows what we are up against more than the rest of us, who've mostly remained inside the compound. From here on, we will more closely monitor our rations. Those who are unable to assist the community will receive fewer rations compared to those who are working. The women who are pregnant or nursing, however, should not have rations cut. If the men who are daily bringing in food for the rest of us become sick or too weak to leave camp, then our detriment will be swift, and I fear we'll not make it through the winter."

In disbelief, I look over at my sister, Anna. Her dull gaze is transfixed on the bishop, but I know she does not understand how his words will affect her. Imagining Anna going without—and even more, someone like Charlie consuming the difference—ignites my fury. I call out over the hum of the community, the majority of whom appear as disturbed by Bishop Lowell's declaration as I am. "My sister and my grandmother—what exactly are they supposed to do when they become the ones too weakened by hunger to get out of bed?"

My *grossmammi* touches my shoulder in warning, the same as I had earlier warned Seth. But like him, I am too enraged to pay her any heed.

Bishop Lowell frowns. "We each must make sacrifices for the community as a whole."

"Yes," I say. "I understand that. What I *don't* get, though, is that my sister can do nothing about her mental state, and my grandmother can do nothing about her age, and yet they are the ones required to make sacrifices."

"Leora." Bishop Lowell peers down at me through his glasses. "I commend you for defending your family, but you must understand that they are not being attacked. I simply cannot see another way of surviving other than cutting back our rations. And if we are to survive, we have to accept the reality of the situation we are in."

Bishop Lowell shifts his attention away from me and leads the community in prayer, signaling our meeting's end. But I don't hear a word. I don't even close my eyes. Instead, I hold Colton's warm body close to my chest and stare at the snow-tipped logs in the distance, composing the perimeter, and recall standing in front of a similar perimeter the first—and only—time Moses and I kissed. I miss him for many reasons, and one of the very least is because I know this meeting would have played out differently if he were here.

❖

I turn to follow *Grossmammi* and Anna back to the cabin, where I imagine Seth is inside, in front of the fire, fuming over Charlie's pointed jibe during the meeting. But just then, Bishop Lowell calls from the platform. "Leora?" He pauses. "May I speak with you a minute?"

Forcing a smile, I glance over my shoulder at him. "Of course."

I call to Anna to wait and pass Colton to her so she can take him in out of the cold. Meanwhile, Bishop Lowell fetches his walking stick and crosses the frozen ground toward me.

"I'd like to talk outside the community," he says. "If you don't mind."

Jabil, near the well, meets my gaze. Even in the weak morning light, I can see his own eyes are veiled with confusion. But then he looks back at Myron and continues their dialogue. My mouth goes dry as I try to understand why Bishop Lowell is singling me out. Is it because I was too forthright during the meeting? The women of the community do not often voice their opinions, whereas I find myself voicing my opinion more and more all the time.

The scrape of his walking stick measures our silence as the bishop and I walk together. I find myself slowing my pace to match his. Sadness fills me as I watch his fingers struggle to open the perimeter's hidden door, leading to the small clearing in the forest, which we hope to turn into a garden plot this spring. Somehow, like *Grossmammi*, I never thought Bishop Lowell would grow old. But the EMP has accelerated the aging process—causing those who needed to mature, like me, to grow up; and yet also making the older generation feeble before their time.

He lets me pass through the gate and then walks through and latches it again. We hike a few yards across the snow-drifted dell. "How are you?" he asks.

I look over, feeling trapped. "What do you mean?"

"You seemed pretty upset during the meeting."

"I'm fine," I murmur quickly, and then soften it with, "Thank you."

"Glad to hear it." Bishop Lowell stabs his walking stick into the snow and turns to face me. "Though it's understandable if you're not. These are troubled times."

I stop in my tracks and look down at him, anxiously waiting to hear what he really brought me here to say. "Forgive me a moment, Leora," he begins, sensing my growing unease, "but I want to speak to you as Jabil's doting uncle, not as your bishop." He smiles at me, and a pair of dimples flash in the age-spotted skin above his beard. "Is that all right?"

My heart thuds for an entirely new reason. Speechless, I nod my assent.

"Gut," he says. "Now, I'm just going to put it plainly, because in my seventy-nine years, I've found that that's the least-complicated way to address complicated things." He takes a breath and then coughs—a ragged, hacking sound. "My nephew loves you. I'm not sure if he's told you that or not, and that's between you and him. But there's another

element to this story that *does* involve me and the community, and I'd like to take care of it while I have the chance."

He picks up the walking stick and rubs the top, shiny as a hickory nut from being handled. "Deacon Zimmerman and Deacon Beiler came yesterday to my cabin and informed me that, given our circumstances, neither of them would like to be bishop if something were to happen to me. It's the first time in my fifty years as bishop that deacons have resigned, but I cannot say I blame them. Nor that I wouldn't do the same if I were in their shoes and using all of my energy just to keep my family alive." He glances over. "Do you see where I'm going with this?"

"I think so." I swallow. "You're saying that Deacon Good could be bishop since the two other deacons won't risk getting their names drawn from the *Ausbund*?"

Bishop Lowell nods. "*Jah*, but there's no 'could be' about it. When I die and Deacon Good becomes bishop, Jabil will take his former place, meaning that—one day—Jabil could be bishop as well." Sighing, he squints as the sun rises over the field, the rays washing orange over the drifts. "I don't know if it's because I'm feeling so tired these days, or because *Gott* has put an urgency in my spirit to get prepared, but I have a sense that this time is soon going to come to pass." He pauses and looks at me with both the compassion of a father and the austerity of a patriarch. "Do you understand the kind of support that will be required from a bishop's wife?"

I shake my head, confused by his words. "Jabil and I, we aren't—"

Holding up his hand, the bishop interrupts me. "I know you're not courting. But that means nothing these days. You could be married tomorrow and sharing a cabin."

My face flushes at the thought. I say, "Bishop Lowell, with all due respect, I don't want to be a bishop's wife. I'm not cut out for that kind of selflessness."

He smiles again and tips his head. "I've been watching you," he says. "These past few years. With your *familye*. And now, with Sal's son. You are more selfless than you think."

I look down, trying to keep from crying. "That's kind of you to say."

"But I'm not just saying it," he intones. "You're a virtuous woman, Miss Ebersole, and that is why Jabil fell in love with you, when he had the other girls vying for his attention. He could see in you what you couldn't even see in yourself." He reaches a hand toward me. "You're a gift to the entire community, Leora. We'd hate to lose you."

I can't hold back my emotion any longer and hide it by turning from the sun toward the gate. If only Bishop Lowell knew that, each time I stand outside the community, I have to fight the urge to run down the mountain and find out—once and for all—if Moses is alive. But maybe this daily struggle is exactly why Bishop Lowell is trying to convince me to stay.

❖

When I return to the cabin, I find that *Grossmammi* and Anna are finishing up breakfast, but Seth is nowhere around. I ask, "Do you know where he is?"

Grossmammi shakes her head and replies in Pennsylvania Dutch, "Looks like he came back, but then left again. In a hurry, too, it seems. He even left the door unlatched."

For the first time, I notice the quilt draping my grandmother's shoulders, and the breath unspooling from her mouth as she hunkers forward to take a bite of gruel. Seth is not always responsible, but he would never normally be so careless as to leave the door ajar, knowing how we strive all day to keep what little warmth we have from escaping.

I tell my family I'll be right back and leave, scoping the premises for my brother.

Someone, in the past half hour, has lit the community bonfire, which Judith Zimmerman is using to make some kind of stock from bones. She stirs the liquid with a wooden ladle, the steam beginning to rise and mix with the frigid air. The copper pot she's using—an heirloom that once held blankets in her cabin in the valley—has turned green for want of polish. No one has time for such vanities now. I smile and nod at Judith, and she smiles wearily in return. In the context of our harried morning, even light conversation, it seems, has become too much work.

A quick pass over the community does not reveal my brother, but I'm not willing to tell anyone about his absence just yet. Disheartened, I return to the cabin and keep busy by cleaning up breakfast and folding clothes. As strange as it sounds, I usually enjoy doing laundry. The chore is so repetitive, my mind can drift from the task at hand and focus on contemplation and prayer. But as I fold Seth's stiff pants, I can't help worrying. I set a stack of clothes on his straw tick mattress, a faded sheet partitioning off his room from the rest of the cabin. My booted foot strikes something. I bend and see the snout of our *vadder's* rifle case peeking out from beneath the bed. The case is empty. I glance over at my sister and my *grossmammi*. Neither seem too concerned about Seth, and I want to keep it that way. Grabbing my *vadder's* old snowshoes, hanging on a peg by the door, I again prepare to leave the cabin.

Grossmammi calls from her chair at the table, "Where're you going?"

I swallow hard, trying to quell the panic rising in my voice. "To look for Seth."

"Outside the compound?"

"I'll ask Jabil to go with me." I have no intention of asking Jabil, and I know I should feel guilty for this falsehood, but I also don't want her to worry while I'm gone.

"Be careful," she says, adjusting the angle of her threadbare *kapp*. "I can't lose you too."

Crossing the room, I lean down and stamp a kiss on the thick, cream-white leaf of her hair, trapping the scent of bacon and smoke. My grandmother's hands on mine are as dry as parchment now that there's no more coconut oil to moisten her skin. I promise her, "I will."

In two hours, the dingy gray world has been transformed by the white on white of a fresh snow. Judith now leans over the cooled kettle of broth while scraping off the film of fat, which she will probably turn into tallow for candles or soap. Jabil is standing beneath a lean-to next to the barn. Snowflakes cover the table like a cloth as he threads what appears to be cow's hair through the cast-iron rings. The three strands will twist together as he turns the crank, becoming one nearly unbreakable rope. I can feel his eyes on me. I dread having a conversation with him, especially considering the conversation I had with his uncle.

Charlie is sitting at the rock table with the men, who are taking turns using the whetstone to sharpen their knives. I must look at him a beat too long because he stands and walks over. I brace myself for confrontation—my default mode whenever he comes around.

"Where's your brother?" he asks. "Haven't seen him since the meeting. His guilty conscience wearing him down?"

I say, "I have no idea what you're talking about."

Reaching into his coat pocket, Charlie holds out his hand. A rifle shell glints gold in the center of his large palm. "Wouldn't have even known he'd stole from me," he says, "if the idiot hadn't dropped this on his way out."

I murmur, staring straight ahead, "How do you know *you* didn't drop it?"

Charlie snorts, pocketing the shell. "These are as rare as hen's teeth and getting more so all the time. Believe me, I wouldn't have been so careless as to drop one in the snow."

I glance at Jabil. He shakes his head, a warning. I turn back to Charlie and meet his gaze head-on. "I don't know where he is."

Charlie scoffs. "Well . . . if you see him, you tell him I'm building some stocks."

"Stocks?" I rear back, incensed. "What's next, a guillotine?"

"He stole from me and needs to be punished."

"And *you're* the one hoarding ammunition while telling the rest of us to use snares."

"It's for our own good," he snaps. "We're keeping the ammunition for emergencies, and I don't think your snot-nosed brother going off on a tantrum counts."

Pivoting in the snow, I leave Charlie before he can say something else. I strike the triangle as if an outlet for my fury, but Jabil intercepts me before his brother Malachi has a chance to open the gate. He touches the snowshoes I'm holding. "You're going out in this?"

"Seth disappeared after the meeting. I thought he'd come back if I gave him some time."

"He *will* come back. But I wouldn't go after him, Leora. It'd hurt his pride."

"I could care *less* about his pride," I say. "He's not thinking straight. He stole ammo from Charlie, and he has *Daed*'s gun. I don't have a good feeling about it. At all."

Jabil glances around. "Well, then I should go with you. Or look for him myself."

I shake my head. "This is something I have to do, Jabil. Alone."

Malachi must be eavesdropping on our conversation from the crow's nest because he pulls the chain hooked to the latch. I see the top of his fleece hat and the tips of his gloves as he waves me through. I wave back and push the gate, the uneven logs plowing lines in the snow.

I stop and turn to Jabil. "I'll never forgive myself if something happens to him."

"He's fourteen, Leora. If he's to succeed at life, you have to let him grow up."

"Yes," I say. "I know that." I drop my snowshoes to the ground. "But not today."

❖

The wind's picked up since I left the compound, spraying snow in my face, the pellet-like flakes as grating as sand. My throat is sore from calling Seth's name. My gloves are coated with ice particles—my frozen breath—from my hands being cupped around my mouth.

"Seth!"

My yell sends more birds into flight. I steady my breathing by biting the inside of my cheek. Where could he be? The silence holds no answers. I continue walking. My *vadder*'s old snowshoes are far too big, so it takes effort to lift and move one forward before setting it down. And then, mercifully, I see Seth's tracks punching through the drifts ahead of me. Two hundred yards away, I come upon my brother's lanky form standing over a dog—no, a coyote. Blood stains the snow melting beneath it, causing steam to rise.

Seth turns while holding our *vadder*'s rifle. His pale eyes remain unfocused even after they are fixed on me. I draw closer. "Stay!" he says hoarsely. "It's still alive."

The coyote's eyes roll in my direction. Panicking, it snarls, showing fangs and flinging its head from side to side. A hopeless effort to escape death.

My brother wipes his face on the sleeve of his coat and gasps, "Why won't it *die*?"

"Why'd you shoot it? Do you want the pelt?"

He shakes his head. "I—I just wanted to prove I could."

My anger rises. "Proving something's a foolish reason to kill."

Seth sneers, "Tell that to Charlie."

"What does *he* have to do with this?"

My brother doesn't answer. "Can you do it?" he rasps.

"What?"

"Finish it off."

"You want me to shoot it."

Seth nods.

I look over as he tries to hand our rifle to me, and then I reach into the pocket of my coat and pull out the small revolver I've carried every day since Moses left.

I tell my brother, "You started this. You should finish it."

He shakes his head, thin voice cracking. "I can't."

I lower the revolver to the coyote's head. The points of its ears, the black pads on its paws, even the russet feathering of its sleek, ashy pelt are so doglike that I have to close my eyes as I pull on the trigger much harder, I am sure, than is needed. The revolver bucks in my hand; my ears throb from the explosion. I realize my eyes are still closed. I open them slowly and see that my shot was true. Fresh blood surrounds the coyote's head. He is quiet and suffering no more. I slide the revolver back into my pocket and look at Seth.

"Now what?" I ask. "You going to carry it back up to the compound and skin it out, or will I need to do that too?"

"I'll carry it," he snaps. I can see by his face that my words have been too much.

"I am sorry for being angry, but where'd you get the bullets in the first place?" I ask this believing I know the answer, and yet wanting to see if my brother tells the truth.

To my surprise, he does not hesitate. "Charlie."

"Charlie."

"Yeah."

"Why does everything revolve around him?"

"He's a jerk."

I tighten my jaw in an effort to keep from saying something I might regret—such as that, lately, Seth's been acting like a jerk too. "Is it because of what he said during the meeting?"

He shrugs, glaring into the snow.

"Whatever happened, Seth, you can't go running off like that. And you *can't* steal."

"*Daed* did."

Run off or steal? I wonder. *Daed* did both. "He was unwell."

"He's a loser."

"Says the thief."

"Better a thief than a coward!"

I roll my eyes. "Says who?"

My brother erupts, *"Everybody!"*

"Define *everybody*."

"Charlie, Henri, Sean."

I give him a pointed look. "The *Englischers*. Two of whom deserted us."

"I'd rather be a deserter with a gun than a Mennonite who gets himself killed."

My sweat's begun to cool now that I'm still, and the dampness chills me to the bone. "You think a rifle and a handful of bullets are going to protect you?"

Seth glances at my coat pocket, where I'm holding the revolver. "Why are *you* carrying?"

"Someone . . . gave it to me."

"Moses." But then his smirk disappears. "You think he's dead?"

I take my hand out of my pocket to fold my arms. "I don't know."

"I think he just doesn't want to come back to us."

My breath catches. "You don't know that. Maybe he can't."

Seth mutters, "Yeah. Just like *Daed* can't."

"Seth, don't be like that."

"Like *what*?"

"Angry." I lean forward and rest a hand on his fingers that are relentlessly picking at a hole in his pants. They stop moving. Seth glances up, his lashes brittle with ice, and in his eyes I see the same hunted look as in the coyote I killed. Sighing, I sit in the snow beside my brother. "It's going to be okay, Seth. These teenage years are the hardest of your life."

"These are the hardest years of *everyone's* life. It's not like it's going to get easier."

It's true. It probably won't. We're quiet for a while as the white falls around us. I knock my shoulder into his. "What if we slip off for a day? Just the two of us."

Seth glances over, his tone incredulous as he says, "Where would we go?"

"I don't know." I pause. "Maybe back to the community? See if there's anything left?"

He shrugs.

"The compound gets a little tight after a while, doesn't it?"

He nods, looking down. "I don't feel like I belong there. I don't think I ever did."

I should tell him I often feel the same way. That I love him and will always be here for him, and yet I fear I've already overstepped my bounds and would therefore cause him to interpret those overused phrases as parental conde- scension rather than sisterly concern.

Rising to my feet, I just say, "Let's go take the coyote back up to the compound and skin it out. We'll talk to *Grossmammi* and see if we can leave in the morning."

But as my brother and I struggle through the snow with the animal's stiffening remains, I recall his words about Moses: *I think he just doesn't want to come back*, an echo of what's been running through my head for months.

❖

The cabin's darkness makes it hard to believe it's early morning, but Seth stands facing the door, a thinly veiled hint for me to hurry up and finish packing. Wanting to oblige him, I stuff a rucksack with jerky, dried apples, socks, a book of matches, and a blanket I first place in a plastic grocery bag to keep it dry in case I drop the rucksack while out in the snow. I walk over to Colton's crib. He is sleeping deeply now, despite cutting a tooth, so the white fir oil I rubbed on his gums must be doing the trick. I brush my fingers across his forehead, about the only portion of him exposed to the cool air. His lips pucker in his dreams.

To my right, the straw tick mattress crackles. I turn and see that Anna is sitting up. Walking over, I touch the side of her face. "Go to sleep," I murmur. "It's all right."

She smiles at me, confused but thankfully not anxious. I had hoped we would be able to slip out without saying good-bye, since Anna cannot comprehend time, and thus, to her, leaving for a day is the same as leaving for good. "We'll be back," I promise, tucking her in.

My sister nods, already soothed by the weight of the blankets. Still watching her, I motion for Seth to go and hear him step outside. I follow and begin to close the door when I'm suddenly touched by the vision of those three sleeping forms, illumined by the fire. I cannot sit an hour in our cabin without feeling the walls closing in, but it's different when I get to leave.

Jabil and Seth are talking when I join them on the path. Seth is holding a pair of snowshoes that Jabil presumably lent to him for the trip. Jabil nods at me. "I told your brother I'll build a fire in your cabin at lunch and then again at supper. Is there anything else you need?"

"No, no." I shake my head. "This is more than enough. Thank you."

He nods but does not look pleased.

"Jabil." I smile, tilting my head. "Seth is coming with me. It'll be all right."

"I just don't know why you have to do this."

I say nothing, for the worry in his eyes tells me he does.

CHAPTER

3

Leora

A PERIODIC SCURRYING in the underbrush or tinny trill of a black-capped chickadee is the only evidence Seth and I have of other living creatures on the mountain. It's hard to gauge if Moses's prediction is true—that six months post-EMP, less than 10 percent of the population remains—or if there are many survivors who have simply learned it's better to lie low than to fight. Either way, I keep one hand in the coat pocket with the revolver as tumbling snow distorts my vision, distorting my sense of direction as well.

The Montana sky is filigreed with clouds, and the sun struggles to shine through the snow-drenched pines, sketching a negative pattern across the white. But the tranquil appearance is deceptive. Wind pounds my upper back, and my toes and fingers tingle, and then grow numb, as my body struggles to circulate blood against the cold. Seth and I don't talk as we force ourselves to transform feet into yards and yards into several miles, and I wonder if he's just as miserable as I am but too stubborn to admit it, a flaw that is keeping me quiet as well.

There is no way to know how far we've come—or how far we have left to go—until the terrain finally begins to level out. Encouraged, my brother and I increase our pace, and soon we come upon the fence that once separated the community from national forest.

"Over here!" Seth calls.

My brother trudges through the drifts blanketing the gap in the stretch of wire and log, but I remain on the other side. My head aches with the memory of riding through that opening on the back of Jabil's mare. How could I have left Moses behind, knowing what he would face? He knew what he would face too, and the impossibility of it pervaded our meeting. But I remind myself not to romanticize that moment; that vulnerability is not such a risk when the odds of a reunion aren't in your favor.

Forcing my eyes to remain dry, I walk through the gap onto community land. The small graveyard is to my left. I stop to look for the place where *Mamm* is buried, to pay my respects, but the snow's so deep, it is impossible to tell. I catch Seth's gaze as he glances away, and grief is as visible there as the day, three years ago, we watched the earthen hole swallow her pine casket. His cheeks are scalded by either cold or embarrassment.

"We should keep walking," he says.

I nod and struggle through the snow until I'm standing beside him. Our snowshoes lift and plant in smooth, circular tandem as we continue trudging across the property. It is strangely beautiful, and calm, covered with unblemished white that hides the worst of the devastation the fires inflicted. We come upon the Lehmans' homestead first. The area is unrecognizable, nothing but jagged mounds of rubble with patches of black peeking through the snow that, upon closer inspection, materialize into charred pieces of log.

Seth and I cross the lane. Three-fourths of the perimeter, in the distance, has collapsed. Whatever is left standing has weathered with time. Field to Table, the makeshift hospital, the schoolhouse, and the pavilion all appear about the same as when we fled up to the mountains, but the latter half of the community—from the Rissers' to the Goods'—is so utterly destroyed, it is like a graveyard relinquished to the elements after its faithful caretakers also died: I know a monument of life and love once existed there, but I cannot find it.

My stomach tightens as I view Moses's plane in the field next to our house. The crop duster's yellow paint is vivid against the snow and ice clinging to the cracked windshield. Decaying vines, left over from summer, climb over the body, as if gradually drawing it back into the frozen earth. The outside of our cabin is licked with charcoal from the flames. Such audacity the gang members had, to try to destroy what we'd already abandoned.

"You all right?" Seth asks, and I'm not sure if he's referring to the plane or to our home.

I nod, and together my brother and I walk up the steps. The majority of the fire damage took place around the front, so the back porch is relatively sound. Seth enters first to ensure no squatters have taken up residence, and it makes me want to cry, seeing how he battles fear in an effort to protect me. But when I follow him inside, I can't imagine anyone living here. The place is nearly uninhabitable, even by apocalyptic standards. A portion of the roof collapsed over the dining room, and two seasons' worth of rain and snow have leaked down through the rafters, saturating the insulation until it got waterlogged and fell, draping the floor in soggy strips. Someone wrenched the kitchen cabinets from the walls and hacked them into kindling, provender for a small fire where the table used to be. The ornate grandfather clock, which metered my adolescence, is gone. Perhaps turned into kindling as well.

I walk over to these ruins—representing hours and hours of my *vadder*'s work—and pick up one of the oil-rubbed bronze cabinet pulls he used because a woman for whom he was making custom cabinets decided she wanted pewter instead. My *mamm* took such satisfaction in those second-hand pulls, hiding her pride so she wouldn't feel guilty for having them.

Seth comes back into the kitchen after searching the rest of the house. "No one's around," he says. "But we shouldn't stay long. Looks like someone's been camping out in your and Anna's old room." He studies me when I don't respond. "Are you crying?"

I shake my head, though I should answer yes. "It's just so . . . hard to believe."

"I know," he agrees. "It's awful. But seriously, we need to get out of here, Lor."

I hear him, but I don't respond. In a daze, I walk across the warped floor into the living room. Water and fire have destroyed this space as well. The braided rug in the center borders the area where I suppose the couch, coffee table, and cedar chest—full of priceless mementos—were burned, the strands of the rug charred into an indistinguishable mess. Besides the cedar chest, I don't mind the damage. In fact, I am almost glad I cannot identify the room where my *mamm* died, as if the physical loss will make the emotional one easier to bear.

The sound of footsteps on the porch rouses me from my stupor. I turn, eyes wide, and see that Seth's gangly frame is outlined by the back door. "Who is it?" I call.

He doesn't answer. Alarmed, I cross the kitchen and look around his shoulder.

Our *vadder* is standing on the porch wearing a moth-eaten wool coat. His arms are filled with kindling. His eyes are clear, but the skin cinches tight over the bare structure of his face. "Seth . . . Leora," he rasps in surprise. "You're here."

I think to myself, *And so are you.*

For years, I prayed for his return, but this is not the return I wanted. I wanted my *mamm* to be here, and well; I wanted my brother and sister to run out to greet him. I wanted our life to be sparkling and perfect so he could see—at first glance—that abandoning us was a mistake.

Instead, we are facing each other on the threshold of this broken house, and I can see that we are all as broken as it. My *vadder* motions to the door, and only now do I realize that Seth and I are subconsciously barring his path. We back up, into the kitchen, as our *vadder* enters the house with the armful of wood. His surprise appearance causes the reminder of his leaving to hang between us, as nebulous as smoke.

He walks around the destroyed cabinets and crouches in front of the woodstove. The flue is rusting, but beyond that, it looks unchanged. Opening the door, he places kindling inside and then stacks the larger pieces on top. I reach into my rucksack and draw out the box of matches, passing it to him. My *vadder* smiles his thanks and strikes a match against the box, cupping his hand around the flame until the fire ignites the wood. The door squeaks as he closes it. He stands and turns to face us. The three of us haven't exchanged a word since he walked into what used to be our home.

My *vadder*, seeing his children struck mute, takes the initiative. "Been here a while?"

Seth and I shake our heads. "No," I reply. "We actually just came."

"How is everyone?" He nudges his head to the left. "On the mountain."

"Okay," I murmur. "Winter's been hard." That's putting it mildly, and he knows it.

Daed looks down. Duct tape serves as laces for his shoes. "I'm sorry I've not been there," he says. "For you."

I reply, "It's okay," but Seth remains quiet. I glance at him in my peripheral vision. His expression looks like it did when he was standing near *mamm*'s grave.

"After you all left," *Daed* continues, "I didn't last long."

"You relapsed?" I ask.

"Yes."

"And then what?" I prod. "You came here?"

"Yes. But I didn't come alone." He pauses. "Moses brought me."

I don't allow myself to believe I heard correctly, and then I tell myself that perhaps the timeline is confused. "You—you came here." I point to the house. "With Moses. After we left."

"He helped me come back." He drags a hand over his face, and yet I can see the sweeping flush of shame. "I was in no shape to walk from Liberty on my own."

I clench a fist to my stomach. "So—he's alive?" My question is a whisper.

My *daed* nods, and that single movement requires me to take a seat on the floor. The wood is mildewed from constantly being wet, but I do not care. I am numb to all but relief.

"He got shot, that night you all left," he explains. "Sal helped him get to the warehouse in town. But then, about the time he started getting better, he could see I was getting worse and told me he'd take me back to Mt. Hebron on his way to a militia."

At this, Seth responds for the first time. "Did he go to the one in Kalispell?"

"Sounds right." *Daed* shrugs. "I can't say for sure."

My brother's grin catches me off guard. "That's where I want to go," he says.

Getting to my feet, I exclaim, "Don't talk like that!"

Mostly this is because Seth's declaration steals my joy surrounding the knowledge that Moses Hughes is alive.

Our *vadder* intervenes by asking if we're hungry. I glance around the destroyed kitchen, trying to see what there could possibly be left to eat. "I got a rabbit this morning," he says.

"Good for you," I reply. "We haven't seen a rabbit in months."

"So," my *vadder* says, smiling slightly. "I take it you're staying for supper?"

I nod and glance over at Seth. After a while, feeling my gaze, he nods too.

❖

A pinesap torch, wedged in a Mason jar like a single stem, blooms in the darkness. My *vadder* pulls up loose floorboards next to the wall where the grandfather clock once stood. He reaches underneath and lifts out an antique Good's Potato Chips tin and twists off the lid. Carefully, he removes a net of coins, the tarnished silver glinting in the palm of his hand. And then he removes a clutch of serving spoons, also silver. There is a small mother of pearl pocketknife I recognize as the one Seth lost summers ago. I am glad my brother is sleeping on the floor of my old room and, therefore, cannot see what I am beginning to understand. All of these items our *vadder* stole from us. The very one who was supposed to provide.

But then he withdraws the final item from the tin: white silk wrapped in butcher paper. My *mudder*'s wedding dress, which she meticulously sewed, although almost no one supported her decision to say her vows to such an unstable man.

My *vadder* passes the package to me. Trembling, I unwrap the paper and scan the cape dress, yellowed at the seams, even in firelight. The silk snags on my fingertips.

"When did you take this?" I ask.

He doesn't say anything at first. "Years ago," he admits. "I would slowly take things from the house and sell them, but I couldn't sell the dress and the knife. Even back then."

His outline blurs. I blink hard and look at my *vadder*, forcing myself to face the pain, separating it from my anger at the one who inflicted it. Then, only then, can I see the pain that is afflicting him, too. There was a reason my *vadder* could not cope when my sister fell and so turned to opioids to dull the ache. Whether it was the imperfect love he experienced in childhood or the imperfect world in which he was raised, something caused him, as an adult, to reach the point where he could not cope. However, all along the way, he was also making choices: forgive and move on or remain. The same choices I am also being presented.

"I forgive you." My words come out tentatively. A whisper. I repeat them and say, "I don't know why you did what you did. I may never know. But I forgive you anyway."

"That means—" Emotion severs my *vadder*'s voice. He looks down. "So much."

I walk closer to him, this broken man, and touch his arm. He cries violently, as if from pent-up release. The same as I have always done. "Look," I say, soothing him. "All things work for good." The silver coins in his hand and the white silk in mine refract the winter moonlight cascading through the hole in the roof. "If you hadn't hidden the dress, it would be burned."

He looks up, wiping his eyes. His smile is bittersweet. "And now, one day," he says, "maybe you can wear it."

❖

My brother says nothing as we prepare to leave, as he has said almost nothing since our arrival. Shutting his heart down toward our *vadder* has become his means of protection, the same as it was for me. In the meantime, my *vadder* and I shuffle around each other, not sure if the words we exchanged last night now require an exchange of physical affection along with a good-bye. But at this point, neither of us are willing to take the risk. So we just smile at each other cautiously as Seth and I descend the back porch stairs.

"You sure you won't come?" I ask for the second time.

He shakes his head. "I'm not ready."

I wonder how long until he is. I say, "I respect that."

"Thank you."

I can tell he is as sincere as I. Halfway down the lane, I turn and wave at our *vadder*, who is still standing on the back porch with that snow-crusted plane stranded out in the field. Only then does my brother snap, "Stop it already, Leora. You're making a fool of yourself."

I glance over in shock, trying to understand how someone who once worshipped our *vadder* could presently abhor him. But then, I *do* understand, don't I? Didn't I feel that same churning animosity when Moses Hughes told me our *vadder* was not dead, as I thought, but alive? That he had been living within miles of his children, who believed themselves orphans?

"Seth," I murmur, reaching out to force him to stop moving. "I've been where you are. I have felt what you're feeling. You do not need to forget everything our *vadder* did; you do not even need to trust him. But if you are ever to find complete healing, you *do* need to forgive."

He is quiet for a while, and then he starts walking away from me. "Don't act like you understand," he snaps. "'Cause you don't."

"Then *help* me understand!" I call this against the wind, and my words are futile in every direction. "I want to be here for you, but I don't know how to do that unless you let me in."

My brother turns, rage in his eyes. "I don't *want* him to come back. I want no part of him. I don't even want to find 'healing' or whatever it is you say."

"Oh, Seth." I begin to cry. "Don't you see? You're only trying to protect yourself."

"No. *You're* the one who needs to see." He pauses. "I'm also trying to protect you."

❖

Seth and I snowshoe for miles in silence. Fury seems to propel my brother so that, even though I have tension of my own, it is hard to keep up. "Slow down," I call. He does not listen but heads off through the woods. "Where are you going?" Again he does not turn. *"Seth!"*

"Would you *just* chill out!" he yells.

His tone, clipped and acerbic, draws me up short. Breathless, I rest my hands on my waist and watch my brother struggle through the snow until the pines close like a curtain behind him. I wait for a moment, unsure how I should proceed, or if I should proceed at all. And yet the memory—of me trying to find Seth through a squall of sleet—is all too fresh. Sighing in frustration, I begin to follow his tracks. Unlike before, it doesn't take me long to find him, but it *does* take all my willpower not to march up and take hold of his hand, as if he's a misbehaving child, and force him to retrace the path that will take us back up the mountain, to safety.

But then I see my brother's destination: the place where he must've come numerous times when he also needed to escape the community. He is standing on an outlook devoid of pine trees, which must've been a vantage point used by hunters before the EMP and perhaps even now. The highway is visible in the distance. Green metal road signs—reduced to hyphens—reflect though the white. It's too far to read them, but I know the arrow pointing one direction says, *Kalispell, 25 miles*; the arrow pointing the opposite direction says, *Liberty, 6 miles*. Below us, through the snowfall, Liberty itself appears: an architect's model of a dystopian city built to scale, the circumference stitched with train tracks straddled by abandoned railway cars. From here, the destruction is not visible.

"It's beautiful," I say, and it strikes me that beauty is not often commented on anymore.

Seth doesn't look back at me, so I walk up until I'm standing beside him on the ridge.

"You okay?" I ask.

He nods, but the tears I saw in his eyes earlier are now dampening his cheeks. "I don't want to go back up there," he replies, wiping his face with the back of his glove. "It's like—" He swallows. "It's like I need to start over again. Somewhere new. Where nobody knows me. Or is always watching what I do . . . to see if I'm gonna turn out just like *him*."

He doesn't have to elaborate. I know who he means. I touch my brother's shoulder, but he draws away. "Sometimes," I begin, "I wish our family could leave too, Seth, but the reality is, there's nowhere to go. We *need* the community. We wouldn't survive without them."

"Then just let *me* leave," he says.

"To go to the militia."

My brother intentionally meets my eyes for the first time in a day. "Yes. Please, Leora."

It both touches and saddens me to hear him plead. "You're too young, Seth."

"In normal life, yeah, I'd say I'm too young, but this isn't normal." Shaking his head, he stares out at Liberty. His voice is subdued as he murmurs, "Nothing really is."

"We'll see," I reply. "Let's just not be hasty about this."

Seth's posture stiffens, as if he knows this is my way of avoiding confrontation and that I have no real intention of letting him go. Abruptly, he turns and starts forcing his way through the trees. I stand still for a moment, watching him, and then follow. He is anger personified: his pace headlong and unflinching, so he will not so much as acknowledge that I am behind him, trying to keep up. We are in the midst of descending the mountain, and about to reach more level ground, when Seth abruptly stops. His hand is raised out to his side, as if in warning.

"What is it?" I whisper, taking a few more steps to span the gap between us.

And then I see why my brother stopped. Ahead, just off the path, a man is sitting against the base of a massive ponderosa. My body tenses as I see the man's rifle, balanced across his lap. He smiles dryly beneath a black hat, obviously enjoying watching us startle and freeze in fear. "Well, well," he says. "Where you two lovebirds off to on this wonderful day?"

My brother's jaw tightens beneath its dusting of facial hair. I take a small step, putting myself just in front of Seth. "We are brother and sister," I tell the man. "We took a trip back to Liberty, and now we're simply trying to make our way up to our community."

Interest flickers across the man's face. "Community, eh? You need to take me there."

Dread corners my mind as I realize my mistake. I've not

only risked my life and my brother's by going through with this venture; I've now risked our entire community. For even if this man is simply a deranged refugee who somehow believes himself the patrolman of these mountains, he is now aware of the group of people who inhabit them. The muscles of my shoulders bunch into knots. "I'm sorry," I reply. "That's not possible."

"Besides," Seth snaps coldly, "who do you think you are that you can ask us where we're going?" If I would not have to turn my gaze, I would give my brother a look.

With his right hand, the man purposefully positions the rifle so that it is pointed directly at us. With his left, he pulls out what looks like a wallet from his jacket pocket. He lets it fall open, revealing some kind of identification card. Holding it up, he states, "I am an informant for the Agricultural Resurgence Commission."

Seth smirks. "Agricultural, huh? Hate to break it to you, but you're not gonna be able to grow anything right now."

Letting the wallet fall closed, the man's riled eyes again shift to my brother. I can see, around his mouth and in the softness padding his jaw, that he is probably only a few years older than Seth. Their tempers are both trigger happy, and I try to gauge how to defuse the situation. "We cannot participate in anything like that," I reply, "but we appreciate the offer."

The man laughs, but his smooth face remains oddly unchanged. "You misunderstand me, sweetheart." He pauses, slipping the wallet back into his jacket pocket.

"This isn't voluntary, and if I say you gotta help, then you gotta help."

"What is this, a joke or something?" My brother speaks yet again.

Fury twists the man's mouth. "You're about to find out just how much of a joke it is." He lifts the rifle to his shoulder. "Either of you make a run for it, and this'll be the day you die." Keeping the rifle trained on us, he gets to his feet.

Somewhere in the woods, a songbird trills a soothing melody that clashes with my pounding heart. All of life, it seems, boils down to two choices: fight and flight. But there's no way we can run in the snow when it's difficult to walk. I hear Seth's breathing quicken and can sense his mounting panic. I grab his arm and grip tightly, mostly out of my own panic and because I know nothing else to do. With my one hand, I am gripping my brother, but with my other, my fingers slowly slide around the revolver, which is in the pocket of my coat.

"Bet you haven't seen one of these in a while, have you?" The man says this in a mocking tone as he brings up a two-way radio with a long antenna protruding from the top. "Hey, base," he calls. "This is Lone Wolf. You copy me?"

A beat of silence passes before the radio crackles to life. "Yeah, we copy. What's up?"

Satisfaction spreads across the man's features as he responds. "You know that Mennonite community we've been looking for . . . to work in the camps?" He stares at me until I feel sick. "I'll be bringing in a couple here soon who can help us find it."

My mind's a race of viewpoints tripping on each other, making it impossible to think. I morally cannot do what I have to do, but *have* and *need* are divided by a thin line, and I suddenly find myself standing on the other side of it.

Nausea causes saliva to pool in my mouth. I watch the man struggle to get the radio back into his right-hand pocket. My body trembles, but my gaze doesn't waver as I smoothly pull the pistol from my own pocket and raise it. The gun is already being lined up with his body before he even notices it.

This time, his eyes are the ones that widen with shock and fear. The wintered world narrows to a heartbeat. The press of my damp fingers on the revolver. A blur of black and white as the man attempts to raise his rifle to meet the threat that is in the hands of the Mennonite girl standing before him.

But his motion is not faster than the bullet that leaves my hand.

❖

The snow-filled air floods with the scent of gunpowder. The shot hits the man center in the chest and nearly throws him off his feet. His rifle drops forward, barrel first, into the snow as his body crumples to the ground. Shaking, I turn to my brother and can only say, "Run, Seth. We have to get away from here." I try to heed my own instructions, but the snow—like a waking nightmare—bogs me down. In the foreground, I can hear the brisk wind streaking through the trees, whose root systems are tethered to the mountain. In the background, just as we are leaving, we hear the radio again crackle to life. "Hey, Lone Wolf, you copy? Where are you?"

Seth and I stand stock-still before turning to look behind us, in the direction of the two-way radio; in the direction of the man who's grown silent—the snow beneath his body stained red, the same as the coyote I killed. But now, I killed a man. Keeling over, I feel the contents of my stomach come up, but there is not much there. I straighten and spit into the snow, my eyes and nose watering as if I'm crying. But I'm not. I'm far too sick and scared to cry.

My brother looks at me, his gaze rife with confusion and loathing. "I'm going to make my way to the militia in Kalispell," he says. "Right now. I couldn't care less if you like it or not. You make your way back to the community, but I'm not going back. *Ever.*"

"I'm sorry, Seth," I murmur. My teeth are chattering. "I—I shouldn't have done that."

It's like he doesn't hear me. Without a backward glance, my brother begins to leave the way we came. Realizing that there is not one thing I can do to stop him or to change his mind, I stare at Seth until the image becomes too painful and I have to close my eyes.

CHAPTER

4

Moses

M Y EYES BLUR as they scan the middle distance, but at first all I can see is a bald eagle rising and falling with the current of wind. Then I notice the shape of someone peering through the diamonds in the airport fence, near the old cell phone waiting area. It could be one of our guys, but I doubt it. There'd be no reason for them to snoop around like that.

Reaching for my gun, I look at the hangar and see Josh is tinkering with the old Cessna. Kalispell Airport's shaped like one long, tapered rectangle. Harold and Dean are monitoring the entrance gates from the traffic control center, and Keith and Robert are positioned at the two farthest points of the grounds. But having guards doesn't mean we're above infiltration. Especially since a majority of us are out scouting for provisions and to see whether there's any sign that order is being restored in the state, or if society's still as lawless as it's been since the EMP.

Even when I shade my eyes, it's almost impossible to see details against the glare of sun reflecting off the snow. One thing's clear, though: it's a man peering in at us, and as skinny as a whippet, but after so many months of people scavenging for food, it's hard to tell if he's not fully grown or just shrunken with starvation. And then he steps back from the gates, as if startled when he spots me watching him. There's something familiar in his self-conscious shuffle. The clouds shift, darkening the airport, and I notice his black hat I've only seen worn by the Mt. Hebron men. I hurry down the plane's icy steps and sprint across the snow-covered tarmac.

"Seth!" I call. "Man, you gotta be crazy! What're you doing here? How'd you find me?"

His face cracks into a wide, relieved grin, and my stomach lurches, seeing a glimpse of Leora. "My *daed* said you were here," he says.

This surprises me. "Did he come up to your new community on the mountain?"

"Nope." He shakes his head. "Leora and I went back down to the valley, to see how bad everything was. We found him there, living in our old house." Seth pauses and looks at the ground. "He told us how you helped him get there."

I wave to Harold and Dean in the tower to let them know all's clear, and then I unlock the gate, hoping Seth won't ask me what kind of state his father was in when I found him at the warehouse—drugged up to the point he was about half out of his mind. But Seth doesn't appear interested in hearing any backstory. Relieved, I step outside the gates and scan the road behind him, but nobody's there, just the empty highway stretching off to the horizon.

"I came alone," he says, seeing the direction of my eyes.

I glance over my shoulder at the hangar's silhouette—the rounded roofline glowing silver—not sure Josh is going to appreciate having a teenager underfoot.

Seth doesn't talk much as we make our way up the snowy path that once led to the airport's busy passenger drop-off zone but now leads to the decimated Concourse A. In fact, he does not talk at all. I can understand his silence. For one, he looks about ready to collapse with exhaustion; for two, he's probably shocked by what he sees. Everything you view daily, you become blinded to over time: a curse if it's beauty, a blessing if it's ugliness.

In this case, it's the latter. I no longer see the rudder of the crashed Bombardier, sticking up from the top of the parking garage. I no longer see one of the three-ton engines burrowed into Concourse C, the force of the impact collapsing the steel beams supporting the roofline's peak and shattering the tempered glass below it so that yards of rubble glitter in the light. All of my senses have become deadened, it seems, because I've even stopped smelling the explosion itself: a toxic mix of burned oil and fuel that stung my nose the first time I got downwind of it.

Josh's reaction when we enter the hangar is just what I expect. He glances up from the plane's engine, and it's like a hand sweeps over his face, transforming his relaxed demeanor into a no-holds-barred scowl.

"Seth's from that Mennonite community I told you about." I hate that I already sound like I'm trying to explain my way out of a fix.

Josh takes off his sunglasses and puts them in a pocket of his navy vest, fitted with more compartments than a fly fisherman's. He looks at Seth. "And why are you here?"

Seth replies, "I came because I heard of a militia."

Josh raises a white eyebrow. "I thought you Mennonites were 'conscientious objectors.'"

I can hear the sneer in Josh's voice. Seth does as well. "I'm not your typical Mennonite."

Josh's mustache twitches. "How old are you?"

"Fourteen."

"You're little for fourteen."

"I'm strong."

I glance between Josh and Seth, trying to predict where this bantering is heading before we get there. Surely Josh isn't seriously considering letting a fourteen-year-old boy stay long-term? Regardless of how overblown our twenty-man "militia" may be in the eyes of those who've lived to tell about it, we do have to defend what we have fought so hard to establish, and no one can defend who is unwilling to kill. Most of us at the airport have no qualms about fighting—maybe because they're all a lot like me, with no roots of any kind.

Either this rootlessness was a decision we purposely made or one that was made for us directly after the EMP. Regardless, we continue pressing forward, determined to survive. But then sometimes, when I'm out at night patrolling and the stars are so clear, my muddled brain can think and I find myself asking, *Why?* What is the motivation fueling our survival to such extremes? And then I realize I know the answer, even if most of us would never want to admit its truth: we are fighting for the belief that one day we'll have roots, and a normal life, again.

❖

I tell Seth, a little tongue-in-cheek, "Be sure to make yourself at home."

He nods, glances around at the traffic control center, and then at the brothers, Nathan and Nehemiah, who have recently switched places with Harold and Dean for the second shift. The brothers' imposing, Carhartt-wearing figures eclipse half of the afternoon light coming in through the bank of windows. One windowpane's been removed to allow for a good shooting position from inside the center, so we can pick off potential invaders before they reach the airport. The others are flecked with bug and bird droppings, which help hide the three bullet holes, splintering weblike patterns across the fourth pane of glass. I don't know the story behind those holes. Maybe nobody here does, though Josh—who was stranded at the airport when the EMP hit—would be the one who could tell it. But he doesn't like to talk about that time period much.

In unison, the brothers turn to the right and nod at me and Seth. We nod back, and I say, "How's it going?" They offer no audible reply, not because they're rude like I first thought, but because the corn-fed brothers are, by far, the shyest of our group. Seth isn't privy to any of this, though, and I can't help smiling as I watch his eyes widen with intimidation. The difference between his Mennonite community and this primitive militia must be as startling to him as Dorothy's transportation from Kansas to Oz.

I inform Seth, "The windows are sloped because it helps with reflections. Josh told me that's also why the ceiling's painted black."

Seth glances up. "Cool."

Just as I saw the airport afresh through Seth's first view of it, it's as if I'm seeing the inside of the traffic control center for the first time. The strewn wreckage from the Bombardier CRJ200—which crash-landed and exploded into flames after the electromagnetic pulse, proving how miraculous my own, softer, crash-landing was—also decimated Concourses C and D. Due to a record winter of snow and ice, the damaged roof over Concourses A and B recently collapsed as well. This, and the cold, forced Josh and our men to leave the concourses and all pile up in the control center, the only inhabitable portion the small airport has left. But, with all our unwashed bodies and clothes trapped in one space, it's not going to be very inhabitable for long.

Seth says to me, "Can I talk to you a minute?"

"Of course."

I lead Seth into the break room we turned into our kitchen. But Brian—who at seventeen is one of our youngest recruits—is standing in the corner, near the defunct microwave and mini fridge. His back's to me, but I can see he's dumping a pumpkin seed packet into his mouth.

"C'mon," I say. "You know we're supposed to be saving those seeds for the chickens." I pause, staring at the empty packet. "What're you going to be eating next, Brian? Mealworms?"

He turns his shaggy head and swallows, wincing slightly as pieces of seeds seem to get hung up in his throat. "Mealworms would probably taste better than anything *you* can cook."

"Whatever," I retort. "Then stop eating what I fix." I angle my head toward the door, and Brian gets the hint. Grumbling, he walks toward it while giving Seth a curious look.

I turn back to Seth. "You hungry?"

"A little," he admits.

I light a fire in the small woodstove one of the guys found in an abandoned house in Kalispell and hauled back to the airport on a sled. Its crooked metal pipe sticks up through one of the glass skylights we broke on purpose so that most of the smoke could get carried off. But *most* is the key word. Taking eggs from the basket, I start cracking them—one by one—against the rim of a glass bowl. "So, Seth," I say. "What's on your mind?"

Seth watches me whisking the eggs a minute, and then he looks up. The expression on his face makes my stomach flip. I set the whisk down in the bowl. "Everybody all right?"

"Everybody's alive," he says, "if that's what you're asking. But this morning . . ." Seth swallows like he might throw up. "Leora and I, we were in the woods when this guy came out of nowhere. He pulled a gun on us and said he was gonna make us go along to some work camp unless we showed him where the community was." His breathing comes hard, as if he's replaying everything, and I know from experience, he'll probably be replaying everything for a long time. "There was no choice," he continues. "I didn't have a gun, but Leora had that pistol of yours she's been carrying in her coat. She pulled it out and shot the guy. Right in the chest."

I raise my eyebrows in surprise. "Did it kill him?"

Seth nods. "It didn't take long."

"So this happened right before you came here?"

Again he nods.

"Where did Leora go?"

"Back to the community, I guess. I don't know. I left after that."

I look away so Seth can't see my frustration. "Did she know where you were going?"

"I told her as much."

Sighing heavily, I set a skillet on the stovetop and spoon out some lard from a tin coffee can. I let the fat warm up, and then I pour the eggs, using a spatula to wipe out the bowl.

Seth says, "She's used to people leaving, if you're wondering if she'll be okay." For the first time, I hear the crackle of anger in his voice, and I try to understand it.

I say mildly, "Are you talking about me?"

"Mostly, yes."

I put the spatula down with some force. "Are you really standing there, judging me for not coming back, when *you're* the one who just left her after she was forced to kill a man?"

His face darkens. "I would've done it myself if I had the gun and not her."

"But she *did*, Seth. She was trying to protect you, and you punished her for it."

Five seconds pass. A pocket of air rises in the cooking eggs and pops.

He says, "That's not the only reason I left. I've been wanting to leave for a long time."

I wonder, over the generations, how many teenagers have attempted to cut off—either physically or emotionally—the only support systems they have left. Though I wasn't a teenager when I did it, I attempted to run away from my life, and the memory of my brother's death, by accepting Grandpa Richard's invitation to come up to Idaho and work on his Bonners Ferry farm. But even then, such a cloistered lifestyle couldn't fill that ache in my gut.

Because of this experience, I understand what even Seth probably doesn't. He left the community because of loneliness and, therefore, needs me to support him although it seems he's trying to push me away. The difference between his experience and mine is that he's going through his turbulent years during some of the most trying times in history, when it's not only imprudent to abandon your support system, but dangerous. On the outside, Seth Ebersole and I might have next to nothing in common, but deep down, he is just a younger version of me.

Leora

Jabil meets me about ten yards outside the community, so I know he must've been watching—or at least had someone else watching—for my return. The snow falls quietly between us, and he studies me below the brim of his black felt hat. His face, in contrast, is the same ashen hue as mine.

"Where's Seth?" he asks by way of a greeting, which is what I anticipated he'd do.

"We had a fight on the mountain. He left and joined the militia." My explanation comes out wooden, and as rehearsed as any scripted lines, but Jabil either doesn't notice or doesn't care.

"The one in Kalispell that the trappers were talking about?"

I nod. "*Daed*'s staying in our old house. He told us Moses is with the militia." I shrug. "I guess Seth left to be with him."

Jabil looks at me for a long time without speaking, so that I start trying to guess what's running through his mind. "People got sick while you were gone, Leora," he finally says.

"Sick?" I stare back at him. "Like how?"

"Flu, I guess. High fever, diarrhea, vomiting, chills . . ." His voice trails off.

"Who's been affected?"

"Your *grossmammi*." He pauses, glancing to the side. "She has it too, but—"

"How bad?" I interrupt, peering around him toward the gates, as if I can see from here.

Jabil moves toward me. "Steady, now." His hands rest on my shoulders, a warm counterweight for the pressure building inside my chest. "My *mamm*'s been checking on her every hour around the clock, and Anna knows to come get her if something changes."

"And who's watching Colton?"

"Judith Zimmerman's offered to take care of him."

I groan in frustration. "I was barely gone for twenty-four hours. What can happen in that time?" But I know exactly what can happen: a pacifist can take a life; a brother can turn his back; a community can implode. I cover my tearing eyes and tell myself to breathe.

Removing the weight from my shoulders, Jabil takes my hand in his. "Come on," he says. "I'll go with you."

❖

Jabil and I walk into my family's cabin, but he respectfully stays by the entrance as I hug Anna and cross the earthen floor to sit on the edge of *Grossmammi*'s bed. Her sallow skin is dry and embroidered with blue veins turned prominent from dehydration. It's hard to look at her, once timeless, now having rapidly grown old. I touch her hand.

"*Grossmammi?*" I whisper. "Are you thirsty?"

Before she can respond, Jabil fills a canning jar with water from the pitcher and hands it to me. I hold the jar to her lips. The liquid dribbles from the sides of her mouth onto her gown. Jabil hands me a dishcloth, and I press it against her chin while I continue letting her drink.

"You—you all right?" she asks.

I rest her hot hand against my forehead and nod against

it, tears threatening to fall. "Yes," I murmur. "I am well." It is a lie, but I won't let *Grossmammi* know what I've done.

"Gut," she murmurs. *"Ich liebe dich." I love you.*

"I love you too." But she's so weak, her eyes are already closing as I respond. I rise too quickly from the floor and have to lean on the bed frame until the darkness clears.

Behind me, Jabil says, "You all right?" an echo of what my grandmother just asked.

However this time, I shake my head no. Jabil helps me across the room to my own low bed. I see Anna in the background, her hands flapping in the firelight like birds: an effort to self-soothe her anxiety. I want to go to her, but I haven't the energy to tell her what I do not know myself. I sit down, and Jabil kneels and wordlessly begins unlacing my boots. His thick, dark hair is flattened from where he was wearing the hat. I stare at his lowered profile, my embarrassment at such an intimate gesture dulled by the fact that I am too fragile to protest.

"You told me that *Grossmammi* has it too, Jabil. Who else is sick?"

He rests his hands on my boots. "Elam Longenecker, young David Good, Esther's newborn, Claudia . . ." I notice how the laces are pulled equally taut.

I remain quiet while trying to process this alarming turn of events. My own event seems nearly trivial in comparison. "How's your uncle handling all this?"

"Not sure." Jabil glances down at my booted foot, still cradled in his hand. "With everything going on, I haven't gotten to talk to him much, but I imagine he feels like I do." He pauses. "The bishop has an overwhelming desire to protect the community—to keep everyone safe—but sometimes, that desire's not enough." Without lifting his gaze, he takes off my boot.

I look away, toward the wall that is so poorly insulated, there are places where I can view the outside. But I do not see this. Instead, I'm envisioning my day-to-day with Jabil in it. How reassuring it would be to have his stable presence to counter the uncertainty of life. I'm so busy contemplating, I do not hear Jabil heading toward the door until the latch clicks as he leaves. The sound, unsettling in its decisiveness, evokes the sound of another door—or rather, a gate—closing me off from the community. For Bishop Lowell would probably not want me here if he discovered I've compromised my pacifist convictions by killing a man. But perhaps he would extend more grace if I had already heeded his advice by entering into a relationship with his nephew Jabil.

Surely there are worse reasons than survival for allowing a heart to love a good man.

❖

I didn't know how much I relied on my brother—or how much strength his presence gave me as I went about my daily household tasks—until he was no longer here to help me complete them. For months, I haven't had to chop wood, haul water, or build a fire in the hearth. Seth took on all these responsibilities without complaining, though he made it clear he did not do any of them with joy. However, in his absence, I am required to do them—and more, since *Grossmammi's* condition has worsened in the past two days.

Her freshly laundered sheets are drying on the rope suspended above the fire, and she's sleeping on the sheets that I had to pull from Seth's bed. It is difficult, in ordinary circumstances, to remain hygienic. But in these circumstances, it seems impossible. The cabin is rife with illness to the point I've had to twice open the door—preferring the drastic temperature drop to adding my own retching to the smell. Anna is quiet throughout it all. Just as I did not realize how much work Seth was doing, I did not know how much Anna actually communicated with me until she became silent.

Someone knocks. I wearily call, "Come in."

The door opens. Judith Zimmerman is standing outside, holding a pint jar covered with a handkerchief. "Do you mind if I leave this?" she says. "It's willow bark tea, for the fever."

"Of course not. That is very thoughtful of you."

For fear of contaminating her, I neither walk toward Judith nor invite her in, but watch as she sets the jar on the snow-covered threshold. She seems to also fear contamination because she doesn't take a breath until she steps back.

I try to smile. "And how is Colton?"

"He's fine," she says. "He's sleeping better now he's cut that new tooth."

"Good. Have you heard how anyone else is doing?"

She folds her shawled arms across her chest. I remember, in that instant, how she looked before, in the valley: her hair always clean and tidy beneath her *kapp*; her dresses without a stain or an unraveled hem. Now, Judith is as I am, or at least as I imagine myself to be, since we have no mirrors and therefore must see ourselves reflected in our neighbors' deprivation.

Judith says, "I guess you didn't hear. Esther's little girl died last night."

I bow my head, throat and eyes burning. "No," I whisper. "I didn't hear." I remember feeling jealous of Esther Martin and her beautiful, perfect family while my own family was holding on to normalcy as well as we could. Such pettiness repulses me. How could I have ever been so blind as to think others needed to suffer so the scales of justice were balanced?

"How is she?" I ask. "Esther?"

"Not good. They can't bury the baby, Claudia, because the ground's frozen solid." After a moment, she adds, "Deacon Good's just come down with it as well."

I look away from her, but not quickly enough to hide my emotion. Once I compose myself, I wipe my face and ask, "And how is Deacon Good's son, David?"

"He might be okay," she says. "It's hardest on the babies and the elderly." Her eyes shift to the darkened space behind me, where my grandmother sleeps. "I—I'm sorry," she says. "I didn't mean—"

I hold up my hand. "It's okay," I murmur. "It's in *Gott*'s hands."

But after Judith leaves, in God's hands or not, I cannot stop crying. The sorrows marking my twenty years have taught that grief demands to be felt. I have been so busy nursing my grandmother and maintaining the household, I haven't had time to process what happened that morning in the woods. And yet here, sitting before the fire, as *Grossmammi* sleeps and Anna sits with a book without turning the pages, the tectonic plates shift. The grief and the confusion and the despair work their way through the crevices, culminating in the seismic sobs that surprise even me. Did my defense of the community bring this plague upon it?

I hear the scuff of the kitchen chair and the whispered footfalls as Anna comes to stand behind me. Her hand strokes my hair, and she begins to sing a fusion of lyric and melody composed from the songs I once sang to her. Leaning back, I take her forearm and sob against her waist as if she is the mother and I am the child, though these roles have long been reversed, and neither of us should have to play the part.

"Oh, Anna," I murmur, tasting salt. "Is *Gott* punishing our people for my sins?"

The vibrations filling my sister's chest abruptly conclude. She leans down and rests one hand against my face. Looking into hers is like looking into our *mudder*'s; even the gesture is reminiscent. Because I so desperately miss that woman, and because if I do not voice my culpability, I fear it will come bursting out, I confess to Anna what I've done.

She absorbs the story as I knew she would, without taking her eyes from me. She is the best possible listener: attuned to my every word, dissecting every meaning, and yet she does not offer advice or reassurance or blame. Instead, when I am done and my sobbing renews, she wraps her arms around me and holds me in front of the firelight. She murmurs against my ear after a while, and though I cannot understand her words, my spirit senses she is praying.

CHAPTER

5

Moses

"YOU ASLEEP?"

I lift my head from the airplane pillow. Josh is standing over me, in front of the double windows on the second floor, so his body is just a cutout in the dark.

I reply, "Not anymore."

"Good. We've got company."

I've not had a night off in weeks, but there's no point bringing that up; Josh would only chide me for complaining, and besides, I'll never be able to go back to sleep knowing what's going on outside. I sigh and glance over at Seth. Snoozing on the cot across from mine, he looks younger and far more innocent than the bristling teenager he transforms into when he's awake.

"How many?" I ask.

"Looks like at least two. Hard to tell."

"Loaded?"

Josh shrugs. "Not sure of that either."

"So what're you gonna do? Pick off the bad guys?"

He nods gravely, even though I'm kidding. He has a self-proclaimed ability to determine, from a distance, the depth of a man's character. Me, on the other hand? I ask, "How come you didn't pick *me* off when I came here? I could've been a thug."

"Nope," Josh says. "I knew."

"How?"

"The way you walked."

"My military bearing."

He laughs and then stifles it, his profile turning to Seth's cot. "No, your limp."

"My limp," I sneer. "You knew I wasn't a thug because of that."

"Yeah, you had this limp and were looking around the airport like a little orphan boy—all you needed was a bandanna on a stick and you would've been Huck Finn."

"Thanks so much," I drawl. "Here I fancied myself with a swagger, like James Dean."

"I would've shot someone with a swagger."

"Well, then, I guess I should be grateful for my limp."

"Yeah," Josh says, completely serious. "You should."

He waits outside in the hall while I get dressed, and then he and I climb two flights of stairs up to the fourth floor. Mark, Donald, and Caleb are already carrying guns and standing in front of the windows. I'm not sure if Josh woke them too, or if they just overheard what's going on and wanted part of the action. Sometimes, believe it or not, we get pretty bored.

"Caleb," Josh says, "you go help Nathan and Nehemiah guard the gates. Mark, you guard the entrance to the center. Don, I want you to guard the fuel."

They nod, exchange some logistical information, and leave to do as instructed. Meanwhile, Josh walks over to the windows and, leaning around the computer on the desk, pops out the cardboard in the far left pane.

"How do you know they're out there?" I ask.

"I thought I saw them earlier, in the distance, when I went to check on the chickens; then Mark saw them tonight. It's hard to hide in snow." He pauses. "Unless you're wearing white."

Despite the anxiety surrounding a possible attack, I can't help grinning while picturing Mr. Sniper Rifle trekking through the blizzard to see how his chickens are faring in the cold.

"Too bad we can't run a heater of some kind in the coop," I mutter, which isn't a coop at all, but the cockpit of the crashed Bombardier CRJ200, which stays pretty cold despite the twenty-five cinder blocks we placed inside to help with solar gain.

Josh nods, and then glances over at me sharply. "You're making fun."

I lift my hands. "I wouldn't dare."

He harrumphs in suspicion and takes out his Sig Sauer P229 from the shoulder holster beneath his vest. Handing the gun to me, he picks up one of the folding chairs circled around the card table and moves it two feet to the right. Standing on it, he pushes up a black tile in the drop-down ceiling and slips out a bolt-action .308 with a scope. It was clearly a rite of passage when Josh no longer waited until I was gone to take the gun from its hiding place, which is easy for him to reach, but not so easy for someone else—even our fellow militants—to spot. He resumes his usual place on the swivel desk chair in front of the window. Snow flurries streak through the void where the glass pane used to be and salt the brim of his cap. He knocks these off and continues to sit, his fists coiled with nerves. After a few seconds, he checks his watch.

"How come yours still works?" I ask, pointing and taking a seat on the folding chair Josh used like a step stool. I must've seen Josh check his watch hundreds of times in the past few months, but some things are so ingrained in my head as normal that, even when they become abnormal, I still don't categorize them as such.

He turns the watch face toward me; the glass disk shimmers in the dark. "It's a USMC-issue Vietnam-era Hamilton mechanical."

"You were in Vietnam?"

He glances out the window, then nods.

I look out the window too. "So was my grandpa."

"What branch?" Josh asks.

"Marines. Fighter pilot."

"Da Nang or Chu Lai?"

"Not sure. Da Nang sounds familiar."

"Later I flew off carriers, but I started in Chu Lai."

Hoping Josh will offer up a few more facts if I confide a few more to him, I continue, "I was there, at my grandpa's farm, before the EMP." I pause. "I stole his crop duster and took off."

Josh removes his eyes from the scope to look at me. "Your grandpa went from being a fighter pilot to a farmer?"

"I know. Talk about a switch, right? After the war, my grandpa moved my grandma, aunt, and dad from their cattle ranch in Texas to a potato farm in Idaho." I've seen grainy, orange-tinged pictures from that time, and my father, Frank, was just a fair-headed, freckle-faced boy who showed no hint of the residual toughness lurking beneath that split-toothed grin.

Josh says, "Why'd you steal his crop duster?"

"I needed to get out of there, like ASAP. My dad wanted me to reenlist."

"Your dad military too?"

"Yeah. He's the garrison commander at Fort Campbell." I push up the sleeves of the sweatshirt Josh gave me since I barely have any clothes. "Two days before the EMP, he called out of the blue and said some 'unnamed' senior enlisted service member was willing to write out a letter of recommendation for me. I had a high ASVAB score and good evaluations, so I probably could've resumed my former rate if I would've retaken the ASVAB. But I was not willing to retake the ASVAB *or* reenlist, and this was something my dad couldn't understand."

My father must've pulled some major rank to get that senior service member to take a second look at me. And despite the fact it was one of the kindest things he'd ever done, I again had to let him down. So I just stood there—in my grandpa's kitchen, with his corded phone pressed against my ear—and stared at the strands of oily flypaper twisting in the open window above the sink. I was quiet for so long that my father asked if I was still on the line. My head cluttered with images from that day in the desert, I told him I had to refuse and replaced the phone in the cradle. I believed some part of my father wished I'd died that day, and not Aaron, who succeeded at everything he put his mind to, whereas sometimes I had trouble putting one foot in front of the other unless I was following in my father's and older brother's steps.

Josh doesn't say anything for a while, and then he gets up and leans out the window with the rifle, using the scope to scan the distance. "There they are," he says. "Look."

I get up from the folding chair and take the rifle from him. Resting it against the edge of the window, I move the scope to the far left corner. Their outlines are crisp and dark, severing the line where sky and snow meet. I hand the rifle back to Josh. He takes it, and I move to the table, letting him resume his former position. He is silent as he peers down the scope, allowing the two men to come closer and closer. Time passes like it's being measured by the clamorous ticking of my pulse. Josh stays still. I'm not even sure he blinks.

"What're you waiting for?" I ask.

"Haven't made up my mind if they're trouble or not."

"Still don't get how you can tell the bad from the good through a scope."

"I'm an expert at reading people."

"How long's it take to become an 'expert'?"

Josh lifts the shoulder not propping the gun. "Twenty years or so."

I look at him as the cold blows through. "You're a sniper?"

"No."

I study him, wondering why I have studied him so many times and never figured him out. But maybe that mystery's part of his job. His vest fitted with numerous pockets. The tiny gold pinkie ring on his right hand bearing a black insignia. The watch he checks out of habit because it must've been imperative that he knew the time as he crisscrossed numerous zones. His nondescript baseball cap. The headset that he keeps in the case hooked to his belt loop. His black leather boots, which seem a little incongruous with his straight-laced appearance. And most of all, the Sig Sauer P229 that Josh keeps in his shoulder holster: the standard gun used by an FAM.

"You're a federal air marshal."

Josh doesn't respond.

"Well, are you or aren't you?"

He looks pained. "I might've done something like that at one time."

I don't buy it. "Were you working when the EMP went off?"

Josh remains focused on the rifle scope. Apparently it's easier to gaze at potential invaders than it is to look directly at me. "No," he says. "I was coming home."

And then he pulls the trigger.

❖

In the morning, Seth climbs to the fourth floor, where Josh and I ended up staying the night to make sure no one else tried to infiltrate the airport. I mumble, "Rise and shine, sleepyhead." Seth grunts in response and stumbles into the break room. He emerges, moments later, with a mug. "Is that coffee?" I ask.

Seth nods.

"That's for the working men."

He takes a sip, watching me. "So put me to work."

"That's pretty risky. What if I ask you to scrub the john?"

"I would do it."

"Yeah, only because you know there is no john."

Seth grins.

Looking at him a moment, I put my arms behind my head. "Tell ya what, I'll let you come on our mission."

His voice cracks with excitement. "Where?"

"Into town. We're going to check out a few places, see if we can find some supplies."

"Can I carry a gun?"

"No."

Glowering, Seth gulps down the coffee.

❖

Sliding down the embankment, our six-man group dusts ourselves off and stands on the road, which isn't a road as much as it's a trail packed into the snow from people walking it. But whoever made the tracks is no longer around. We pass three more mile markers before we reach the small Kalispell suburb—one of the few places, according to our map, our militia hasn't explored. As always, we split up into teams of two: one man entering the house and one man covering for him in case it's occupied by drifters. Brian and Dean, Nehemiah and Beanpole Joe pair off. I look at Seth. "You're coming with me."

He walks over, and together we approach the first house, with the mailbox number 34514. It's a cedar-sided A-frame with unstained, rectangular patches bracketing the windows, which suggest that the house's wooden shutters were removed for firewood. Wind chimes twirl on the porch, and a bald curly willow is in the yard, festooned with a bird feeder like an ornament on a forlorn Christmas tree.

Seth says, gesturing to the teams, "How come *they* get to carry guns?"

"Because they know how to use them."

He stiffens. "I know how to use them."

"Sorry, kid, but I'm not willing to take your word for it. Friendly fire's a deadly thing."

Argument closed, we crunch up the driveway and cut left where the sidewalk must be. Ice veins the glass storm door that is closed and, amazingly enough, intact. I push the black button and pull it open—the squeak of hinges reminding me of an entirely different season and time. There is no front door behind it, as it too was probably removed and burned for firewood.

Drawing my gun, I enter the house. The majority of the windows are broken, so the interior is nearly as cold as the outside. Dirt smears the carpet at the entrance, and footsteps march back and forth throughout, so it looks like someone was living here before winter set in, since dirt is now packed beneath layers of snow. Just like the other houses, there are no shelves, books, tables, chairs, wooden picture frames, curtains, or tablecloths. Even the trim work and wooden blades of the fans have been removed and burned for firewood. But you can only expend so much energy finding fuel for a fire before it becomes clear that food is as important as warmth. When both of these necessities are removed, it's difficult to survive for long.

I come out of the hallway and see Seth still standing by the door. "You coming?"

He takes two steps inside. "What are you looking for?"

I stride into the kitchen—the slush on my boots turning the linoleum's grime to mud—and peer into the open cupboards. "Oil, canned goods, toiletries, blankets, ammunition."

"Do you ever find anything?"

"Sometimes." I shrug. "It depends if it's already been ransacked."

"Has this place been ransacked?"

"Looks like it."

A magnetic dry-erase board is stuck to the side of the fridge. Someone had kept up with the calendar—large black Xs crossing off each day—until November 15. I wonder if that's when the occupants decided to leave or when they were forced from their home.

I tug open the drawer below the oven. It's empty, so I pull it out and peer underneath. Nothing but charred bread crumbs. My stomach growls in visceral response at the thought of bread. I pass the time searching the appliance-filled but bare kitchen, thinking of a striped steak sizzling on the grill; of chocolate and mint saltwater taffy being pulled apart—oily and loose—on that machine in Gatlinburg; of strawberries in my grandpa's garden, so ripe and sun-sweet, they burst in my mouth.

The basement door's also been removed. I walk down the rickety steps with Seth following behind me. "The idea's to be thorough," I explain, whispering as if there's someone here to disturb. "To find the stuff even the owners forgot about, or thought they could hide."

Most of the daylight in the basement's been covered up by the grayish snow piled outside the French doors. A large flat-screen TV is mounted on the wall. A plastic and metal foosball table sits untouched in the corner. The wooden pool table's been hacked into pieces. The cues are gone, but the pool balls make a colorful triangle in the rack on the floor. I walk into the mechanical room, where the water heater and breaker box are stored. I reach behind the water heater—a favorite hiding place—but my hand comes away gloved with dust.

Seth calls from the main room, "Hey, Moses . . . check this out."

I leave and cross the floor to where he's standing. The wall is inscribed with three letters, all caps: *ARC*, along with a straight line and two smaller lines branching off it.

Seth says, "You know what that means?"

"No clue."

Nehemiah, Beanpole Joe, Brian, and Dean are already waiting when we exit the A-frame. They are standing on the curve of the cul-de-sac. Their backs are to us and they're facing the houses, discussing something. As we approach, I call out, "Did y'all have better luck?"

They turn. Brian says, "Not sure you'd call it luck."

Nehemiah asks me, "You didn't find anything?"

"We found some graffiti, but that was about it."

The men look at each other.

Brian adds, "You didn't find anything *beneath* the graffiti?"

"No." My patience wears a little thin. Clearing his throat, Dean looks at Seth. Finally understanding their hesitation, I say, "It's all right. He can hear too."

Dean, once a buttoned-up tax assessor for Flathead County, nods. "Looks like this ARC group came in and killed two of the families."

"Shot right through the head," Brian adds. "All of them. Mafia-style."

Nehemiah says, "So we went and checked out the rest of the houses. All six had *ARC* written on a wall somewhere, but only two houses had bodies inside them."

"Any clue what that means?" I ask.

Beanpole Joe adjusts the strap of his gun. "Maybe they
let some go?"

"Or," Dean counters, "they forced them to go with."

Nehemiah says, "Maybe the ones who refused to go got
shot."

"I think I know what ARC stands for," Seth says, startling us all so much that we look at him simultaneously.

"What?" I prod.

"Agricultural Resurgence Commission. That's the name
of the organization in charge of the work camps. This informant told us about them. He said he'd shoot us if we didn't
go with."

"So . . . what happened?" Nehemiah asks. "How'd you
get away?"

"I shot him first."

Brian turns and claps Seth's shoulder. "Dude."

I give Seth a disappointed look. He won the men's respect
by providing them with key information, but he sure lost
mine by telling a lie.

Leora

I empty the chamber pot in the outhouse. Though I know
I should immediately return to *Grossmammi*'s bedside,
I find myself taking my time as I pass the community fire
and the other cabins, subconsciously aching for fellowship
but too exhausted to seek it out. And then I spot Esther
Martin, hanging clothes on the line. This would not be so

incongruous if she weren't barefoot in frigid temperatures, and if her *unkapped* hair weren't tousled down her back.

Our community is unusually quiet because of the illness, and therefore it appears that Esther's behavior hasn't warranted any attention until now. I walk over and murmur softly, "Esther?" I set the chamber pot down in the snow, but I do not touch her. Esther's bloodshot hazel eyes are void of emotion, calling to mind the night I discovered Anna walking in the field.

Esther turns from me to hang another garment: a tiny white gown. Claudia's. I look down the line and see her dresses, sweaters, and bonnets. This woman is giving voice to her grief by washing her deceased daughter's clothes. My throat tightens. I walk over and stand beside Esther. "Come," I say, reaching for the worn cloth diaper. "Let me do that for you."

Wordlessly, Esther lets me take the cloth. Her fingertips are icy as they brush my skin. I hang the diaper on the line, securing it with the wooden clothespin she is holding out. I quickly fill the rest of the line with laundry, and then wrap my arm around Esther's back, opening the door to the cabin and drawing her in. Her husband, Benuel, is not home, but her three young children—James, five; Mary, three; and Tabitha, eighteen months—look up from the floor of the cabin, where they're playing, completely unconcerned over their *mudder's* absence.

I help Esther into bed and pull the quilts over her. She begins to shiver, her lips tinged blue with cold, so I add another log to the fire smoldering in the hearth. I wipe the children's grubby faces and hands with a washcloth and stack the lunch dishes on the sideboard. I don't have time to do anything else, not with my grandmother suffering in our cabin four doors down.

I walk to the bed to let Esther know I'm going for help, but her shivering's abated and she is already falling asleep. Leaving the cabin, I begin to cross the compound to Judith's when I notice Charlie and Jabil talking together under the lean-to next to the barn.

I approach them and ask, "Have you seen Benuel?"

Charlie says, "We just got back. He was out hunting with me."

"Could you tell him his wife needs immediate attention?"

Jabil turns to me. "Everything okay?"

I nod, wanting to protect this woman I barely know, though she's been my neighbor for years. "I don't think she's doing very well."

"And Eunice?"

I look away from him, determined not to break down in front of Charlie. "Okay," I reply, though I'm not sure of this at all.

Charlie says, "Your brother still not back?"

My body language hardens into a shield. "No. He left to join the militia in Kalispell."

Charlie's eyebrows lift beneath the front of his fur hat. "Really." His entire opinion is summed up in that one word. "The men and I actually found the body of a soldier in the woods today," he adds. "Or what was left of him." He pulls out a card and passes it to me.

I have no choice but to take it, though I am sure my face blanches as I look into the pencil-sketched face of the man I killed in the woods. "Was he part of the militia too?" I ask, hoping my facade of ignorance will hide what I know for fact.

"Doesn't look like it," says Charlie. "The card has some kind of agricultural seal."

"Interesting," I reply, though my mouth is sandpapered with anxiety. "Do you mind if I show this around? Ask if anyone knows anything?"

Charlie shrugs. "Be my guest."

I turn from them both. My fingers tremble as I hold the dead boy's ID in my hands.

❖

Grossmammi Eunice's breathing becomes labored around dinnertime. The room swells with the struggle until my own panicked breathing overtakes the sound. I set the platter of cabbage fried in bacon grease on the table. Anna doesn't dish up her plate like usual but watches me, innately sensing something is wrong. *"Esse,"* I say to her while gesturing to the food.

I walk over to our grandmother. I rest my hand on her forehead. Her skin is dry and hot; her features warped as if she's crying in her sleep, but there are no tears. I turn her wrist over. The rapid pulse vibrates against my fingers. *"Grossmammi?"* I call. "Can you hear me?"

No response. I call her name again and lean forward to lift her eyelid. Her eyes are rolled upward, just the bottom portion of the iris and pupil visible. I rise from the bed and turn toward Anna. "I'll be right back," I murmur. It takes no effort to steady my voice. A preternatural calm has descended upon me, which I experience during each life-and-death event.

I leave the cabin and walk over to the Snyders'. I knock on the door and a voice says, "Come in." I enter reluctantly, fearing I am spreading the illness to them. The family is sitting down to supper. Mrs. Snyder smiles and says, "Evening, Leora." Her warm greeting and smile, for some reason, make me want to cry.

Jabil rises from the head of the table. "Is your grandmother . . . ?" He does not finish.

Looking down, I murmur, "She's gotten worse."

Jabil pushes back the chair and motions for me to follow him out. He lets me exit the cabin first, then pulls the door shut behind us. We face each other on the narrow porch. The night sky is strangely starless—the low-hanging clouds like gray sheets, weighted with snow.

He looks at me with concern. "What can I do to help?"

Taking a breath, I allow my desperation to usurp my pride. "I—I'm not sure she's going to make it, Jabil." Those words, thought but never spoken, conjure forth the ending that I've known for days. "I think Seth would like to be here—" I swallow thickly—"when she goes."

"Of course, of course." He nods after each phrase. Absently, he reaches out and touches my arm. "So I should go to the airport in Kalispell?"

"Yes." I look down. "I'm sorry, Jabil. I know that's so much to ask." My buckskin slippers are wet from walking through the snow. I may have been calm, but I didn't have the presence of mind to change into boots before I left the cabin. The image blurs as my eyes flood with tears. Jabil places a hand on my chin, lifting my gaze to meet his.

"I'll leave tonight," he says, "and try to have him here by morning."

"No. That's impossible." My voice breaks.

"It's nothing. I want to do this—" his calloused thumb strokes my cheek—"for you."

CHAPTER

6

Moses

JOSH AND I ARE, once again, sitting up in the traffic control center, passing the small hours by passing a thermos of coffee back and forth, which we use to refill our mugs. The hot beverage tastes stronger than the standard one-quarter cup of grounds.

I ask, "Did you leave any coffee for the other guys?"

Josh gives me his annoyed look, which means the rules he made don't apply to him. "It's almost the last of it," he says, "so just be happy I'm sharing with you." He takes another sip and adds, "This guy from Carter County gave me a sack of bur oak acorns in exchange for salt. Said if you boil and bake the acorns, they're about as close to coffee as you can get."

"Sounds like you got the raw end of that deal."

His head snaps up. "Hey—don't question my bartering skills."

I lift my hands. "I won't, as long as you don't force me to drink the stuff."

"Believe me. You're going to be eating your words once I'm done." After our coffee's down to its dregs, he asks, "What's this I hear about Seth killing a soldier?"

"Who knows." I lift my shoulders. "He also told me his sister's the one who did it."

"Interesting." But I can tell Josh isn't all that interested in a teenage boy's efforts to prove himself a man. "And the soldier was part of an agricultural resurgence project?"

"We have no idea who he was. But it looks like EMP survivors are being forced from their homes into work camps, where they grow food for an organization of some kind."

Josh shifts in the rolling chair. "And who organized it?"

"No clue about that either. Maybe the ones who set off the EMP? Maybe a homegrown terrorist group, trying to use the labor of other refugees to survive?"

We are silent for a while. Josh and I have learned to pace our conversations, since we've got to spend the whole night finding topics stimulating enough to keep each other awake. Pouring more coffee from the thermos, I say, "Sometimes I wonder what our purpose is."

He glances over in the dark. "Our purpose as humans or as a group?"

"Both, I guess."

He doesn't reply right away, and I wonder if I've offended him, but then he says, "Sometimes I wonder that too." Leaning forward, he slides his mug on the span of desk between two of the blank-faced computer screens. He sits back and gestures to the bullet holes branching across the fourth window pane. "I was here," he says. "That day those shots were fired. Some of the travelers stranded at the airport just lost it when the food ran out. They thought the airport personnel were hoarding everything up here, so they got together and stormed the place."

"How did you respond?"

Josh shakes his head. "Most of the travelers were carrying weapons made from stuff they'd found around the airport. They were out for blood, Moses. You could see it in their eyes. It was down to us or them." He pauses. "But the crazy part is that, slowly but surely, the rest of us started turning on each other too." He rolls the chair forward. His pinkie ring flashes as his long fingers tap across the computer keyboard in that *ASDF JKL;* pattern that's equal parts familiar and strange. He asks, "You ever heard that phrase, 'It's a dog-eat-dog world'?"

"Sure."

"Well, it was kind of like that—kill or be killed—so I did what I had to. The same as in Vietnam or when those stranded travelers stormed the center. I decided, after burying the last person, the only way to thrive in a communal setting was by creating a strict chain of command."

"So that's why you established the militia."

He nods. "But even now, I feel like I'm just holding my breath, watching and waiting for that tipping point, when everything starts spiraling again." Josh looks out through that cracked glass to the snow-covered airport. "Are we supposed to keep doing what we're doing—living day to day, trying to keep ourselves alive—or should we be doing something more?"

"Like establishing a new form of government?"

Reaching up, he reshapes the brim of his ball cap. "At this point, I have no idea what we're supposed to be establishing, but I *do* know that what I'm doing here's not making the kind of difference I swore I was going to make to counter taking all those lives to save mine."

I pour the rest of the rich coffee into his mug, but Josh lets it sit where it is. "Maybe," I say, "you're making more of a difference than you think."

❖

Nehemiah's large frame blots out the doorway to the hall as, in the distance, the rooster cuts loose again, relentlessly announcing dawn before its visible arrival. "Moses," he says, "there's some man named Jaybell outside the gates. He said he needs to talk to you."

I glance over at Josh. "You mind if I run down a minute?"

"Nah," he says. "Our shift's almost over anyway."

I rise from the chair, hobbling slightly until my joints start loosening up when I reach the first landing in the flight of stairs. I'm too young to ache like an old man. But then, I bet not everyone's survived a bombing, plane crash, and gut shot, so I'm lucky I don't feel worse.

I exit through the fire escape. Jabil hears the crunch of my boots on the snow and looks up through the gates as I approach. I try not to wonder why he's here, and yet I know he wouldn't be coming all this way to tell me something good. "Moses," he says and nods.

"Jabil." Our exchange isn't a greeting as much as it is a duel of names.

Taking out my key, I insert it into the padlock and

twist hard, shattering the ice that has sealed over the metal. Nehemiah and Joel are standing ten yards off—far enough to give us privacy but close enough to intervene. I should've told them Jabil won't fight with his fists.

Jabil glances around as he steps inside the gates. Even in the dark, and even though he cannot see much of anything, I can still perceive his scorn. "I heard you're now part of a militia."

I laugh to prove I'm not perturbed. "Guess you could call us that. Though most of us are here because we've got nowhere else to go."

"What do you all do? Besides—" he makes a dismissive gesture—"shoot people?"

I have neither the energy nor the time to let him bait me into an argument. "We're also trying to get a vintage Cessna running so we can see how far the EMP reached."

Jabil nods, but the corner of his mouth lifts in a sardonic grin. I can see my revelation through his viewpoint: I've been hanging with homeless guys and piddling with planes while he's probably trying to keep a community from starving.

Eager to switch topics, I say, "So, how's everybody on the mountain?"

Jabil's jaw throbs. "Not good. The flu hit. Four people have died so far."

My heart speeds up; I can't stop myself from asking, "And the Ebersoles?"

His gaze lifts to my face. "Eunice is bad," he says. "I don't think she's going to make it. Leora sent me here to tell Seth." He stops and studies me. "He *is* here, right?"

"Yes," I murmur, "he's here. I just can't believe all of this happened so fast."

"Not so fast," Jabil retorts. "You've been gone awhile."

"I had no choice."

He steps closer, his breath streaming white against the darkness. "If you cared about Leora half as much as you think you do, then you would've come back."

"I only stayed away because I thought you'd take care of her . . . were the *best* for her."

Jabil speaks, his voice cold and hoarse, anger sparking in his eyes. "Night after night, I've followed her out of the community. Night after night, she stands there, freezing in the dark, waiting for you to come back while I'm—" he thumps his chest—"I'm waiting right there."

"Then maybe you should stop waiting."

"You don't deserve her!"

I look at him and slowly shake my head. "I never said I did."

❖

I pass Jabil the refilled thermos of coffee, which Josh doesn't know I took. He thanks me and accepts it—a peace offering— but I can tell he's still frustrated. I'd be too, if I were him.

I turn to Seth. "Thanks for coming," I say. "It's been good . . . having you here."

He nods curtly, caught between dread of losing his

grandmother and frustration that he has to leave. "Save a place for me," he says. "I'll be back."

"Will do, man," I reply, clapping his thin shoulder, but I hope he doesn't come back. Though for the most part I've enjoyed having him around, I don't think—well, I *know* that the guys in our militia aren't the best role models for someone like Seth, who's so eager to learn the ways of the world, he absorbs every good and bad thing he's taught.

I watch Jabil and Seth depart until their shrinking figures are extinguished by the glare of the rising sun, and then I force myself to turn away. I want to leave with them. Of course I do. I want to lay eyes on Leora myself and make sure she's okay. But I can't. I know it's part fear that keeps me landlocked to this airport, telling myself I have a purpose here when the reality is, I'm not sure what my purpose is—or like Josh and I discussed, what our purpose is as a group. And yet how could I show my face now, when the community has lost so much?

Entering the traffic control center, I go up two flights and try to catch some shut-eye on my floor, though my circadian rhythms are so messed up from guard duty that I have a hard time sleeping beyond catnaps during the day, but I will be sure to wake up starving in the middle of the night. However, even after the majority of the guys stop cutting up and leave, my mind's eye burns with the image of Seth's empty cot. This makes me think of his sister and the horror she must be facing as she's about to lose another foundational pillar of her already-devastated life. And I *still* won't go back to her? *Coward.* I mash the airline pillow beneath my head and cover myself with the airline blanket, though it's like trying to get warm beneath a paper towel. I *can't* go back to her. Sal told me—that day she had her crazy grandmother about kill me while tending my wounds—I was brave for holding off that gang. I suppose, all things considered, I was. But another, lesser part of me wanted to be left behind.

It was all fine and good, having that whirlwind intimacy with Leora when all of life was falling apart, but could I be the kind of man who was content with the unending rhythm of life, secluded on a mountain? I wasn't sure I could, so I played the hero because it was easier than me finding out I hadn't grown up as much as I thought, and then—even worse—Leora finding out that she was disappointed in who I am. Yes, all things considered, it was easier to just let fault-less, reliable Jabil go back with Seth. Nice and tidy, these things of the heart.

I try to sleep for about two more hours, and then throw myself into my work in an effort to distract myself. The only problem is, manual labor is not very distracting: a body can shovel snow, chop firewood, or haul melted water up to the fourth floor of the center while the mind continues working double-time.

Josh comes over from the hangar as I'm trying to clear the pathway from the traffic control center's emergency exit to the gate, even as more snow's falling, reclaiming the asphalt as soon as I uncover it. "What are you doing?" he asks.

I look up at him. I'm wearing no hat, and sweat pastes

my hair to my forehead, despite the cold. "Keeping out of trouble."

"Isn't there a more productive way?"

"Nope."

Josh sighs with the world-weariness of a father trying not to get exasperated with his son, which is what I've become to him, and what—as strange as it is—he's become to me.

He says, "Is this because of Seth?"

I shrug and lift the shovel, cracking the ice, and then scoop it up and toss it away in an effort to reach the snow trapped beneath. "No."

Josh folds his arms. "Is it because of the guy who came?"

I glance up. A line of sweat drips, stinging, into my eye. I blink hard, clearing my vision, and straighten, leaning on the shovel. Blood *thwump-thwump*s in my ears. "Seth has a sister."

A smile splits Josh's face, the skin crinkling around his aviator glasses. "A sister."

"Her name's Leora. Jabil, the guy who came for Seth, wants to marry her." I think about saying more but don't. Josh doesn't seem the type to salivate over drama.

But to my surprise, he prods, "And you don't want him to."

"Marry her?" I shake my head. "No."

"But you don't want to marry her yourself."

"No."

"Why not?"

"Because I'm not cut out for it."

"Sounds to me like you're scared."

"Says the guy who got divorced."

Josh lifts his hand. "Hey. Don't meddle."

"Then don't meddle with *me*!"

Reaching out, he takes my shovel and tosses it on the snow. "I want to talk to you a minute," he says. "Seriously. Man to man."

"Glad we cleared that up."

Josh looks at me, his gaze hard. "Stop hiding behind your mouth. That's just fear too."

"Sorry," I mumble and have a flashback to me as a child, apologizing to my dad for the very same thing. Maybe I hide behind my mouth because it draws attention away from how inferior I feel next to guys like them.

"It's all right," he says. "But I've been on this earth twice as long as you, so I know a thing or two more about it." He pauses and takes off his aviators, hooking the ear stem over his coat and pressing them down. "I don't want you ending up like me," he says. "Holed up in some airport, waiting for somebody to come back to you, who doesn't seem to care that you're gone."

"Who you waiting on?"

Josh studies his boots. Despite the slush, the steel toes are buffed to a shine. "My wife."

"But you're not married anymore."

He glances to the side. "No. Not on paper."

"Does she know you're here?"

"She should. She was on her way to pick me up when everything happened." He shrugs. "I'd flown in for our son's wedding. He was marrying a girl who lives near Flathead Lake."

"So you've just been waiting here the entire time, thinking she's still going to come pick you up or something?"

Josh flinches, and I realize, too late, that my words were harsher than I intended. "In the beginning," he says, "yes. I figured we had a better chance of finding each other if I stayed put." He exhales. "I've lost hope, though. It was stupid of me to ever think it was possible. Honestly, I doubt any of my family's even alive, but what I wouldn't give to see them again." He swallows hard; his eyes gleam. "Nothing like everything falling apart to put your priorities in line."

I clap him on the shoulder. "Least you've got them in line now."

He nods. "Just take my life as a warning: I used to be fearful of showing those I cared about just how much I loved them. Man, if you've got someone to love, don't be like me."

Such a difference between last fall—when Sal brought me here to the warehouse, and blood leaked through my stitches and splattered on the hot concrete—and now: ice sheathing the rusty railing and the stairs covered in so much snow, they better resemble a slope. It's probably not my smartest move, returning to Liberty, but Josh told me I wasn't going to be worth anything until I saw for myself how the community is doing. And how Leora's doing, in particular. But before I make my way back up to the compound, I have to find Sal.

The day I discovered Luke Ebersole upstairs in the warehouse, I sensed he wasn't going to make it unless his riddled body had the chance to withdraw from the drugs. I wasn't sure how everything worked because I stayed on the main floor with the refugees who were there for room and board alone, but I got the feeling Luke must've owed someone something, and I didn't want to get tangled up in that by busting him out of there.

Because of that furtive maneuver—the two of us sick and weak and nearly falling down those rusty fire escape stairs—I never got the chance to properly thank Sal for saving my life. This debt has always bothered me, and I figure coming here to tell her about the sickness and seeing if she wants to come along to see her son, Colton, might pay her back, at least in a small way, for how she helped me. Plus, her medical knowledge could be of use.

I have to knock on the door twice before Papina, the wizened gatekeeper, opens it. She stares for a long time, as if trying to place who I am. And then she leans forward, grips my shoulders, and presses a whiskered kiss to each cheek. She never showed a hint of affection while I stayed here, so the action startles me, to say the least. "Is Sal here?" I ask.

Nodding, Papina leads me into another room. A cheap metal filing cabinet stands along the left wall. On the floor is a mattress layered with blankets. An orange recliner is to the right. Sal sits in this recliner, reading a Louis L'Amour

Western with dog-eared pages. One leg dangles over the recliner's sagging arm. She glances up. The book falls closed. She stares across the room at me like she's seeing a ghost.

I shift my weight, trying to come up with an icebreaker and yet finding none. "I'm sorry I didn't say good-bye." I shrug. "I would've left a note . . ."

"But you had no paper."

I nod.

"Doesn't matter," she says, but I can tell it does.

"I'm going up to the community. Wondered if you'd like to come with."

She hesitates. "I don't want to upset Colton, showing up just to disappear again."

"Sal . . ." I deepen my voice and wait until she looks up. "I think you should come."

Her facial features shift in surprise, and then grow pale. "Why? What happened?"

"Flu or something's going around up there. It sounds bad."

"*How* bad?"

"People have died from it."

"Why didn't somebody send for me before?"

"I just learned about it myself. I thought you should know."

She stares at me a moment, as if deciding how to react, then says, "Thank you."

❖

Due to the screen of evergreens, the community's not as easy to find as you might expect. But I am grateful for the obscurity. If it's difficult for *me* to find—who learned of the general vicinity from Seth—it will be equally difficult for the ARC. Sal and I approach the compound's wall, which doesn't appear nearly as formidable as the one we built down in the valley. An iron triangle hangs outside it, the same as it did down there. Who had the forethought to take it down and pack it along with everything else? Even some of the wooden signs made it.

My stomach tightens, seeing those words—*Warning: Property Under Surveillance*—painted by Leora's hand, and I recall each conversation, and touch, that followed after I gave her those pieces of wood. How do I come back here to show my support while also letting her know I'm not the type of man she wants to have around?

Striking the triangle, Sal calls out, "Anybody here?"

I stare at the silver bark papering the logs and can feel the snow soaking through both layers of my pants. The gate, where we're waiting, is about a foot taller than I am, but the wall towers above it. Everything is built from birch, and it appears the door was simply cut out after the perimeter was built, then reattached. I assume the community used ropes to lever the massive logs into place with a mixture of horsepower and manpower. Wish I could've been here to help. Then again, who knows how many hammers Charlie threw the second time around.

Sal moves forward to strike the triangle again when we hear someone trudging through the snow on the perimeter's other side. The person calls, "Who is it?" I never would've thought Charlie's gruff voice could sound like music to my ears.

"Moses."

A few seconds of silence pass, followed by him responding in a somewhat disbelieving tone, "You're alive?"

A grin puts feeling back in my frozen face. "Don't think I'd be talking to you if I wasn't."

Charlie begins fumbling with the latch. He drags the gate open through the new layer of snow and comes out through the shadowed entrance. I'm shocked by his appearance. Charlie's always been this overblown caricature of strength, but he's lost so much weight, he looks like a scarecrow version of his former self, swallowed in his old Salvation Army clothes.

Embracing me, he beats my back as if helping someone who's choking. "You came."

"Of course." I don't know how to interpret the break in his voice, and so I don't have the guts to tell him I'm not staying.

Charlie pushes me away and lightly smacks my bearded cheek. "You're thin."

"I was just about to say the same about you."

"What've you been eating?"

"Lobster and cold duck." I roll my eyes. "It's such a drag."

"Bully for you. We ate our lobsters two months back and turned their shells into meal."

"Ah," I sigh, "the finer things in life. What've y'all been eating besides meal?"

"Not much." Glancing behind me, he nods at Sal. "Your son's doing good, though."

She lowers her head—her tangled dark hair sweeping across her face—and I can tell that she's fighting not to cry. To draw attention away from her, I say, "I heard y'all have the flu."

"Yeah, man," Charlie says. "Talk about a drag."

"Who all has it?"

"Who doesn't? I just got over it myself."

"How many deaths?"

Charlie looks down. "Sixteen. And we're losing more all the time."

Sal breathes, "No."

"Dehydration," he says. "That's what's getting them. Because they can't keep anything down long enough." He pauses. "You *still* sure you want to come in?"

Sal nods immediately, but I pause, knowing I can't return to the militia until the risk of contaminating my men is past. However, I could never just walk away, knowing what's inside. I nod as well, and Charlie steps to the right to let Sal and me move past him.

Placed in a circular pattern, thirty yards apart, the cabins appear like the set of a play, even down to the clotheslines strung between them that seem more for decoration than everyday use. Someone—possibly Charlie—recently attempted to shovel a pathway between the cabins, but the snow is packed so high outside the last five doors, it seems those families haven't gotten out for days. The community itself is so devoid of people, I would think it deserted if I couldn't see a pair of boots leaning against the door outside one of the shoveled cabins. No one would leave boots behind. Sal asks Charlie, "Where's the Ebersoles' cabin?"

Charlie points to the cabin next to the one with the boots. "But Colton's not staying there," he says. "He's staying with the Zimmermans because Eunice is so bad."

Frowning slightly, Sal says, "Which one's theirs?"

Charlie points that cabin out as well, and Sal walks toward it. She knocks and the door opens, revealing a sallow thread of a woman in a drab brown dress. A few seconds pass, and the woman extends her arm, inviting Sal inside. I stare at the door after Sal closes it between us and I hear the rudimentary latch slide into place.

Not sure where to go, since Charlie's disappeared too, I stand on the platform tucked inside that circus ring of cabins, waiting the same as Sal and I waited outside the gate. The wind rocks a wooden bucket on a rope suspended above a well, the fibers binding the rope creaking against the strain. A sloe-eyed Guernsey bellows in the paddock beside the barn. Her protruding hip bones make her look far too scrawny to produce milk. The barn seems solid, even though I'm sure the men had neither the materials they needed nor the time to construct it well.

Then Jabil appears, coming out of the Ebersoles' cabin, and a cold bolt of jealousy runs me through. He walks toward the well, a spring they dug out, its rim stacked with rocks. The top is layered with boards to keep dirt and animals from tainting the water. His plodding steps hesitate when he sees me standing on the platform, but I can't read his expression since it's hidden by his wool hat—a warmer version of the straw one he used to wear. He lifts the gloved hand not holding the bucket. "I had a feeling you might show up," he says. It doesn't sound like it was a good one. From the bucket, Jabil lifts a large rock tied with a rope and tosses it into the spring. The thin plate of ice covering the water cracks. Jabil hauls up the rock and lowers the bucket. It returns, water darkening the wood and sloshing over the rim.

Without looking at me, he says, "Eunice is dying, Moses."

I wince, though I already knew. "I'm so sorry to hear that."

"Thanks." He nods. "But I'm not the one who's taking it hard."

Concern makes it difficult to speak. "Leora and Seth—are . . . they okay?"

"Not really. It's a good thing Anna doesn't understand."

"Is there anything I can do?"

Jabil studies me a moment, his eyes scanning my face. I see a resignation in his own that I don't understand. "Yes." His grip tightens on the bucket. "Come with me."

CHAPTER

7

Leora

I CAN SEE ANOTHER MAN standing in the filament of light visible between Jabil's body and the doorframe. Straightening, I squint but can't make out the man's features due to the distance and the gloom. But the atmosphere of the room changes as tangibly as the pressure drops before a storm. My body responds to this unseen shift. The hair rises on my arms, and sweat breaks out on my skin beneath the many layers I'm wearing to help insulate myself against cold. Jabil steps into the room and sets the bucket of water on the table. The other man steps in behind him, and I perceive that it's him: Moses. Looking down, I take a breath, desperately trying to maintain control. Everyone but *Grossmammi* is watching me, even Anna.

Tell me, what are you supposed to say or do when you come face-to-face with someone you love—or *have* loved—but never thought you would meet again? I lift my gaze to Moses's. "How are you?" I ask. "It's been a long time."

Words are insufficient, but they are all I have. All *we* have. I want to embrace him, and strike him, and kiss him as hard as I kissed him that night in front of the fire. I can do nothing. I can *say* nothing but parlor talk to this man who saved our community and then broke my heart by not coming back—by not returning to me as he promised he would.

Moses clears his throat. The room is silent except for *Grossmammi*'s unending death rattle: a composition that unpredictably crescendos and decrescendos, like the classical music our driver, Ronnie, used to listen to when he would take us into town.

"I'm doing well," he says. "Thank you, Leora." He pauses and stares at his boots, a puddle of melted snow pooling around them, which will turn our earthen floor to mud. I am calloused, I find, as I mutely rejoice in his discomfort, but I know enough to realize it cannot be a balm for mine. "I am sorry not to find you under better circumstances," he adds.

I reply, "She will soon be at peace," and reach for my grandmother's hand.

Her skin is cold, and growing bluer by the hour, as her failing body uses the last of its energy. I glance up, looking over at Moses and Jabil, and marvel at the difference between my grandmother and me: my twenty-year-old body is at the peak of its performance; however, the heart within me is so full of disappointment and sorrow that it already feels dead. Will it—will *I*—ever find peace?

Just as I never knew how much responsibility my brother assumed until he left, I also never knew how much security I found in my grandmother until she died. For hours after she seamlessly slipped from one life to the next, I sit up beside her and cry while watching my brother and sister sleep. They look young and beautifully naive in the firelight. I see that Seth tucked the dividing sheet behind his headboard, so I wouldn't feel alone as I kept watch. This display of thoughtfulness makes me weep harder. He and I haven't had the chance to talk about what happened on the mountain, nor about his experience among the militia in Kalispell, but I have been observing him. All day, Seth tended our grandmother's dire physical needs with a sensitivity that took my breath. Or, rather, let me catch my breath for the first time in a week.

Wiping my face, I rise from the mattress and pull the bedsheet over my grandmother's body, that single gesture seeming to confirm her demise even more than the moment her pulse slowed beneath my hand. I move into the kitchen and open one of the drawers in the rustic cupboard Jabil made. Feeling along the back, my fingers touch the edge of the dead soldier's identification card. I pull it out and angle the picture to best catch the light. His swarthy features haunt me, as does the horrific comparison of what he must look like now. Every day, I do this; every day, I force myself to face what I have done, though I surely don't need to keep the card as part of my penance, for—wanted or not—his shocked expression will forever remain.

Returning the card to the drawer, I push the wooden utensil divider to the back, pinning the card into place. I pull my worn sweater off the back of the kitchen chair and spread it across the floor in front of the fire. Lying down on top of the meager padding, I curl my body toward the heat in an effort to thaw the foreboding that has crept over my spirit regarding so many things. Most of all, though, is the harsh reality that Seth may be growing up, but Anna never will. How am I supposed to care for her on my own? Yes, the community has been good to my family, and will continue to be, as long as it's possible for them to do so. And yet the members of our community are barely able to care for those beneath their own roofs. I cannot blame them for their partiality. If the situation were in my hands, I would likewise lean toward helping the ones who share my blood.

Someone rests a hand on my shoulder. I awaken, trapped in that fluid amalgam between dreaming and consciousness. Turning from my right hip to my back, I look up. Brown eyes instead of Moses's blue, dark hair instead of blond, a scar cleaving the smooth, square chin, as if dividing into hemispheres the unsmiling face. Jabil. I immediately sit up from the damp floor, where I somehow slept all night, and his calloused fingers pull away.

"I came to check on you," he says. "Seth let me in."

Mortified, I look at the table, where my brother and sister are sitting at breakfast. I glance over at the bed. The sheet is still covering *Grossmammi*'s body. "I—I'm sorry," I stammer. "I didn't hear you knock."

"It's okay," Jabil soothes. "I see that it's over now. You can rest."

Pain blocks my throat. I stare at the gray coals of the fire pit. "How are we going to bury everybody?" I ask. "There are too many. The ground's too hard."

"We're looking into it," he says. "I don't want you to worry."

"But—" I lower my voice and Jabil leans down, innately sensing my need for Seth and Anna not to overhear—"what am I supposed to do until we figure it out?"

His jaw throbs. I can tell he's as unsettled as I am. "Charlie found a cave when he was trapping."

At my shocked expression, he looks to the side.

"I'm sorry, Jabil. It's just so—"

"Philistine? Barbaric?" he interrupts. "I know that. But the deceased are being stored in the barn right now, as your grandmother will be. Is that truly any better? The cave is the only solution, Leora. My uncle and I have been going over this for days."

"What about Deacon Good? Have you asked him?"

Jabil flinches at the name.

"Don't tell me," I say. "He passed away too?"

"No," he replies. "But he's not well. Deacon Good must've caught it caring for his son."

"Then how come *I'm* not sick? How come *you're* not sick? We've all been exposed. Why does the illness pick and choose who it's going to cut down?" Tears spill from my eyes. I wipe them with my palms, but more tears immediately replace them. In my anger, I forgot to moderate the tone of my voice. I glance over at my sister and brother. Seth has reached across the table to try to soothe Anna's stimming hands.

Jabil lifts his shoulder in a gesture of incomprehension. "I don't know," he says. "I don't know why this's happened, but we've got to get through it." He pauses, crouching, and lifts my chin until my panicked gaze meets his. "We have no other choice, Leora. It's going to get worse before it gets better. But it *will* get better," he promises. "The winter will pass and spring will come, and we will have an entire season to get prepared."

"'To get prepared'!" I cry. "Do you even hear yourself? We wait all year for spring and summer, but we spend spring and summer just hoping we can store up enough food to get through until the harvest season comes again."

"That is our life now!" Jabil says. "Do you hear me, Leora?" He rocks my shoulders firmly in his hands. "That is our life. But it will be a good one; it will possibly even be a better one because we will *never* take it for granted."

I lean forward, pressing my wet face against his wool coat, which never fully dries. Shifting his body, he puts an arm around my waist, scooping me and the sweater up from the hearth. I curl my arm around his neck while acutely aware of how filthy I am, since I haven't had the chance to bathe while caring for *Grossmammi*. He adjusts his grip— his fingers poised on the piano keys of my ribs—and walks toward my bed.

Over his shoulder, I see Seth and Anna watching us, their eyes wide. I want to go to them. I want to tell them it's all going to be all right. But despite Jabil's declaration of hope, I don't know anything. Jabil's heart thrums against my side, the beat a reverberation of my own. He lays me on the bed and pulls the quilts over my body. Our eyes meet, and even after everything that's happened, I can see the glimmer of desire in his. I look away to hide my fear.

He asks into the silence, "Do you love him?"

His frankness stuns. "I don't know," I murmur, picking at the quilt. It is the truth.

Jabil tucks the blanket around my legs, entrapping the warmth. "I'm going to give you all the space you need. But I'm staying right here." He pauses. "Because Moses is not the type who does."

Moses

Two days after the death of *Grossmammi* Eunice, Deacon Good dies from the same disease.

Grossmammi's death was heartbreaking. But she was ninety years old. At forty-five, Deacon Good was considered, in the old world, a man still in his prime. He also left behind a wife and their brood of children, half of whom are too young to know they are now fatherless.

With his death, the community can no longer dismiss this mysterious flu as something that only kills young children and the elderly.

Bishop Lowell stands on the platform. His face has been pared of all excess flesh, making his cheekbones knobby and eyes sunken, so I can nearly see the definition of his skull. "Thank you for coming today," he begins. "We have tried to avoid a group meeting, to keep those who are ill from infecting everyone else. But it seems we have moved beyond that cautionary measure, so we will have to enforce a new one." He pauses. "We are quarantined. No one can leave without a written pass." He looks to the side and takes off his black hat. "But we have neither pencils nor paper." His smile is as thin as his hair. "So you can only leave with *verbal* permission, which will be given by me or . . ." He looks out at the community to the two deacons who are so pointedly avoiding his gaze. He turns from them to Jabil, who nods, that single motion placing him in Deacon Good's shoes. Donning his hat, the bishop clears his throat. "Or it will be given by Jabil." He stops speaking, his bloodshot eyes beseeching his nephew. "Could you tell them about our burial plans?"

Jabil steps onto the platform and concisely explains that this morning he and a few men were planning to use sleds to transport the deceased to a nearby cave, but those plans have been postponed until tomorrow so that Hannah Good and her children have time to prepare Deacon Good's body and, more importantly, to grieve.

At this news, Esther Martin—who has been inconsolable since losing her infant daughter, Claudia—begins to weep. Leora puts an arm around the woman's frail body, but I notice she is crying too. She leans close to Esther Martin's ear and asks something. Esther nods. Leora addresses the bishop, "Will there still be a service?"

"Of course," Bishop Lowell says. "But we will have a service here, before the men depart, so that everyone can attend. The journey to the cave is long and difficult."

Benuel Martin, Esther's husband, asks with an edge to his voice, "And what if someone else dies tomorrow, how long are we going to postpone the burial then?"

Jabil glances at his uncle, who wearily lifts a consenting hand. "This is a very trying situation," Jabil says to the grieving father, and then turns his attention back to the group. "For everyone involved. I understand that you all have been waiting to bury your loved ones, and I understand that this waiting period has been agonizing for you." He pauses and looks down, then reaches up and presses the bridge of his nose. "These are unprecedented times. There is no rule book, no *Ordnung*, no hierarchy of bishops to tell us how to proceed, so we will need your grace—and your patience—as my uncle and I try to navigate these uncharted waters."

Soon afterward, the community disperses. The Goods' cabin is silent as I pass; there is no mournful dirge resounding from the poorly insulated space, though I suspect that if Hannah Good could set aside her duties as a single mother and open the floodgate of her emotions, the young widow would mourn her husband the way he deserves.

But nobody is receiving what they deserve.

I find Sal standing by the Zimmermans' cabin—two

over from the Goods'—with Colton on her hip. The child is snotty-nosed but happy and red-cheeked, cuddled against his mother as if no time's been lost. Smiling, I walk toward her. "Looks like someone's glad to have you back."

She kisses the top of his capped head and then glares around the community. "I thought it'd be better for him up here. I thought Leora would keep him safe."

"Hey, now." I reach out and touch Sal's shoulder. "She did the best she could."

"Well," she says, "it wasn't good enough. I wouldn't have even known about the flu if you hadn't come for me. I mean, Colton . . . he could've . . ." She covers her face with a dirty hand. I move toward her, understanding that the anger she is directing toward everyone flows from the same current of anger she is directing toward herself. It's one thing to be separated from your child when you can tell yourself he is warm, dry, and well; it's an entirely different matter when you see the condition in which he's lived without you.

I wrap my arm around Sal's back and pull her into a loose hug. She leans against me for one second, emitting a sob that racks her small frame, and then straightens and smooths back a greasy hank of hair, and I can tell she's dammed up her current of anger, which causes me to wonder what she would look like if it suddenly broke loose.

Smiling shakily at me, Sal begins to walk around the Zimmermans' cabin, where she's been staying since we came. "You moving to Leora's tonight?" I ask.

"I guess." Her shrug is redundant. "Just until Colton and I can leave."

"You're taking him to the warehouse?" I ask, surprised.

She nods. "There's no way I'm letting him stay here."

I wait until she and Colton are inside before heading back toward the barn to see if I can help build the numerous coffins when Jabil appears out of nowhere.

He seizes my upper arm. "Come with me."

When Deacon Snyder speaks, you do as you're told. The closer we get to the small building, the more potent the smell of smoke becomes. I can see the steady plume of gray rising from the roof and streaking across the sky as it hits an atmosphere shift, making the smoke appear like clouds. "Go inside," Jabil says, so I enter the smokehouse. He steps in behind me, leaving the door ajar so we don't asphyxiate. He wraps his bicep with his left hand and uses his right to prop his anvil chin, watching me with such intensity, I try not to flinch.

"What are your intentions?" he says.

He looks so serious, I have to fight not to laugh. "What are you talking about?"

"Listen," he says, "I'm trying to be reasonable here. I let you see Leora, thinking you came back for her, and then you treat her like she means nothing to you."

"Her grandmother was dying. What was I supposed to say?"

He levels me in his gaze. "It's more like, what you shouldn't *do*, Moses."

I shake my head. "I'm so confused right now."

"I just saw you with Sal! You flirt with every girl around!"

I hold his gaze with the same intensity, which is some feat, considering my eyes are watering from the smoke. "I wasn't *flirting* with her, Jabil. It's called being a friend."

"I don't *hug* my friends," he says.

"That's because you're Amish!"

Jabil doesn't break the stare. "I'll give you the benefit of the doubt," he says. "But you and I both know you're not staying. You're just coming here to appease your conscience, and then you'll head out again when you feel like enough of a hero that you can leave."

I make a snorting sound. "That's pretty harsh."

He finally looks away, staring down at the floor littered with cedar chips that smolder and burn. "Maybe. But I'm just calling it like it is."

Leora

I didn't sleep well last night, dreading the burial service for our loved ones, which will take place this morning. However, my heartache is not the only reason I could not rest, or I suppose my heartache stems from two different forms of grief.

The truth is, Moses Hughes has come back, but he has not come back to me. If he *had*, he would've sought me out over the past few days, touched my hand, given me a signal that let me know the memory of us holding each other kept him going all these months too.

Instead, I have nothing but his acute discomfort as he stood in our cabin, and I'm not sure if this confirms his feelings for me or denies them. Getting out of bed, I cross the floor toward the fire and crouch to warm my hands. Seth and Anna are still asleep. It's hard to gauge when to awaken, since no windows allow daylight inside. I look at Sal, who's sitting at the table, letting Colton feed himself breakfast mush, though his little fingers are struggling to hold the spoon. He is used to being fed by me. *"Mamm."* He keeps saying, *"Mamm,"* and looks in my direction, beckoning. But I don't let myself go to him, knowing Sal would see any help as encroachment.

Carefully, I ask, "Did he sleep okay for you?"

Sal pulls a face. "No."

"Poor thing."

"I hope you're talking about me. *I* was the one up comforting him most of the night."

Her words are breezy, and yet the tension hangs between us. After a moment, she tugs a chain from her sweater and leans forward so that the pendant dangles in front of Colton. But then I see it's not a pendant, as the child reaches for the large ring and pulls it into his mouth. I stare at it, hypnotized by the loop's gentle sway. I feel myself rising and stepping closer. "Where—where'd you get that?" I ask.

Sal straightens, the ring knocking back into her chest.

Her eyes snap to mine, and the challenge in them makes me think her casual gesture has intent. Pulling out the stretched neck of her sweater, she drops the chain and ring inside. "I took it from Moses before we went to the warehouse," she says. "My grandmother's like a magpie when it comes to shiny things."

"Then why—" I tilt my head—"didn't you give it back?"

"Because he left before I could."

Something indiscernible floods me. Envy? Anger? Remorse? I pull out the kitchen chair opposite hers. "My *daed* told me that Moses got shot."

Sal adjusts Colton's grip on the spoon. "Yeah. At the perimeter, when the gang came in. I dragged him over to Field to Table, where I'd been hiding. He was bleeding bad, so I looked around and found a sewing kit under one of the shelves. I sewed him up and put pressure on his wound. He wouldn't be alive if not for me." She lifts her gaze, chin thrust out. There were moments, in the valley, when I felt close to her. But right now, she's looking at me like a rival.

"Thank you for saving him," I murmur.

She lifts an eyebrow. "I didn't save him for you."

I'm not sure what to say to this. Is the territoriality I'm sensing from her because she likes Moses, or does it reflect the fact that, for months, I mothered her son?

"Sal." I swallow, unsure if kindness—like help—will only hinder the situation. "I want you to know it's been an honor to care for Colton, but you're his mother and always will be."

"I'm not worried," she says and lightly shrugs. "He knows who I am."

Using the spoon to clean Colton's mouth, Sal scrapes back the kitchen chair and pulls on her coat and hat and then his. She wraps a blanket around her bundled son, and the two of them depart with Colton saying, *"Mamm, Mamm,"* and reaching one arm out of the blanket toward me. I cannot blame him; I have been his caregiver for almost half his life. But Sal blames me. I can see it in her eyes, as if I purposely tried to teach him what to call me, though children somehow learn all on their own. Sal slams the door but doesn't latch it. Frigid air blasts through the breach, and the temperature of the cabin plummets. I walk over and close the door. My chest aches as tears sting. I miss her companionship, but I have to wonder if Sal and I were ever truly friends.

Over the years, I have attended about a dozen funeral services overseen by Bishop Lowell. Most notable, of course, was my own mother's, though I have a hard time recalling much about that day except for how hot it was and how many smiles I had to give to reassure everyone our orphaned family needed no outside help, all while my insides were roiling with dread. This funeral is very different. I have never been to one so poorly attended, which is appalling, considering how many people died in our community. But I know that a majority of the mourners are recuperating from the same illness that took their kin. I am not sure why the rest of our family has been spared, but I do not take it for granted. I find myself wanting to tell Anna and Seth to hold their breath as we stand huddled around the podium, where Bishop Lowell is offering succor to those, like us, who are fraught with grief.

He begins by opening his worn German Bible and reading from the book of John: *"Das Licht leuchtet in der Finsternis, und die Finsternis hat es nicht überwunden."* His breath frosts the poetic words. *The light shines in the darkness, and the darkness has not overcome it.*

I think he's going to flip to more touch-oiled pages, continue quoting more passages, but unlike the times before, that is the only one. Closing the Bible, Bishop Lowell tucks it under his arm and looks up at us through bent spectacles. "I know," he says, "as your bishop, that I should tell you all things happen for a reason, and that *Gott* will turn all things for good. And he will." He nods emphatically. "He will overcome the darkness." The bishop pauses, studying the families: the Zimmermans, Goods, Rissers, Lehmans, Snyders, and Ebersoles. Each soul bears the trials of the past year, like scars. "But I also want you to know that *Gott* hates this. That he weeps with you. That he—the giver and author and sustainer of life—does not rejoice in these temporal deaths." Bishop Lowell stares at the platform upon which he stands, and I can see that he is crying. "He weeps with you," he repeats, and then steps off the platform and opens his arms. Initially we are confused by the gesture. Our stoic background has never encouraged physical affection, and yet here this revered bishop—this patriarch of the Mt. Hebron community—is standing before us, asking us to embrace.

And so we do. I am the first to move forward. I stand at Bishop Lowell's side, wrapping my arm around his hunched back, and the bishop leans down to rest his hoary head against mine. I begin to cry as well, as my broken spirit responds to the secure embrace of a father, for I can feel in his embrace the embrace of my heavenly Father as well, who mourns the loss and the pain just as we mourn, even though he can see the finished plan.

❖

Moses, Jabil, and Charlie begin unloading the caskets from the sleds. I step forward to take the smallest of the nineteen coffins. Jabil passes it to me as if the child inside is merely asleep.

Neither Esther herself nor her husband, Benuel, could come. Esther is incapacitated by grief, and Benuel recently came down with the illness that claimed their infant Claudia's life. I am incapacitated by grief as well, and yet losing my grandmother—whose circle of life was naturally drawing to a close—is not the same as losing a child whose circle never had the chance to begin. Therefore, I promised Esther I'd perform this task, which I am honored she entrusted to me, since I know the heartache of burying a loved one.

I somberly carry the coffin to the mouth of the cave. The landscape, through my tear-filled eyes, blurs into a white backdrop stippled with midwinter brown. I stoop to enter the darkness. The air is musty with trapped smoke. I am shuffling toward the back when I hear someone come in behind me. I look to see Moses, his features illumined by a pine resin torch. The interior of the cavern, abruptly splashed in amber light, reveals a woven blanket and a bowl scooped out of the dirt, the improvised fire pit filled with wood ash and bones. Moses squats. A cinder falls off his torch and lands on the blanket. He curses and stomps it out.

Moses says, "Sorry," and then glances at me with a sheep-ish smile. It's the first time we've looked directly at each other since he came back.

"It's all right," I murmur. "You think people are camping here?"

Standing, he dusts off the knees of his pants. "They were at some point, at least."

"We can't block the entrance," I say. "What if they need to get in?"

Jabil and Charlie finish bringing a coffin into the cave and set it down. Folding his arms, Charlie says, "I know one thing: I'm not carting all those caskets back to the barn."

"He's right, Leora," Jabil says. "We can't. Plus, we have no idea if people are still staying here. Maybe they just for-got their stuff."

"Shouldn't we wait?" I ask. "See if they do . . . come back?"

"Too risky," Jabil says. "We have no idea who they are."

Moses adds, "Nobody's going to want to sleep in a tomb anyway, so it's either block the gap to protect the bodies or don't bury any of them here."

I exhale in frustration. "But we already promised the families we would."

"Let's get the show on the road, then." Charlie claps his hands. "I'm starving."

I look at him in disbelief. "Charlie," I say, "you're about the only brute in the world who could be in the middle of transporting caskets to a cave and think about hunger."

He shrugs but appears embarrassed enough to mollify me. The men leave to retrieve the rest of the caskets from the sleds, but I stay toward the back with Claudia's. Taking the blanket from the cave floor, I shake off the dirt and drape it over the tiny pine box. I close my eyes and say a prayer for the Martin family's healing—not because it's something Esther asked me to do but because I would want a prayer said at my daughter's graveside, if I had to entrust someone to do what I could not.

CHAPTER

8

Leora

I WATCH THE COALS gradually fade from orange to black beneath the cast-iron pot in our hearth. Anna stirs beside me. Sal's holding Colton on *Grossmammi*'s old mattress. Meanwhile, the bishop's words from this morning play over and over inside my mind: "*Gott* hates this." But if he hates it so much, why does he let it happen? Giving up on sleep, I rise to stoke the fire. But right then, the curtain pulls back from around Seth's room. I lie back down but observe him cross the floor in his long johns and socks. He adds two more logs to the fire. A smaller one, beneath, tumbles from the pile, casting a handful of dice-sized embers that land inches from the blanket draping Sal's straw tick bed. Cursing beneath his breath, Seth takes hold of the poker, rolls the smoking log into place, and brushes the embers with the fireplace broom.

I sit up again and whisper, "That's exactly what Moses said today."

My brother startles, then recovers fast enough to retort, "That's because I learned how to cuss from him."

I don't let him get a rise out of me. "What else did you learn at the militia?"

"Nothing." He stabs the log with the poker, stirring sparks. "There wasn't time."

"Thank God for that."

"What?" He sneers. "That there wasn't enough time? Or that I didn't learn?"

I shrug, smoothing the quilts over my lap. "Both, I guess."

"Stop trying to protect me, Leora. It didn't work the last time."

I was foolish to think Seth would never use our experience in the woods for leverage. "You're still alive, aren't you?" I can't keep the frustration from my voice. "Our community's still here. We're not all getting carted off to some work camp."

"Maybe I didn't want protecting that day."

I stand. "You're too young to know what you want."

"I know that I want you to get a life and leave mine alone!"

As Seth intended, his command pushes me away. I stalk across the room in three steps. By the door, I pull on my coat and boots. My fingers are shaking too badly to tie the frayed laces.

"Where are you going?" Apology is trapped in the changing timbre of his voice.

I turn, hand on the latch, freedom at my fingertips. "To live my own life."

❖

I stand at the barn's threshold, breathing in the odor of freshly cut wood and waste. All but one cow and Jabil's horse got eaten months ago because we couldn't sustain the animals through winter and, if malnourished, there would not be much use for them come spring. It is strange to remember the time, before the EMP, when eating a horse would have been as horrific as eating the family dog. It is not so horrific now. I see horses like I see any other livestock in our community—means to an end, which always culminates in keeping us from going hungry. "Moses?" I call out, my voice a decibel above a whisper. "You here?"

A scuffling in the loft. Fear of rejection pours through me, but after Seth's tirade, I fear not living my life more. Pulse pounding, I make my way to the ladder and scale it. My eyes struggle to adjust. I can discern the outline of a man: his bearded face and broad shoulders.

"Sorry to wake you," I murmur. "I just have to talk."

The man pulls something over his head and pushes a button. A headlamp, illuminating Charlie's face. He squints at me in confusion. "About me being a brute?"

I shield my eyes from the light, hoping I'm also shielding my embarrassment. "No, um . . . I—I don't need to talk," I stammer. "Thought you were somebody else."

"Ah." Charlie nods knowingly and turns, using his headlamp to spotlight Moses, sleeping in the straw on the other side of the loft.

"It's okay. Really," I plead with Charlie. "I'll just . . . go."

"Stay right there." Stooping to keep from smacking his head on the rafters, Charlie crosses the loft, takes Moses's coat that he's using like a blanket, and uses it to smack him on the back of the head. Moses flips over and jerks the coat from him.

"What's your problem?" he roars.

Charlie straightens up as much as he can. "You've got a guest."

Moses glares, obviously believing Charlie's lying. Charlie turns his headlamp on me. I try to smile but I'm near tears.

"It's a bad time," I whisper.

Moses jumps up, hitting his head on the rafters. He presses the knot. "No! Stay!"

I look down at the ladder, not sure if I should listen. Moses doesn't give me time to decide. He walks over and gently wraps my wrist, moving me to the center of the loft. Moses and I blink in the glare of Charlie's headlamp. Moses clears his throat. Charlie just keeps looking at us. Moses pointedly says, "Some privacy would be nice."

"Oh, yeah. Sure." Charlie switches off the headlamp. I absently wonder how many batteries he has stockpiled. Charlie grabs his boots and walks to the edge. Clambering down the ladder, he jumps the last few feet, the impact like a small bomb going off. "I'm gonna sleep down here," he says. "In the tack room. I . . . I sleep sound."

The barn falls silent. I rub my arms for comfort and warmth, not sure why I came. Moses walks over, forcing me to either be rude or face him. "Won't you get in trouble?" he asks.

"For being here, you mean?"

He nods.

My laughter is pitched with nerves. "Only if they find me."

"Then why'd you come?"

I tug on the cuffs of my coat. "I wanted to talk about Seth."

"About Seth." I'm not sure if I hear Moses's skepticism or only imagine it.

"Yeah. He seems a little—" I pause—"off."

"He's trying to figure things out, Leora. Give him time."

"And space, apparently. He told me to get a life."

Moses whistles softly. "What'd you say to that?"

"Nothing. Right away. Before I left I told him I was . . . was going to do what he said."

Moonlight sieves through the barn boards, striping Moses's face. After a while, he says, "Seth told me about the man he killed." He pauses, watching me. "Did he really do that?"

"No," I murmur. "*I* did." I swallow hard. "I killed him to—to save us."

Moses doesn't respond, and I wait here, sick with the knowledge that I can't take that thoughtless confession back. And then he leans forward and touches my hair. "I'm sorry," he says. "In a perfect world, you would've never had to make that choice."

I stare at the floor of the loft to hide my remorse, and then I remember what Seth said. Looking up, I reach out to press my right hand to Moses's chest. The erratic thumping beneath my palm articulates everything he won't say. His hand still in my hair, Moses pulls the baling twine tying off my plait. The tresses loosen, damp and waved from my bath, the soap wafting of rendered fat and coals: the bar a consolation gift from Judith Zimmerman. His arms come around me; his hand on the back of my head presses my mouth toward his. But then he withdraws, and at the same time, pushes me away. "Leora—" he rasps. "I'm not staying."

My chest aches with the realization that Jabil was right. "I'm not asking you for anything." My voice breaks. "I never have. I just want to be—" What *do* I want? To be whole? Desired? Loved? I settle for the one term that encompasses them all. "Held."

Moses continues staring at that same patch of loft, but then he lifts his head. Tears stand in his eyes. "I don't know why you want to be with me," he whispers.

"You wouldn't say that—" reaching out, I cradle his face, his scars—"if you could see yourself the way I do."

Moses

I am free-falling—eyes closed, arms spread, pants fluttering against my shins as the wind buffets my ears so hard they sting—and then, as always, I jerk awake before I strike the desert floor. Arms tighten around me. I thrash, searching for escape. A voice, in my ear: "It's okay; it's okay." My entire body stills. I turn my head, feeling a current of warm breath against my cheek.

Leora. It all comes rushing back, as vivid and adrenaline-inducing as the dream. We did nothing more than hold each other through the dark hours of the night, but I know we can't expect the others to believe that. "You—you shouldn't be here," I say, to protect her reputation, but also to protect *me* from feeling when I know that feeling so much for someone can only bring pain.

I can tell that she takes my words seriously, because she does as my worst self intended. Her arms stiffen and loosen their grip. She withdraws, turns from me—her loose hair cloaking her face so that she becomes one with the shadows around her. "Why'd you let me stay?" she asks. "If you don't want me here?"

I am at a loss, for I'm aware the truth would be just as hurtful as a lie. And then a gunshot splinters the pastoral quiet, changing the course of my thoughts. In the darkness, inside the community, I know it changes the course of everything.

"What was that?" Leora asks, breathless, but it's just a reaction. She knows.

I grab my revolver and flip out the chamber to make sure it's loaded, though I made sure it was loaded last night. "I'll go—" Another shot fragments my sentence. Leora and I look at each other. "Stay here," I say, holstering my gun. "I'll check it out."

"I'm *not* staying here!" she cries. "That could be my family!"

I nod, and we take turns scrambling down the ladder to the ground. I take hold of my weapon, easing open the barn door with my foot. The rim of the horizon above the trees is traced with light, but the black sky's still full of stars. I make sense of my surroundings by noting the contrast of the icy path against the log buildings. Snow cossets everything in a pure hush. Did I imagine the gunshot? Was it some echo from my dreams? But no, I remind myself, Leora heard it too.

She exits behind me. Bishop Lowell shambles past without his cane, the whites of his eyes bright with panic. He is so focused on his mission, he doesn't stop when he sees us leaving the barn. He just continues hobbling toward the gate when the hinges creak open and a man appears in front of it, his outline darker than the gloom. The man lifts his arms. I can see the gun—its long barrel glinting—but the bishop continues right toward him. And then I see what *he* is seeing: the prone body marked out in the snow in front of the gate. Malachi, Jabil's younger brother and Bishop Lowell's brother's son, was on duty tonight and has been shot.

The stranger's barrel swings in that direction, preparing to finish the job. I see this all in slow motion, the same as I saw everything in slow motion the day my brother died. Perhaps it's my mind's way of slowing time down so I can think clearly enough to make the right decision, or maybe my mind's not thinking clearly at all. Regardless, this time warp presents an ultimatum: let the bishop die trying to protect his nephew, or shoot a stranger when I know the bishop would rather die than be protected at such a cost.

Choice made, time resumes its maniacal sprint, leaving me with one gesture, one mark, one chance to get it right. I pull the trigger, and the bullet rips through falling snow, smashing into the chest of the man, who clutches it and crumples. But so does Bishop Lowell.

Ears ringing, I sprint toward him. There's no question the man who shot the bishop is dead, and my veins flood with a sated fury, which will soon need quenched again. Jabil comes running up the path. He's not wearing a coat. Then again, neither am I. "What happened?" he asks, clearly torn between going to his uncle's and his brother's aid.

But Malachi's now sitting up, holding his shoulder, making it obvious his uncle's injuries are far more severe. Jabil's eyes dart between Leora and me—a question visible in their depths. But what can I tell him that he doesn't already understand?

Malachi begins to speak, his words halting as if he's in shock, "The guy asked if he could come in, but I—I told him I couldn't open the gate. So he—he told me he and his daughter were freezing. That we'd blocked their cave. I couldn't see her in the dark, so I went outside the gate to check it out, and that—that's when he shot me."

"We blocked their cave?" Leora asks.

I touch her shoulder. "It was probably just a lure."

"We don't know that." She glances through the open gate. "She could be out there."

Charlie hovers over us, wearing his headlamp. He's breathing hard. Apparently his claim about sleeping soundly is true. His light shines on the soles of Jabil's boots as he kneels next to the bishop. The laces are untied, the worn treads clotted with snow.

"Das Licht leuchtet in der Finsternis," Bishop Lowell murmurs.

Jabil whimpers, "No, no, Uncle. I—I can't do this without you," and I learn the truth: this is not just Jabil's uncle; this is the last tie to his deceased father. Jabil presses his hands over the stomach wound. But it's clear the bishop doesn't stand a chance. I turn from Jabil's tears, seeing how they dampen the bishop's shirt.

"You will be a wonderful bishop, Jabil." I glance back and see the bishop's hair, which I thought stark white, has a yellow hue as it's spread across the snow.

Jabil sobs as the bishop begins to struggle. Standing, I move back to give Jabil and his uncle privacy. Leora looks up, one hand supporting Jabil's quaking shoulder. She shakes her head softly—wiping tears from her eyes with her other hand—and that's when I learn the leader of the community is dead. Soon, Jabil Snyder will take his place.

Bishop Lowell's body is lying on the bed he shared with his wife, Verna, who's used the past few hours since his death to bathe her husband, comb his hair, and then employ Jabil and me to help dress him in his best suit. The bishop's square, age-spotted hands are interlaced over the German Bible he read from one day ago: *"The light shines in the darkness, and the darkness has not overcome it."* The fulfillment of that promise now seems impossible as we sit at the table in the muted light of a candle, guttering and smoking against the darkness.

Jabil says, "We could check out the cave in the morning, when we bury him."

Leora straightens. "This can't wait 'til morning."

Jabil glances at the rocking chair, where his aunt is sitting still, her thousand-yard stare transfixed on her husband's drawn face. "I'm not leaving her like this."

Shadows take flight as Leora sets her mug down and lifts one hand to her chest. "There's no way a little girl could survive without shelter."

"But we're not even sure that guy's daughter exists."

"And we're not sure she doesn't." Leora stands from the chair. "I'll look for her myself."

Jabil says, "Hold on now," and turns to me, an interloper to the max. "You go with her."

"Sure." I glance over, but Leora doesn't meet my eyes. "That is, if she'll let me."

"Come if you want." However, her tone and body language contradict this invitation. I should've never let my guard down last night, for both our sakes. I should have never looked at Leora, held her, let her see that hidden portion of my heart as I told her about all I've seen. I knew that dream world could last only so long before the waking and the reality crashed back in.

❖

Leora and I snowshoe through the forest, the untouched path before us floodlit by the headlamp Charlie let me borrow. Charlie's rank layers of clothes, which he also lent, aren't enough to keep me from freezing, and I shiver as we approach the cave. Wolves howl from the ridge, calling to mind that coyote or wolf Leora and I kicked up when we hiked to the fire tower last summer. There is just as much unspoken tension between us as there was back then. But I don't know how to gauge what she's feeling, so I remain quiet, which doesn't resolve anything.

The front of the cave is blocked with a few large rocks we guys found inside and rolled to the opening and stacked. I shut off the headlamp to conserve the battery, like I promised Charlie I would. We shiver in the falling snow. The rock is a chilled marble slab against my back and has to be against hers. I ask, "You cold?"

"*Jah,*" Leora says. "But if I'm this cold, how's a child doing . . . out there?"

"You have to remember—"

She interrupts, "I *know* you think that guy made a daughter up so he could get inside, but I've got this feeling about it, Moses. I think she's real."

We wait for what must be a good hour. Leora spends it intermittently calling out to the child and stomping her feet in an effort to warm up. My eyes have adjusted to the blackness, and the constellations appear so crystal clear, it's as if they're part of a connect-the-dots illustration, etched across the sky. Then I hear something. I reach for Leora's hand, and she squeezes my fingers before letting go. She hears it too. I think, at first, it's an animal, but then another branch cracks, too heavy for a wolf or deer. We can hear the person getting closer. My heart pounds.

I whisper, "Should I turn on my headlamp?"

Leora nods, so I push the button. My dilated pupils contract against the light. My hand drops down to my revolver, but I see it's nothing more than a child—swallowed in a camo coat that brushes the ground—as she squints against the artificial brilliance. I release my grip on the gun and turn the headlamp to the side. She remains standing in front of us, her eyes screwed tight, bracing herself. She says something, but her words are muffled by the collar of her coat.

"It's okay," Leora murmurs, extending a hand. "We won't hurt you."

The girl tosses a stick on the snow and her hat falls off, brown curls springing free to take on lives of their own. Round freckles splotch her coffee skin, as if concentrated drops of color on her cheekbones and nose. "Do it," she says.

"What?" I'm genuinely confused.

Her eyes open. "Whatever you're here for."

Leora says, "We're here to make sure you're all right."

The girl just looks at the stick, lying on the ground in front of her.

"We have this place," I explain. "Where you can stay. Not far from here."

She folds her arms. "What's in it for you?"

I say, "What's in it for me's knowing you're not getting eaten by bears!"

A hint of a smile tugs at her mouth. "They got food?"

"Some." Leora takes a step. The girl flinches until Leora reaches down for her hat.

She snatches it back from her. "Bring the food here," she demands.

"You have no shelter."

"Yes, I do."

I say, "We blocked your cave with rocks."

"Yeah." She glances behind us. "Why'd you do that?"

"We used it for a tomb."

"For, like, dead people? Where am I suppose'ta sleep?"

"At the compound," I say. "As far's I can tell, you don't have much choice."

The girl frowns, twisting the hat. "How'll my dad find me if I'm not here?"

My stomach sinks. How do you tell a child her father is dead—and even worse, that you are the one who killed him? I ask, "How long's he been gone?"

She looks to the side. "Just tonight. He told me to wait. That he'd bring back food."

"Do you have any left?"

"No. I'm hungry."

The wolves cut loose again. She glances at the forest, which is as black as pitch compared to the light. Her eyes turn to me. "Could we leave him a message?"

I clarify, "Your dad?"

She nods.

I look at Leora, who says, "We don't have anything to write with."

"Could you bring back a note?"

"Yes," Leora says, her voice breaking. "We'll come back."

She asks, "You got somethin' on ya I can eat?"

I check Charlie's coat pockets and find a shriveled piece of venison jerky he must've forgotten about. The girl grabs it from me before I can hand it to her. Her face has the sharp, focused intensity of a starving dog as she swallows the meat almost whole, and then glances up and tries to smile. "Thanks," she says.

I smile back. "Sure thing."

Leora asks, "What's your name?"

"Angel?" The girl poses this as a question, so I assume this is not her real name, but one she's put on like she's put on her dad's coat.

"How'd you and your dad get here, Angel?"

"What you think we did?" she says to Leora. "We walked."

"No, I mean *why* did you come here?"

Angel shrugs. "We had to get out."

I guess that's the answer most of us could give these days.

CHAPTER

9

Leora

"WAKE UP." I open my eyes at the sound of the terse voice and see Sal standing over my bed, holding something. I blink hard, narrowing my gaze, trying to pinpoint the item in the dim light. It's the ID from that soldier I killed. My exhausted mind struggles to comprehend how Sal could've found the card in the drawer. She flicks it onto the bed and folds her arms.

"Where'd you get it?" she asks.

"Why were you going through my stuff?" I am more confused than perturbed.

Her lips flatten over her teeth. "I was cleaning."

"Who cleans first thing in the morning?"

"Those with a kid who gets up at the crack of dawn."

Glancing over her shoulder, I see Colton—bedecked in his wool snowsuit and matching hat to combat the chill—levering his spherical bulk by pulling himself up on the table's leg.

"I went to make breakfast," she says, "and found mice droppings in the silverware drawer."

"Great," I mutter. "How can mice even survive up here?"

"Who knows? Maybe you guys brought them with." After a pause, Sal resumes her interrogation. "So . . . how'd you get the card?"

I should've known she wouldn't let up. I evasively reply, "It was given to me."

"By my cousin?"

"I—I didn't know you had a cousin." I stare at her. My head pounds.

"You never asked. His name's Alex Ramirez." She points. "It says so right on the card."

My throat is dry. Swallowing, I wipe my palms on the quilt and look over at Anna, who's curled up on the opposite side of the mattress. Seth's dividing sheet is pulled around his bed, and Angel's sleeping on the pallet that I quickly made up when we came in so early this morning. I say, "We're going to wake everybody up." Rising from the bed, I walk over to the kitchen table. Sal comes in behind me. I take hold of the spindles of the chair. "When did you see him last?"

"Alex? I'm not sure," she says. "One night at the warehouse, but that was weeks ago."

Through tears, I look up at her, gauging if I should lie. But I can't. I owe her the truth, and maybe telling it will serve as part of my atonement. "He was going to turn us in," I murmur.

Colton totters away from the table and buries his face against my skirted legs, rubbing his round baby cheeks on them. Once he regains his balance, he lifts his arms, wanting held. I bend and pick him up—like I've done so many times—but then I look over and see Sal.

Her wary eyes flick from her son up to me. She says, "He was going to turn *who* in?"

"The community. Seth and I, we came across your cousin in the woods. He said he'd shoot us unless we told him where the community was." I look away. The memory of that moment is clear: the snow, the shift in weight as I withdrew the gun from my coat pocket, the surprise on the man's face when I pulled the trigger—a surprise which surely mirrored my own.

Sal flinches. "What'd you do?"

"I had no choice, Sal." I force myself to hold her gaze.

Her hand comes up to her mouth. Her eyes, above it, are wide. "You—"

I nod. "I shot him. He died right away."

"Oh, Leora," she rasps. There are no tears. No anger. Only fear. She reaches for her son and takes him away from me. Another shift in weight. "You have *no* idea what you've done."

❖

The firelight cuts in and out as I pace in front of the hearth. Sal continues stuffing the clean cloth diapers and few articles of clothing I made for Colton into her backpack and then zips it shut. "Wake up," she calls to Angel, the same as she called to me less than an hour ago. When the child doesn't respond, she walks over to the pallet on the floor and bends to pull on one of her socked feet. "You need to get dressed," she says.

Angel lifts her head, looks up between us in confusion, and lies back down.

"You can't take her!" I cry. "She doesn't even know who you are!"

Sal gives me a look. "She came with you, didn't she?"

"That's different. I told her we'd let her dad know where she is."

The look deepens. "And I'll tell her I'm taking her back to him."

"But Liberty isn't safe."

"It's now safer than here."

Crossing my arms in front of my chest, I carefully control my breathing. I wait until I feel steady enough to say, "Your uncle won't find out what I've done."

"You don't know that, Leora. You really don't. He has ways of finding out everything."

"But that doesn't mean anybody else is in danger."

"You're wrong about that, too." Sal pauses. "Everybody in your circle's at risk."

I turn from her, trying to hide my fear. My voice catches. "Sal. What am I going to do?"

"I don't know. But I'm not putting Colton at risk while you figure it out."

My body begins to shake with adrenaline. "Do you think I should warn the community?"

"That's up to you," she says.

"They don't believe in killing, even in self-defense."

"So you think they'd kick you out?"

I murmur honestly, "I don't know."

"Well. Bishop Jabil sure wouldn't kick you out if you were his wife."

I look back at her and, despite the darkness, can see a cool calculation on Sal's face that alarms me. Is she suggesting this so I remain safe, or so Moses and I no longer have a chance?

I declare, as a reminder to her and to myself, "I'll only marry for love."

Sal shrugs, lifting a brow. "The risk, in that case, is yours."

"There is a risk either way."

Moses

I climb down from the barn loft and see Jabil's in the stall, cleaning the hooves of his mare. Moving to the horse's back leg, he trails a hand down her shank. The mare lifts the hoof, and he begins cleaning that one as well.

I ask, "You hitching up the horse to take your uncle's casket to the cave?"

He nods. "You slept right through his service."

"Sorry. I could ride with you to the cave now, though, and help you unload it."

"Thanks," he says in a way that makes me unsure if I'd be welcome.

"We found the girl last night," I continue. "Near the cave. The one whose dad I killed."

"I heard. She okay?"

"Yeah, she seemed fine . . . besides being hungry and cold."

"That's a relief." A couple of seconds pass before Jabil continues. "Charlie's not too happy about the girl being brought back. He's already complaining about having another mouth to feed."

"You're kidding me."

He exhales. "I wish."

"Well, you're going to wear yourself right out if keeping Charlie happy's your goal."

"It's not. But he's also done so much for our community." Jabil switches the hoof pick for a currycomb and begins dragging it over the mare's matted coat. "I don't want him to leave. Truth is—" he glances over for the first time since our conversation started—"I'm not any good at leading. I'm only good at supporting those who do."

I wasn't expecting this from him. I especially wasn't expecting him to confide this to *me*. But Jabil probably got as little sleep as I did last night, and the deprivation's loosening his tongue. "Your father and uncle were leaders," I say. "I'm sure it's somewhere in your blood."

Hooking the currycomb on a nail, Jabil picks up a brush. He looks tired as he runs it over the mare's protruding ribs. "How am I supposed to do the hard things—make the hard decisions required of a bishop? I can't even work up the nerve to put down a starving horse, when we're starving too."

"Maybe one of the other deacons will take your uncle's place."

"They resigned. *Nobody* wants to take his place."

"Not sure if I should congratulate you or offer my condolences."

Jabil throws an old saddle pad over the mare's back. Tufts of hair flutter in the morning sun slanting through the barn's open door. "Saw Leora come in here last night," he says. "Was she still with you when Malachi got shot?"

"Yeah." I shift uncomfortably. "But nothing happened."

He mutters, "You're lucky it didn't."

"I respect her, Jabil."

Straightening his back, he turns. "That doesn't sound like respect to me."

"What would *you* have done? Thrown her out?"

The fight leaves him. "I couldn't do that." He sighs. "Like I said: I'm a bad leader. Unable to separate myself enough to do the hard things that need done."

❖

I'm feeling out of sorts. I don't know my place enough around the community to start on a project, and yet I don't want to just sit around all day, doing nothing. Sal comes walking over as if she can sense this. "Hey," she says, "I'm about to ask if I can leave with Colton and Angel."

I move to let her stand near the fire. "Heading back to the metropolis of Liberty?"

She nods and holds her hands over the flames. "I wondered if you'd like to come along."

Her invitation seems off. I say, "You want me to help out with the kids or something?"

"It wouldn't hurt. We could split up once we reach the road."

Sal and I turn when we hear the barn door open. Jabil comes out through it, propping the door with a piece of wood that he wedges into place with his boot. He props the other door as well and motions to someone inside the barn. Myron Beiler drives the sled through the opening. Jabil ties his mare to a hitching post, and the men walk over to Bishop Lowell's former residence. Jabil soon comes back out, carrying one end of his uncle's coffin. Myron Beiler has the other end. The two men carry the coffin over to the sled and load it carefully in the back.

I watch the community members slowly gather around the sled—the women, and even some of the men, making a point to touch the coffin and say their tearful good-byes. Jabil must sense my presence because he pivots toward the fire, but he does not acknowledge me. I return the cold stare. Jabil didn't have the courtesy to tell me my offer of help wasn't wanted; he's just letting me see for myself that Myron is going along to the cave instead.

Sal looks at Jabil too. "Quarantine or not, aren't you ready to get out of here?" she asks.

"Yeah," I reply, not letting myself think of Leora. "I am."

Sal

Moses hasn't said one word since we left the compound. I take that back; he's said three: "I got it," which was his reply when I offered to help him pull the sled because I didn't want him to think I'm a freeloader and regret escorting us down to the highway. I know why he's been quiet. I saw his face when we were leaving, before Jabil and Myron even had the chance to maneuver the bishop's casket through the gates, and I saw Leora's too.

All morning, she'd been on the verge of crying as she stood in the cabin, watching me pack up Colton's clothes and toys she'd somehow scrounged together from whatever threadbare stuff she owned. But then, when Moses pulled that sled out through the gates—Angel holding Colton on her lap, the quilt Leora insisted we take wrapped around them—Leora just crumpled.

There's no other word for it. It's like she was standing there, waving to our strange little group, and the next second, her knees were in the snow. Moses saw this too. He'd turned around to take one more look, but he didn't go to her when she fell. He just about-faced, as if the sight of her hurt him. The skin flushed above his beard, and the blue of his eyes turned to water. He moved forward with the sled, and the gate shut behind us—dividing Leora from Moses the same as they've been divided since they met. Tell me, how am I supposed to compete with star-crossed lovers? The force Jabil used to close those gates showed he felt the same.

Leora

Halfway down the mountain I stand, looking over the ridge. There is such a hollowness in my chest, it's as if the man who walked off two days ago left with a part of me too. I don't know when—or if—Moses is coming back. He didn't even say good-bye, and I try to comfort myself by thinking this is not because I don't mean enough to him, but because I mean too much. Deep down, however, I admit I feel foolish for entertaining this thought. Suddenly, he shows up after months of not seeing him, and the whole time I never knew if he was dead or alive. Then, like an apparition, he is gone—once again out of my life, and once again leaving me with nothing but confusion that causes me to wonder if Sal's manipulative suggestion concerning Jabil is right.

Face chapped with grief, I lift my snowshoes and struggle through the drifts that have shifted during my brief spell in the woods. As I draw close to the community, I can see the dark form of a horse at the wood's edge, outside of the perimeter fence. I walk toward it and can tell, within a few yards, that it is Jabil's mare. Jabil holds the horse loosely by the halter, his forehead bowed low and resting on the mare's neck. I continue toward them, but neither Jabil nor his horse notice me. I see the glint of a knife in his free hand, and my heart aches at the realization of what he's about to do. Jabil brings the knife up to the mare's throat. I cry out, "Jabil, don't!"

Startled, he turns to look at me, his eyes wild with desperation. "I have no choice, Leora," he rasps. "We are starving. We have to find food."

I'm not aware that I am crying again until I taste the salt of my tears. This isn't just the slaughtering of the horse, which belonged to Jabil's father. This is the end of our civilized humanity. Burying our dead in caves and choosing between feeding our own children and feeding the daughter of a stranger: have we forfeited our souls in exchange for survival?

I step closer to Jabil and gently peel his gloved fingers away from the knife's hilt. He turns to me. His eyes close. "I have to," he says again.

"I know," I murmur. "But why don't you get Charlie or one of the other guys to do it?"

"No." His answer is firm. "It wouldn't be right. I must do it myself."

I step back and watch as Jabil places the knife against the underside of the mare's neck. Tears flowing from clenched eyes, he pulls hard across her throat. Blood instantly rushes out of the wound, drenching Jabil's arm. The horse stumbles and then goes down with force. Jabil kneels by her head and caresses her mane. After a few short bursts of movement, she lies still. Jabil's head remains down, and his back shudders as he weeps.

I step slowly forward and rest my hand on his shoulder. "I am sorry. I'm so, so sorry."

He murmurs, "I am a wimp."

"No, Jabil . . . you are human."

❖

I walk behind the sled. Contrasted by snow, my bloodied footsteps fit perfectly inside the bloodied footsteps of the men using their own power to haul the last two hundred pounds of meat to the compound. The gates—flanked by pine resin torches—creak open to admit us. The men strain against the ropes. Shadows shape-shift across the compound facade, as five pairs of booted feet dig for traction. The runners begin to move, and the sled slides though the gates.

Relief of a winter's survival floods each square foot of the compound, as effervescent and heady as ginger mead. The majority of the women stand around the fire near the spring, conversing and staring in wonder at the horse's back straps, which drip fat onto the coals beneath the spit. The children feel this relief as well. Layered in dirty clothes and with uncombed hair, they play tag while darting in and out of the firelight like woodland nymphs. My sister, Anna, is among them, laughing with joy. My spirit rings with the sound.

Esther Martin breaks away from the women and walks down the snowy path. Though thin and pale, her eyes shine with a clarity I haven't seen since before her Claudia's death. "Thank you," she says, pressing a warm stone mug into my hands. "For everything."

I take the mug by the handle and breathe in the bittersweet scent of spruce needle tea. "You're welcome, Esther," I murmur. "I only wish I could've done more."

"We *all* wish that." She looks away before saying, "I've decided—if I'm going to love the ones in front of me well— I have to stop yearning for the ones who are already gone."

Her words scald my throat. I swallow them down hard. "I think you're right," I reply.

Commotion erupts near the fire. Turning, we see Jabil signaling the meat is done. He lowers that hand, and the community—following their leader—grows quiet. He looks over, finding me in the crowd so effortlessly, I sense he's always been aware of my place inside it.

"My dear people," he begins, "thank you for entrusting me with your care. *Gott* has, once again, provided for us, and I pray for his divine guidance as I lead you in the days ahead."

Outside the walls, the wolves begin to howl as they are no doubt drawn in by the scent of the entrails left in the wake of our slaughter. The circle of life has never been so easy to see. I lift my mug to Jabil, and a smile creases the lines around his eyes. For the first time, we are pulling toward something, together. A team.

CHAPTER
10

Moses

MONTHS HAVE PASSED since we've come upon any signs of the rumored Agricultural Resurgence Commission, causing us to wonder if they moved on, disbanded, or weren't much of a group at all. However, when I enter the two-story house—smiling at the ironic *Welcome!* sign greeting me—I see the blinds are pulled down over French doors, fracturing what little light can make it through the gaps. But the dark letters *ARC* are easy to spot on the wall next to the fireplace.

Heart thudding, I look down the porch steps, searching for Nehemiah, who was going to try entering the house through the basement door. I walk—gun in hand—through the foyer, living room, and dining room. A showy parade of ants marches across the carpet in the living space to the tile in the kitchen. What they're finding to eat is a mystery. A spray of bullet holes runs from the ceiling down to the baseboard, the aftermath covering the tile with silt.

I walk around the stainless steel–topped island and view a bony middle-aged man wearing camo shorts and a T-shirt, slumped against the cupboard doors with a tire iron by his open hand. Blood covers the floor around him in a near-perfect circle. I sense he's dead, but I lean down to check for a pulse anyway, resting my hand on the island. The movable island shifts with my weight, and I have to brace the man to keep him from falling.

Alarmed, I notice his body is warm.

A floorboard creaks upstairs. Nehemiah couldn't have finished exploring the basement already. I lower the man to the tile and stand.

Making my way to the bottom of the steps, I listen. The center of the carpet is patterned with dirt. I don't hear anything else, so I slowly begin to move up the staircase. Suddenly, a bullet whizzes past my head, punching a hole in the drywall beside me. The guy didn't really aim, but more or less stuck the gun around the corner and took a shot. I quickly place three shots in the wall where I think he must be, hoping to hit him on the other side. I hear him run across the floor, and I am confident enough he is trying to flee that I quickly leap up the stairs. I reach the top just in time to see him exit out the window in the bedroom farthest down the hall.

"Stop!" I yell, as if he will listen.

I descend the stairs in a few large bounds and nearly wipe out at the base, trying to get to the door in time to see where he runs. But I am halfway across the kitchen when I hear shots ring from outside. I run into the backyard and see the man who shot at me and fled sprawled next to the trampoline. Nehemiah steps out from the basement. His wide face is colorless.

"I heard the shots," he says. "I was getting ready to come in when he ran out."

"You made the right choice," I say. "Looks like he killed a man inside."

I walk into the yard and look at the soldier lying facedown in the grass. Crouching, I search through the pockets of his uniform. Sure enough, he's carrying a wallet with a handwritten ID for the Agricultural Resurgence Commission, just like Seth Ebersole said. I wonder how many of these ARC soldiers are out there, killing and spreading fear in an effort to make the few remaining refugees obey them without a fight, like the man inside attempted. The fact that I entered the house when I did is chilling. A few minutes earlier, and the outcome would've probably been different. Most of all, though, I wonder where the organization camps.

After a while, I walk back over to Nehemiah and offer him the soldier's gun and military-style boots. But Nehemiah shakes his head. "Does it ever get easier?" he asks.

I look at him, this twenty-year-old who would much prefer to be cutting a field on his dad's farm: the back of his neck scalded with sunshine, the callouses of his hands filled with dirt.

"No." I glance down at my feet, knowing I'll heartlessly wear the soldier's shoes if Nehemiah won't accept them. "It never does."

Leora

I never thought I would long for the cold after such a harsh winter, but as I pick my way across the compound, I find myself yearning for the once-frozen pathways the warmth of spring has thawed to mud. The mire sucks at my shoes, making each step as exaggerated as Christian's in *Pilgrim's Progress* when he was trying to manually extract himself from the Slough of Despond. Jabil intercepts me when I've almost reached my cabin. I stop so abruptly to avoid falling into him that the water splashes over the rim of the bucket and dapples the dirty fabric of my dress.

"Morning." He nods. "You'd better get over there. Your *vadder* wants to talk to you."

In shock, I look toward the gate and see my *vadder*: the man representing one half of the broken partnership that—despite its failings—gave me life. I almost do not recognize him. He is clean-shaven, his thin hair cropped short. Though not new, his T-shirt and jeans appear fresh, making me self-conscious of the two cape dresses I've been alternating since August.

Taking a breath, I ask, "When did he come back?"

Jabil shrugs. "Just now, I guess. Charlie came to tell me he was here."

I stare down at the bucket gripped in my hands. The water's trembling surface reflects my pale face. "I—I need to clean up first."

Stepping closer, Jabil takes hold of the bucket's horsehair rope. "I'll take this to your cabin." His thumb traces the top of my hand. "I won't let him hurt you, Leora."

This seems presumptuous, since there are more ways than just one to inflict pain. But when I glance up, the look in Jabil's eyes tells me he would do everything in his power to fulfill that promise. Smiling nervously, I let him take the bucket and turn toward the gate. My *vadder* is already looking my way. His hand lifts in greeting. My nails carve crescents into my palms.

"Leora," he calls as I draw closer. "Good to see you."

I nod at him curtly. "Good to see you too." Surprising as it is, it is not a lie.

"Thanks. I—I'm clean now." He has enough self-respect to stammer over the declaration.

"That's great."

"I am. Really," he insists, sensing my disbelief. "I got better after you and Seth left."

I cross my arms in front of me for reinforcement, as everything from that horrific day comes back. Regardless, tears spill from my eyes. I wipe them away with my fist.

His eyebrows lower. "Everything all right?"

I shake my head, wondering which catastrophe I should break to him first: that I committed murder, or that his mother died. "You should've been with us, *Daed*."

"I know." He looks down. "I'm sorry. I wish I could make it up."

"I don't want you to make *anything* up; I just want you to be here when I need you."

He pauses, absorbing this, and then he looks at me. His countenance appears softer, relaxing the taut angles of his face. "I guess that's better than you not wanting me around."

Instead of replying, I turn toward the gate. Charlie stands

there—legs splayed and eyes narrowed—like he's already regretting letting my *vadder* in.

I turn back to him. "So you're here for a while?"

"If you'll have me."

"We don't have enough room in the cabin. You'll have to sleep in the barn." This isn't true, since *Grossmammi*'s bed is empty, but I haven't the fortitude to share such a tight space.

"That's fine," he says. "I've slept in worse."

"Have you been staying at our old house this whole time?"

"No, just over winter. Then I moved to the fairgrounds when it started warming up. There's a camp there now." He pauses. "I saw your friend Sal. With her baby and little girl."

My *friend*. Friendship doesn't seem the way to quantify our relationship, considering how we parted. "The little girl's not hers." My pulse quickens as I say this, and it's as if the increased blood flow spreads the flush of anxiety up my neck. "Did you hear anything from her uncle?"

"Mike?" My *daed* seems puzzled. "He's there, at the camp, all the time."

I glance back at the gate. Charlie has returned to his post. "Is Mike looking for anybody?"

"I'm not sure what you're getting at."

Wetting my lips, I say, "Is he looking for the person who shot his son?"

Something flickers across the surface of my *vadder*'s careful expression. "Alex?"

Sweat breaks out across my body. "I killed him. I killed him that day Seth and I left you."

❖

The moon, inviting and ripe, glints off the lines of quart jars carefully placed over each plant, and the centipede of hoop houses constructed over the long, single raised bed. Our greenhouses destroyed in the valley fire, Jabil and I had to improvise by bending branches into hoops, and then we covered these hoops with a series of large, thirteen-gallon trash bags someone retrieved from Field to Table before we left.

Small pine resin torches glow inside the houses and will be replaced throughout the night—a ritual as solemn as the changing of the guard. With my face pressed against the plastic, I can see the tiny green shoots pushing through the dirt: each a promise of the harvest season when—for a while, at least—our people will no longer have to live in fear of want.

Side by side, Jabil and I continue walking. My bare feet sink into the earth, padded with moss, and I can feel my weary body releasing the tension coiled in my shoulders and spine. Jabil crouches and holds out his lamp. Silver-pink night crawlers dart like lightning into the soil, recently turned for yet another planting of seeds. Jabil secures a squiggly handful of worms, grabbing them before they can disappear into the ground, and drops them in his tin bucket to be used for his fishing trip in the morning. "Quite the date, isn't it?" he says, laughing.

I do not laugh. For weeks, Jabil and I have been taking these nightly walks after the rest of the community quiets down. It's a time for us to talk about our day and the plan for the coming week. And though we've often seemed as effortlessly conjoined as a long-married couple trying to reconnect after tucking our unruly children in bed, I have never considered any of these walks *dates*. Furthermore, Jabil's never said anything to confirm the shift in our relationship, even if—every now and then—he looks at me like he wants to.

Jabil presently stands, his smile slipping. "Did I say something wrong?"

I shake my head. "Of course not."

His fingertips, feather light, brush against my cheek. "Then what is it?"

"Nothing."

But it's *everything*. I tell my heart to still, my mind to focus on the man standing before me rather than replaying the image of the man I imagined I would spend my life with, who has since abandoned me twice. When Jabil takes my hand, I let him. I even go so far as to lace my fingers through his. His grip tightens gratefully. In his other hand, he carries the bucket of night crawlers, and I imagine the two of us being watched by that brilliant lunar eye.

We walk farther from the compound than we have all spring. Jabil pulls apart pine branches and steps underneath them. "I did this for you," he says and shows me another patch of cleared earth. I glance at it, trying to understand.

And then he kneels, just as he knelt before. Setting down the lamp, he presses his thumb into the soil. Next to the indentation, I can see it: the tiny bud. "I planted wild-flowers," he says. "Judith had a pack. I traded with her."

I kneel, then, beside him in the dirt, not caring that it is scalloping the hem of my freshly laundered dress. I touch the plant. The promise of new life, of beauty and hope awakening. Through the screened moonlight, I look over at Jabil. I see the insecurity, and the vulnerability, as he waits to find out how I will receive his gift.

"Thank you. I'm sure the flowers will be beautiful."

He nods and leans forward, resting the top of his head against mine. "I was going to wait until they were in bloom," he says. "To show you. But we never know, do we? If we have time."

"No," I murmur. "We don't."

Our lips touch. Unlike before, with Moses, there are no crumbling walls, no fire, no shaking or fear. Instead there is peace, tranquility, the coolness of night air brushing the back of my neck. Jabil and I pull away from each other, and then he rises on one knee and pushes off. He reaches down for my hand. "Marry me?"

I look up at him. This proposal is so different: an inversion of every *Englisch* one I have ever heard. But my life is not what it once was. And neither is his. "Yes," I whisper. "I will."

Jabil pulls me to my feet and encases me in his arms so wholly, I could never break free, even if I wanted to. After a moment, he asks, "Should I have talked to your *vadder* first?"

I turn my head against the expanse of his chest. I think of him, my *vadder*, sleeping in the barn loft with Charlie. He is here, with us, and yet I treat him as I would treat any man who is an acquaintance—with deference while always remaining on guard. I laugh a little, albeit sadly at the thought, as I reply, "There's no need."

Jabil nods. Then, hand in hand, he leads me back to the community. The pine torches remain lit: a practice we started after Bishop Lowell's death, when we realized darkness makes us vulnerable. This time, a different vulnerability overtakes me. But Jabil merely escorts me to my door and says good-bye without a kiss. I enter the cabin and lie down in my muddied clothes next to my sister. I stare up at the ceiling, knowing I'm going to be staring at a similar ceiling when I enter the cabin next door as Bishop Snyder's bride. Warm tears roll down my cheekbones, tracing the shape of my face, though I tell myself this is what I want. That there is no need to cry.

Moses

Josh and I stand before the map taped to a wall in his hangar. A grid stripes the northwestern section of Montana, primary-colored pushpins marking the areas the militia has explored. Three weeks have passed since Nehemiah shot the ARC soldier, but we've still not found their camp.

Josh says, "Every time you guys go out, your odds of not coming back grow."

"I know that."

"We've no clue where they are. The ARC could even be out of state. And what do we do when we find them? It's not like we can overthrow them like an army."

"I've thought of that as well."

Swearing softly, Josh bends the bill of his ball cap in his hands. "This whole thing's so beyond me, it's ridiculous. I mean, was the ARC orchestrated by a terrorist group? Was it orchestrated by our government to—to try to reestablish what we lost after the grid shut down?"

I pick a handful of tacks out of the coffee cup on the stained concrete floor and push them into the areas I want to fly over once the Cessna's finished: Missoula, Helena, Butte. Then to the north, Glacier National Park. Finding the camp's like finding a needle in a haystack, but an aerial view's sure better than trying to find it on foot. I look over at Josh. "This wacky conspiracy theorist from the community told me that detention camps were getting built way back, and that there were dark forces in our own government, preparing for a day like this."

Sighing heavily, Josh says, "Maybe it's not just a theory." He puts on his cap and walks past the Cessna to stare out through the hangar's open door. "I lost friends for the sake of freedom," he says. "Not to mention my own family." His voice breaks. "What was it all for?"

I come over and stand beside him. "Don't lose faith. Nothing is wasted."

He looks at me. "You might think differently when you're as old and grouchy as me."

"What about when you saved the lives of the airport staff? Don't you know that wasn't wasted, even if it didn't turn out the way you planned? Or when you waited here, for months, hoping your ex-wife would come back? Or when you let all of us stranded guys hole up here?" We're not the touchy-feely type, but Josh seems so despondent, I put my arm around his shoulders. "You're a good man. The world, broken as it is, needs people like you."

He lowers his head, the ball cap shielding his face. I stand in support beside him—not expecting either of us to say anything else—when he breaks the silence. "The same goes for you, Moses." He pauses. "Don't try to forget Leora because you think she deserves a better man."

I ask Josh, "Sure you're not just trying to get rid of me?"

"If I wanted to get rid of you," he says, "I would've already done it."

He punctuates his sentence with a grin and takes another forkful of eggs. The two of us are sitting in front of the computers at the traffic control center's desk, squinting against the glare of sunlight flashing through the bank of windows. We're eating breakfast, the same as we've eaten breakfast together every morning that we haven't just completed a night shift and, instead of eating, are more interested in sleeping off our exhaustion on airport cots two floors below.

But this morning's different. The Cessna is finished. Or as finished as it can be, considering the limited tools and education Josh has had to work with—little details I am choosing to forget at the moment.

I continue, "You don't want to take it somewhere first?"

"I *did* take it somewhere."

"Yeah. A five-minute loop."

"What?" he asks. "Don't you trust my mechanic skills?"

"You're not a mechanic."

"And *you're* not a pilot. Your point is?"

"My point is: this sounds like a recipe for disaster."

Josh takes another sip of his infamous acorn coffee and winces like it's all he can do not to spit it out. I ask, "Why do you put yourself through that?"

"If you don't give your body a treat once in a while, it starves itself."

"Seeing your face every time you take a sip of that stuff would hardly lead me to call it a treat. You will end up poisoning your body before it can starve."

He nods, knocking the brew back. "That's exactly why this trip appeals to you, isn't it?"

"What? You think I'm going off in search of real coffee?"

"No, a recipe for disaster is just what you like."

Looking down at the desk, I pick at the burnt edge where a hot kettle melted the Formica. But I still can't hide my grin. "Guess you could say it's in my blood."

After breakfast, Josh and I walk out to the hangar. Our shadows stretch tall, bisected between tarmac and grass.

I see two of our men patrolling the perimeter—the distance turning them to specks. We tug apart the hangar doors and stride across the cement flooring. Opening the door to the plane, I toss my backpack up onto the seat, and it's like a glitch in the matrix: a déjà vu of when I tossed that backpack up onto the seat the day I stole Grandpa Richard's crop duster.

Josh says, "You've got twenty-two and a half gallons of usable fuel, which should be plenty to get you to Anaconda and back. But you don't want to give the plane too much throttle, or you'll burn it—"

"Josh," I say. "I know. We've been over this. It's all right."

"And don't fly too low, or anyone with a rifle will be trying to shoot you down." He adds, as an afterthought, "Don't be stupid, Moses. I don't want to have gone through all this work just to have you crashing this plane on your first trip."

I punch him lightly on the arm. "I'll bring it back in one piece."

"Bring yourself back in one piece too."

I look over at Josh and then climb up into the plane to give us some privacy to blink the water from our eyes. I study the coordinates we've mapped out and the Cessna's configuration of switches and gauges, trying to remember what Grandpa taught me and Aaron all those summers ago, when Grandma was so busy canning, she didn't know what was taking place in the barn.

I flip the ignition switch—the propeller flinging dust as I set the propeller control—and watch the orange tachometer arrow climb. I yell over the noise, "I'll bring 'er back!"

"You'd better," he says, shutting the door. "I'll have your hide if you don't!"

In lieu of a wave, Josh salutes me as I taxi out of the hangar. A stubborn lump in my throat, I salute back and shift my focus to the runway's grid of expansion joints outlined with weeds. I glance down, checking to make sure the oil pressure and oil temperature are right, and that there's a proper correlation between the intake manifold and the torque the engine's developing. Once I reach the runway threshold, I advance the throttle to full, pull back slowly on the yoke, and feel that unmistakable dip in my stomach as the plane lifts and the earth falls away.

I head south from the airport in Kalispell. I will fly over Polson, Superior, Missoula, Philipsburg, and Anaconda, searching each city for any sign of the Agricultural Resurgence Commission's camp. Within five minutes, I fly over the mountain range where Leora and the rest of the community live, and it astounds me that they are so close when the distance between us feels like the other side of the nation. I bring the plane down and can see the cabins. From this vantage point, they are nothing but Monopoly houses circled by a wall that looks as inhibiting as toothpicks. I glimpse a woman standing beyond this wall, working alone in the garden. She rises from the dirt when she hears the noise, a hand to her brow as if to more clearly see the plane.

Not until I pass over Superior have I convinced myself to keep the plane heading south instead of turning around to see if that was Leora, the woman who, despite Josh's suggestion, I am determined to forget. I fix my gaze on the horizon and on the sheets of stratocumulus drifting across the plane, as I descend at five hundred feet per minute. The "sardine can"—as Josh deemed the Cessna—rattles and bobs with the turbulence. My eardrums ache with the pressure. Sweat gathers on my back. I'm so concentrated on flying, all other focus drifts.

Seconds or eons pass before I'm ready to bring my airspeed down again. As the clouds part and clear, the bird's-eye view becomes a startling reality. Buildings and houses are obliterated to rubble. Cars are blackened by fire, the glass windows and windshields busted out. Telephone poles are broken or chopped down, causing the electrical lines strung between them to drag across the grass. In Missoula, an entire block is decimated. An apartment's facade is missing, exposing the rebar reinforcing the concrete structure and the plumbing and ductwork. I hope no one was living inside the apartment when the bomb went off.

More than anything, though, I notice the mysterious lack of people. A few traces of smoke are visible amid the miles of ruins, but not the ones who set the fires to blaze. There is no sign of reconstruction, no sign of life resuming its ordinary American pace. There is only desolation to remind me that the world is not the same as before, and maybe never will be again.

CHAPTER

11

Leora

THE RAINS HAVE BEEN STEADY all spring, encouraging the morels to sprout through the sandy soil, giving them opportunity for growth. I spot a large one sprouting beneath a pine, stop and crouch, plucking the strange, spongelike entity from the moss. A few smaller ones are growing around it, and I begin to gather those as well. Jabil kneels but does not gather, and I sense he is focused on me and not on our task. "You are so beautiful," he says.

I smile. "We're supposed to be working."

"We can work anytime." He leans closer to brush a loose eyelash from my cheek.

"Isn't it going to seem suspicious when we return to the community with so few morels?"

"We'll just say we couldn't find any."

I laugh but the sound stalls in my throat. "A bishop who lies."

"It's not a lie," he insists, putting an arm around me, "if we're not looking."

Rocking back on my heels, I rise with the basket, and Jabil's arm falls away. I glance at the sun pouring, warm, through the grove of pines. All day, I have been unsettled, and I know Jabil—despite his compliments and affection—senses this. For weeks, I have been able to put my childish dreams aside, concerning what one in love should resemble and feel, and have been able to focus on Jabil, whom I can easily think of as my fiancé but am still unable to contemplate as my husband. But then, this morning, when I was out tending the garden, a plane flew overhead. It was a small red plane—so different from the one that crashed in our field—and yet the image of it caused me to miss Moses with a physical ache that made me realize some hope, buried deep within, is refusing to die. Why? I wonder. Why can't I give up? Why can't I *grow* up and wholeheartedly embrace this man?

I turn and look at him now, his dark eyes shining with worry. "Jabil Snyder," I say, "thank you for loving me, even when sometimes I'm undeserving."

My fiancé stands and puts his arms around me, drawing me back. "You are *always* deserving," he says. "And I look forward to the day when you know it . . . here."

His fingertip touches the front of my cape dress. My heart pounds as his breathing changes. He turns my face toward him, one hand supporting my throat, and seals his mouth over mine. His urgency makes the kiss different from before, and for the first time, I can imagine the transition from fiancé to husband, and the magic available through that change. The basket falls from my hands, the hard-won morels tumbling across the earth. But neither of us cares.

Moses

A good tailwind propels me back toward Kalispell, making the miles pass far more quickly than on my way here, when I had to fight the headwind buffeting against the plane. But though it's easier to fly, I'm still fighting my return. I dread Josh's disappointment when I have to tell him about the trip. So I decide to make a detour to at least delay the inevitable. Using basic math, I divide the distance by the gallons of fuel I have left. A cushion of thirty minutes allows me to make it to Bonners Ferry and back. I know it would be more useful to check out the area around Glacier National Park instead of saving that for another day, but somehow I am compelled to turn west instead. I admit, within a few miles, that I have subconsciously been planning this detour from the time I climbed into the plane.

In less than an hour, I am circling over Bonners Ferry, and I'm shocked at how different it looks, though I'm not sure if it's different or simply recollected through the soft focus of hindsight. Spring growth covers the majority of the desolation. This time, I do spot a few people camping in the woods, the smoke from their bonfire rising in a column. I bring the plane down low, and they glance up as if it's a giant bird of prey—part wonder, double parts fear. I wave out the window, and they pause before waving back. If they know I come in peace, maybe they won't want to shoot my plane down, if they somehow have ammunition.

The creek wends through the bottomland, and the green

of the grass is intensified by the contrast of sky. A bald eagle pair perches in a decaying tree to my left. It amazes me to see how humanity seems to be the only thing harmed by the EMP. If anything, nature is thriving and taking its territory back. I pass the Best Western restaurant and casino, where my grandpa and I used to stop in the summers after Grandma died and we got tired of looking at each other, not to mention tired of eating our own cooking. The building's structure looks remarkably untouched, but the first floor windows and glass panels above the indoor pool have been shattered, revealing the pool's painted-blue tiles dirtied with leaves.

Turning downwind, I slow the plane to eighty-five knots and power the engine down to around two thousand rpms. I see my grandpa's farm up ahead—the once-comb-straight rows now a tangle of yellow star thistle and oxeye daisy, the latter straining their faces toward the sun.

I flip the carburetor heat on and power back to fifteen hundred rpms. I hold the nose level until the airspeed drops, and then I extend ten degrees of flaps. Every spare thought is pared away as I coordinate my turn with the rudder pedals. One miscalculation could send me into a spin. Flying low, toward the yard, I spot the model 1940s Spitfire airplane attached to the top of the thick wooden post serving as the mailbox's backbone. I can remember Grandpa Richard spinning the propeller of that glorified toy whenever he'd walk down the lane to fetch the *Bonners Ferry Herald* and bills. I understand that, more than likely, I will never watch him do such a civilian task again. What I have learned is this: some things you expect to be destroyed aren't, and some things you expect to survive never do.

Once the threshold of the lawn is forty-five degrees behind me, I apply another ten degrees of flaps. This brings my airspeed down even more. Beside the barn, on my left, is the Quonset hut where the crop duster used to be stored, along with a mishmash of farming tools Grandma didn't want to see from her kitchen. The brick rancher, flanked with white pillars and shutters, appears in person the same as it does in my mind's eye. Pinning down the front porch are the massive ceramic planters, which Grandma had me and Aaron place because, she claimed, our backs were young. I almost expect her curtains—something flowered and blue—to be flapping in the breeze. Their pattern was similar to the apron she always wore and used for everything from shielding me from Grandpa—when he'd come after me with a switch for something like sneaking his Red Man tobacco—to wiping dirt from my face when Aaron and I came in from playing horse.

Past and present, childhood and adulthood, converge as I use pitch to maintain my approach speed and the rudder pedals to keep the plane aligned with the makeshift, overgrown runway. This time, unlike when I crash-landed in Leora's field, everything goes smoothly. A few feet off the ground, I ease off the yoke until I reach taxi speed and turn the plane in the front yard, mashing the long grass beneath the tires, leaving behind an indentation, like a crop circle.

And then, just like that, I'm here at the refuge I felt I had to escape, rather than facing my fears like a man and sorting them out. I hop down from the plane and listen to the wind sweeping across the Idahoan prairie. The sound is a relief after the plane engine's incessant whine. A jackrabbit, with ears longer than old-school antennas, bounds away as I cut through the grass of the yard, my arms lifted out like I'm wading through water. Though I should be thinking about what I'm going to eat tonight, for once survival's not the first thing on my mind.

I approach the house and see the manual door is lifted on the double garage, an addition my grandpa built after he and Grandma reached the age where falling on ice became a hazard. My heart jumps around in my chest as I enter and see my grandpa's old pickup truck—the undercarriage eaten with rust from those years it sat outside—next to my grandma's sedan. Both of these vehicles, which I once rode in without thinking, are relics from another age.

I walk up the cement steps and open the door, calling my grandfather's name. No response. I step onto the linoleum in the kitchen and feel weird wearing my shoes when Grandma spent years harping at me and Aaron (and sometimes even her husband) to take them off. I almost expect to see one of her crocheted washrags spread out to dry on the rim of the soapstone sink, and my grandmother's blue bird figurines perched on the window ledge, catching the midmorning light and covering the eggshell wall in a maritime tinge. Of course, all of this is gone. Not from looters having desecrated the home, like you'd think, but because—the week after her funeral—my grandpa removed everything but her pictures, while the rest of the family was holed up at the Best Western, unsure if our reclusive patriarch needed us to go or stay.

He soon made it obvious, in his passive-aggressive manner, that he preferred us to go. He gave us boxes of mementos to take back with us: yarn picture frames in Christmas colors, encasing younger versions of ourselves; a somewhat cheesy depiction of a farm scene that my grandmother had tried to paint from a calendar print; sensible women's shoes, scarves, and dresses with padded shoulders and round brass buttons that could've doubled as kitchen knobs. What he thought his special ops grandsons could've done with such items, I don't know.

My father, though far from sentimental, was furious that my grandpa didn't keep these things. But Grandpa Richard didn't get rid of everything because he felt it was time to move on. The fact was, though he and his wife picked on each other for all the ways they were different, he could barely live without her, and so he couldn't stand to live with the physical, daily reminders that everything she'd touched was still with him but she, herself, was gone.

I continue across the kitchen. A coating of dust, as thick as scattered flour, covers every surface. I refuse to let myself understand what this lack of disturbance means and call my grandfather's name again, almost in defiance. A gingham place mat and a ghostly white ring mark the spot where my grandfather used to sit at the kitchen table. A pile of

Bonners Ferry Herald papers is to the right, and I remember how he was holding one of those as he came out onto the front porch, hitching up the strap of his bib overalls, and saw me circling above the farm in his stolen crop duster. He waved the paper at me; I remember that. Like he was both chiding me for taking the plane without permission and saying good-bye.

After a few more steps toward the hallway, I am suddenly hit with my worst fear. My eyes fill as I bring my sleeve up to my nose to lessen the stench. My stomach tightens. I force myself to leave the situation by going back to those carefree days, fifteen years ago, when my grandparents would take us out of our parents' hair.

Back then, Richard and Mary Edna Hughes were in their late sixties—feeling good and getting around fine. The house, in the summers, smelled of baking zucchini bread and my grandfather's boot polish, overlaid with that rich earth that always clung to the heels.

I slowly make my way along the hall, punctuated with pictures, whose careful documentation stopped after my grandma died, and my grandpa didn't have the heart to update or touch. I pass the bathroom. I can tell from the increasing odor that the body is in the bedroom, one door over. I am torn between just turning away—holding on to memories of him alive, working in the fields—and going farther. I decide I have to know what happened. I take off my button-up shirt and tie it around my nose and mouth like a bandanna before entering the room.

Grandpa's body is in bed, as I guessed it would be, tucked under blankets. One of them I recognize as the ancient ragbag quilt Grandma didn't care if we destroyed, so she let me and Aaron haul it out to our tent that we'd set up in the front yard because we—much to our grandfather's chagrin—wanted to play Army. I walk closer and touch the quilt's frayed edge, wondering if Grandpa recognized it as well when he climbed beneath. I hope he did. I hope it called to mind happier times, when life wasn't reduced to how many pieces of wood you can cut for warmth or how many pounds of potatoes you can dig before your strength gives out. Did he know it was the end when he died? Or did he simply . . . fall asleep in one world and wake up in the next? Most likely he knew, but I will hold on to the hope that he did not.

His white hair and the tip of his hand are the only portions visible. My chest shudders with sobs at the sight. I instinctively reach out, wanting to pull the blanket back, as if doing so could bring back the grandpa I knew, who was like another father to me. Or more like a father than the one I had. But I stop myself, just in time. I surmise from his state and from the state of the house that he must have died early in winter. The brutal Idaho cold kept him mostly frozen until spring's warmth came, allowing his body to start the process of returning to the earth.

The cause of death torments my mind as I stand here, bitter tears stinging my eyes. Did he die shortly after the EMP, or did he languish through some of the winter? I so wish I could believe he died of natural causes, that he didn't freeze or starve, though common sense tells me otherwise. I should have come for him sooner, even if I would have died in the process of trying to reach him. I should have figured out a way. Beside him, lying on top of the covers, are two framed pictures. The left is of my grandparents on their wedding day, before he was shipped out. The right is a more recent photo, probably taken at Good Shepherd for the church directory. I love that it's recent, because I can see my grandma's rinsed white hair, permanently waved, and her large square glasses with the tint that she said helped protect her blue eyes from the sun. I see my grandpa. His hand cups my grandma's padded shoulder, like they were newlyweds, rather than having lived through so much trial and joy. Leaning across the body, I pick up the left frame and turn it over.

I push up the tiny plastic arms to pull out the back. I remove the cardboard, and the other pictures fall into my hand: a chronology of the life he spent with my grandmother. There they are with me and Aaron, the summer after high school graduation, when we decided to come up and help with the harvest. There they are on their golden anniversary, dressed to the nines while holding flutes of champagne, even though my grandpa hated the taste. My eyes burn when I see the picture of my family—my mom and dad and brother—and I remember so clearly the night it was taken. How I wouldn't even smile because I'd rather be playing paintball with my friends.

There are a few other pictures, some stuck together by heat and time, and then I come upon the one I was looking for. In it, my grandfather is standing, his 1963 USMC sateen shirt billowing in the wind, his hair—later inherited by Aaron—so thick and oiled that the darkness of its hue hasn't faded in the picture, though the picture itself has. My grandmother, his wartime bride, appears soft and inviting, and I recall how she was always eager to bandage my wounds even if she'd also swat me out of her kitchen.

Like so many others during that time, they'd come together because that unity made them feel they wouldn't break apart. Surely my grandfather must've worried he wouldn't make it back to her—who, unbeknownst to him, was already carrying his child, my father. And though, when he *did* come back, he wasn't the same man who left, judging by these pictures gathered in my hands—and judging by the way I would sometimes catch them looking at each other or holding hands on the center console while they drove to church—I know that their love ran deep.

Fifty-some years later, my grandfather, when he died, was holding neither his medals of valor—though he had many—nor the roster of the men he'd saved. No, he was reaching for the picture of his bride, and of the family they'd created when the entire world felt a hopeless case.

I kneel then, in that bedroom they shared, decaying in every way imaginable, and see what my grandpa must've seen, all those years back. Everything in this life fades to dust except for the love we give while we live it. I came back here to rescue my grandfather—or at the very least, to say good-bye—but instead, even though he is gone, I feel that he is somehow rescuing *me*. His death is teaching me I cannot keep withholding my heart from someone simply because I want to keep her from experiencing pain. Yes, if I pursue Leora, she will no doubt experience more pain than if she were alone, or with Jabil. But the joy of companionship—of daily love—far exceeds the pain. I slowly go back through the stack of pictures once again.

My grandfather lived a worthy life—a life that started out as conflicted between duty and desire as my own remains. But in the end, obviously in the end, he realized that his family was his anchor to this earth. Yes, some of that understanding took place because he experienced such heartache—witnessing the devastation and the bloodshed of war. There is also no doubt he would have fallen into ruin if it weren't for my grandmother and my father, waiting for him back home, eager to help him reclaim his place in life. But they *were* there, for him.

Despite the ways he failed my father—the way he withdrew himself sometimes, when the memories overpowered the present—and therefore my own father failed *me*, I do not have to fail my own son or my daughter or my wife. I know that, at the end of this temporal journey, all we have are these snapshots of moments. One day, we will yearn to relive each as we lie in our beds—or in the grass or in a patch of woods somewhere, just trying to survive—and if

I know that, if I understand that, I will yearn to make each moment count.

Once I bury my grandfather in the backyard—beneath the curly willow, where he used to place peelings of apple and orange to draw in the orange-chested Baltimore orioles and simply sit there in the grass, his hands on his knees, to savor the beauty of watching them eat—I am going to make my moments count by flying this Cessna back to Kalispell. There, I will tell Josh I have to leave the militia and our mission to locate the ARC. And then I'm going to hike up to that community and take Leora Ebersole in my arms, telling her that I have loved her from the beginning of the end. And this time, I am not going to crash-land into her life just to leave it.

❖

A group of people emerges from the traffic control center when I fly toward the airport. I panic, at first, fearing the airport's been overrun in the past two days. And then I look closer—my eyes squinted in confusion and disbelief—and see that the people are not adults, but children. *Children* are sprinting across the grass in between the center and the runway. They stop when they reach the tarmac and wave, both arms extended as if embracing the hot afternoon sky. I touch down and taxi, bringing the Cessna to a halt. I shut off the engine and gaze out the window.

The children have stopped waving. Instead, they stand in a disorganized line, staring at the body of the plane as if they anticipate another life form, an alien, to step out. Jumping down, I stride across the tarmac toward them. They don't scatter like I expect, but wait. They are dirty, these children, but not with the kind of dirt Aaron and I were always covered with when we were kids. This is the kind of layered grime that's hard to wash off, that's been accumulating daily for months. Their hair is also uncombed and uncut, their clothing nothing but a hodgepodge of rags barely covering their skin, making me relieved the temp's warmed up. What did they do before?

I smile uneasily. "Josh know you're here?" I ask. None of them answers me.

Then I hear his voice. "Welcome back, comrade."

I turn to see Josh striding out of the hangar. The children turn to look as well. Their wide eyes follow him, but their bodies remain still, as if they're accustomed to bracing themselves for anything. I walk across the tarmac. "What's this?" I whisper. "A reboot of *Lord of the Flies*?"

Josh nudges his head to the side. "Let's talk over there."

We move into the hangar, my eyes smarting as they struggle to adjust to the dimness. I say, "You need some skylights."

"Get right on that," Josh quips and then turns toward me. "So . . . how'd the plane run?"

"Like a top." I pause. "But there was no sign of the ARC."

"Too bad. Guess we'll just have to take 'er up again."

I decide, sensing his pensiveness, not to bring up the fact that I won't be taking her up again. Instead, I look out at the kids. The tallest boy—no more than twelve or thirteen, and thin as a stick—has picked up one of the smaller girls, wearing a pair of wraparound pink glasses and her brown hair cropped short. Josh says, "That's Emmanuel. Holding Elizabeth, his little sister."

"But where'd they all come from?"

"They walked. Emmanuel led them here, from town."

"What town?"

Josh shrugs. "They don't tell me much. It was hard enough, just getting their names."

"Where are their parents?"

Another shrug. "Who knows? Maybe they don't have any. Or maybe their parents thought the family would stand a better chance, splitting up."

"Or maybe the parents starved, keeping them alive."

"True," Josh says. "We might be seeing more of this."

"I already have." I tell Josh about the little girl, Angel, we found outside the cave, and her dad I killed, who was only breaking into the community because he was desperate for food.

He shakes his head. "Sometimes I think about buffets, ya know? 'All you can eat.' It disgusted me, whenever I'd go there, and see all the food left on people's plates."

I say, "Imagine if we had it now."

We watch the children for a moment: ten of them, and they are as quiet as mice. I wonder what—or who—they've been hiding from so that even their playtime's altered.

"Any siblings besides Emmanuel and his sister?" I ask.

"Three other sets." Josh points out two little boys,

sticking grass down each other's shirts. "Maybe four. Hard to tell. They all begin looking alike after a while."

"They need baths."

Josh snorts, picking at his grizzled beard. "And haircuts. They have lice."

I pause. "Are you going to let them stay?"

"We're a militia, not a day care. Brian and Dean have already reminded me of that, telling me the kids have to leave. I know they do." He sighs. "It's not even safe, having them around. But then, I think that my grandkids could be over there in Washington State, completely orphaned, and I hope that if that's the case, then somebody will take them in."

"Like . . . if you're doing right by these, someone will do right by yours over there?"

"Yeah." He swats the air. "Karma or something."

"There's nothing wrong with that."

"I know," Josh says again. "But it's like I've been so focused on our militia, on survival, that I've forgotten what it's like to be kind."

❖

Someone is pushing against my back. I lift my head and see Josh. He bends down and sets a steaming cup beside me. I groan. "That does *not* smell like coffee."

"It does the trick."

I sit up, massaging my face, numb and ridged with the pattern in the carpet. Marco, the little boy with the overactive bladder, is catching Zs on my cot. I don't even want to *think* about that. I take a sip of Josh's "coffee" and croon a remake of the old Folgers jingle: "The best part of waking up is acorns in your cup."

"Ha, ha," he says.

"Hey. I'm not complaining."

"Could've fooled me."

I take another sip and find the acorn coffee tastes better once I get over the shock of ingesting something that doesn't match the hot, black liquid I see. Still, the concoction can't replace caffeine's boosting effects, and today, I'm really going to miss them.

Josh and I spent the majority of last night trying to catch a few minutes of shut-eye in between shifts. Marco was one of three kids who wet the bed. Five had night terrors, which is no wonder, considering what they've been through.

Josh, meanwhile, sat at the air traffic control center's desk with Elizabeth, Emmanuel's little sister, who was too frightened to go back to sleep. He held her against his chest, his stocking feet resting between two of the computers, and told her stories about his childhood as the son of an oil engineer. Josh never lived in one place for long, and before being sent to a military academy, he got to explore all the world's major sights: the Great Wall of China, Leaning Tower of Pisa, Eiffel Tower, the Incan temples of Peru. He described each in detail, using more hand motions than a pantomime. I listened to him drone on and on until the little girl's head bobbed forward, the short sides of her dirty-brown hair brushing her face.

Josh didn't move from the chair after she fell asleep. He just stayed like that for a long time, staring out at the stars suspended above the runway strip, and I wondered if he was again worrying about his own grandchildren and hoping that, just as he was comforting Elizabeth, someone might be kind enough to comfort them.

Josh says, interrupting my sleep-deprived daze, "Where can we take the kids?"

Standing up, I glance east through the center's windows, the rising sun like an orange tack, pinpointing the direction where Mt. Hebron Community would be. The Lost Children, as I've begun to think of the kids, fell asleep once it got light—switching from restlessness to REM so abruptly, it was like someone had flipped a switch. This made me realize the reason they'd had such a hard time going to sleep was because they'd been sleeping during the day and traveling at night. Emmanuel must've deduced that the roads and woods would be safer to travel, concealed by darkness. How he fed and protected so many children boggles my mind. I am overwhelmed, and they've only been part of my responsibility for less than a day. "I don't know," I murmur in reply to Josh. "Can't take them to the community. They're barely able to take care of themselves."

"There's nowhere else?"

"Not really. Unless Sal has some connections."

"Who's he?"

"She," I correct him. "Sal's a friend. She took Angel with her down to some camp."

"You know where it is?"

"No. But I could find out, and then bring the kids back if it looks promising."

Josh sighs, glancing over at Elizabeth, who is sleeping on his cot while still wearing her wraparound glasses. Like me, he slept on the floor. "That little girl, right there," he says. "She just wrecks me, Moses." He sniffs and turns away. "I want us to do right by her. And them."

I smile at him, a cutthroat federal air marshal with a heart of gold. "We will," I promise. "We have no other choice."

CHAPTER

12

Moses

THE CAMP'S LOCATED inside the old fairgrounds. The rusted, curlicue entrance gates are reinforced with new barbed wire and beefy-looking guys, toting attitudes as overblown as their guns. They pat me down more thoroughly than post-9/11 TSA, removing my pistol from my holster, my knife from my boot, and then making me remove my boots themselves.

"Can I keep my pants?" I ask as I hand over the boots. They don't crack a smile, so I try a more straightforward approach. "What are you guys going to do with them?"

Thing One tags my boots and lines them up on a crude shoe rack outside the gates, like I'm about to enter a grown-up playground.

Thing Two hands me the tab. "Nothing. It's in case you want to do something and run."

"But I can leave, right?" I ask.

Thing One nods. "Just don't lose your tab."

"Or . . . I might what? Get high heels?"

Thing One's face stays the same, but I see the skin pleat around his eyes. Just a little. But Thing Two is all business. He holds up a piece of paper, sketched with the face of a young man. *MISSING*, it reads, along with the name *Alex Ramirez*. "Have you seen this guy?" he asks.

"Nope," I say, hoping this isn't the ARC soldier Leora killed.

❖

Bracketing either side of the driveway, the fairground's grass portion is fastened down with tents formed from branches and different-patterned blankets and tarps. I imagine, if viewed from above, the campsite would appear like a patchwork bordered with green. The families watch me from their campsites, dispersed with no pattern or plan. They are circled around small fires and bring spoons up to their mouths with such speed, it's like they're expecting someone to steal the utensils along with the food. I nod at them. They don't nod back, but continue watching me with wary, territorial eyes. The whitewashed buildings to my left and right—where it looks like auctions and fund-raisers were once held—are filled with men.

Some warning bell starts dinging inside my chest. I turn around to look at the gate and see it's been closed behind me. One of the guys strides to the sliding door of the FFA/4-H building and leans against it, smoking a handmade cigarette while scoping out the premises.

"Need something?" he asks.

"Yeah." Pebbles from the lane prick the soles of my bare feet as I walk closer. "I'm looking for someone. Her name's Sal. She's the niece of Mike Ramirez. The, um—" I'm at a loss as to how I should describe his shady business dealings—"boss man."

He nods and gestures loosely down the lane. "She's over there," he says. "Working."

My face remains blank, but inside I'm wondering what kind of work she could be doing, surrounded by all these characters. I'm relieved when I approach the cleared area and see her running some sort of outdoor café. This is where I imagine the farmers' market used to be: the vendors gathered round like brightly dressed gypsies, displaying—from the backs of earth-friendly vehicles or under kiosks that protected the items from the sun—goat soap, bird feeders, unpasteurized cider, organic baked goods, and coolers of grass-fed beef and MSG-free jerky.

Picnic tables are now set up, and Sal's grilling cuts of red meat over an open fire—her dark hair bound by a white kerchief bearing the same checked pattern as the material tied around her waist. Colton is nearby, raking dirt into a mound with a fork. His features have sharpened. A lot of his baby fat has been chiseled away, either because he's walking—and also probably running—or because he's not getting enough to eat. But at least he's with his mother.

"Sal!" I call.

She looks up, her brows stitched together, pulling her face into a frown. But her default expression doesn't change when she sees me. She just sets down the tongs she's using to turn the meat and wipes grease on her apron, the gesture adding more streaks to the palette of stains.

She walks closer and nods. "Moses."

"Hey." I smile.

She turns to the side, chafing a hand on the back of her neck. "What are you doing here?"

"I came to see if you're settled." I pause when I see her look. "What's wrong with that?"

"Nothing," she says. "I just don't think that's why you're here."

"I *have* been wondering about you, Sal. I hated that you wouldn't let me bring you and the kids into Liberty." I pause, wondering how to begin. "But, uh, you got room for more?"

"More kids?" She laughs when I nod. "You think I'm, like, a patron saint of orphans?"

I grin, folding my arms. "Well, aren't you?"

Her eyes widen. "Um, no."

I say, "You took Angel in."

"That's different. The community didn't want her around. I know a little of how that feels." Sal glances over her shoulder, and for the first time, I notice the girl from the cave, washing clothes against a piece of corrugated metal framed with wood. "Angel told me her dad was hiding in the woods 'cause some guy wanted to take her as payment for a debt."

I grimace. "Who?"

Shrugging, Sal rolls her eyes. "I know nothing for sure, obviously, since her dad's dead, and Uncle Mike's not about to tell me a thing. But I think it might've been him." She glances around again, and I see her squinting toward the buildings, as if scanning for a face. "That's why no more kids can come here. I feel it's all I can do to keep Angel safe."

I gesture to the steaks, sizzling on the grill, and to the

men waiting inside the buildings, like they're eager to get up to nothing good. "He involved in this too?"

"Yeah," she says, clearly annoyed. "His men bring food; I distribute it to the people staying here, and to the ones staying at the warehouse, and the kids and I get to eat what's left."

"Where does he get it?"

"Who knows? It comes like that." She gestures to the sacks leaning against an outbuilding. "The families get rice and beans. The meat is for the gang."

I walk over and see the fifty-pound sacks are stamped with the letters *ARC*. My stomach turns as this riddle starts falling into place, as seamlessly aligned as Tetris pieces. "Sal," I murmur, returning to her side. "You and these families have *got* to get out of here. ARC stands for the Agricultural Resurgence Commission. They're an organization of some kind who have sent soldiers out to pillage the countryside and force refugees into work camps."

"Look around you," she says. "Nobody's being forced to stay. And I sure don't mind working if the kids and I get shelter and food. Besides—" Sal looks at the ground between her feet, bare the same as mine, making it difficult for her to run—"where are we going to go if we don't stay here?"

Leora

I'm beating rugs—the weight drooping the clothesline—when a gradual expansion of sound sweeps toward me from the gate. Holding the broom, I turn, squint through the spiraling dust, and see Moses walking into our compound. Dirty children are following behind him in two straggled rows. Another, older, man draws up the rear. A shotgun is cocked loosely over his arm, so I'm unable to tell if these children are in the midst of being protected or imprisoned.

I meet Moses's eyes through the settling haze. He holds up his hand in a greeting or a signal that he will soon explain. But *I* am the one who must explain. To distract myself, I look away from him toward the newcomers. The children have clustered together and are peering around with trepidation, like they'd much prefer to be outside the gates. Jabil steps down from the watchtower. I know my fiancé well enough to notice the unease ironing the narrow line of his mouth. He stares at the children and then at Moses, as if trying—and surely failing, as I have done—to understand why they are here.

Jabil signals to Moses, and the two men walk down the path toward me. The white-haired man, meanwhile, sets down his gun and opens a canvas sack I didn't notice him carrying. He loosens the drawstring and takes out two chickens—Ameraucanas, judging by their falconlike heads and the rooster's showy, calico plumage. Anna leaves our pitiful yard and picks up the hen before it has the chance to squawk. Her rag baby is sprawled on its back by my feet.

Wanting to neutralize any potential altercation, I lean my horsehair broom against the exterior of the cabin and look at the men as our three paths intersect. "May I join you?" I ask.

Jabil glances at me, his insecurity apparent. Moses smiles and says, "Sure."

The men separate, opening a space for me between them, and we walk down the narrow pathway toward the outskirts of the compound. "Where are the children from?" I ask.

Moses glances over. "No clue. Josh said they just showed up at the airport in Kalispell."

"Are they orphans?"

"Seems like it."

Jabil says, "They can't stay here. We have neither food nor room."

Moses nods. "I know that. Josh and I talked it over and decided that if you help these kids, we'll help you expand the compound and bring in food quarterly."

"Decided?" Jabil says, his eyebrows raised.

"Relax." Moses smiles again. "Nobody's trying to usurp your authority."

But Jabil doesn't respond, merely opens the hidden door that leads to the garden. I file through first, the men following behind me.

Closing the door, Jabil asks Moses, "How would you bring in food?"

"We're growing a garden," he says. "We've got chickens. We've got men who can hunt."

"How do you know it'd be enough?"

Moses sighs, knifing fingers through his hair. "It'd be

enough, all right? And it'll sure be more than you're gonna get on your own, without helping these kids out. Besides, it's not like I *wanted* to come here. I first tried taking them to Liberty, where Sal's staying, but it looks like the camp down there's part of the Agricultural Resurgence Commission."

"The—the ARC?" I stammer.

Moses glances over, my secret between us. "Yes. Looks like Mike Ramirez is their middleman. The people are already congregated. They can go in and out now—" he shrugs—"but there's barbed wire around the fence and a lock on the gate, so I say it's a matter of time."

"Did you warn Sal?" I ask.

Moses nods. "I don't think she'll let herself believe me. It's easier, staying right there."

Breathing through my panic, I stride over to the garden and crouch to hide the fact that my legs are suddenly weak. I let the tilled soil sift through my fingers in an effort to soothe myself. The cocoa-like powder falls away, leaving bits of stone behind.

I hear Jabil, behind me: "The community won't go for it."

Moses mumbles, "You mean *Charlie* won't go for it."

"Of course he won't. You know he didn't even want Angel to stay."

Moses says, "When we were trying to figure out what to do about the gang, you told me we'd find protection in the shadow of God's wings, and now you're trying to find that protection in Charlie." He pauses. "Let me tell you, they're not the same. You should cut him loose."

"It's easy for *you* to say that," Jabil snaps. "Just dropping kids off and leaving again."

"I'm not leaving."

My head snaps up. I look at Moses.

"I'm not leaving," he repeats, staring at me.

Clearing his throat, Jabil maneuvers around Moses to offer me his hand. The stone fragments bite into my palm. We only see our true selves once we are sifted. Is my future husband's true self the one who would abandon orphans, or the one willing to take in my orphaned family? Not wanting to answer this, I drop the stones and allow him to pull me to my feet.

Moses

The sound of Charlie yelling "Timber!" ricochets through the forest. Judging by his enthusiasm, it's like he's wanted to be a lumberjack all his life. But the yell and the collapse are nearly overpowered as men sink axes into Douglas fir and Engelmann spruce. Needles rain down as more straight, softwood trunks fall to the blunt force of axes, spraying the ground with the scent of resin. During this chaos, Jabil and I are standing side by side fifty yards away. We're sizing up a massive pine, soaring into the air. But we have no clue where to begin.

"Well. Let's get to it," Jabil says, like the project is up for debate.

I take my gun from the holster and set it on a nearby

stump. Jabil and I don't say anything as he uses an ax to cut a wedge, manipulating the tree trunk in the direction it should fall. Then I pick up the left side of the two-man saw, and he and I start. The blade bites into the trunk, which is about four feet around, but as he continues pulling, I am unable to maintain my grip. Instead of working together, we begin working *against* each other—the saw's uneven tempo incapable of cutting the wood in a straight line and getting so out of hand that it's actually dangerous to hold.

Finally, I glance over at Jabil, keeping the saw braced, so that it doesn't let go and hurt either of us. "Buddy," I say, "I don't know what your problem is, but I can tell you've got one."

Jabil doesn't respond right away, just keeps chewing the saw into the trunk's flesh, so I have no choice but to keep working. "I have a problem, all right," he says, out of breath. "I have a problem with the fact you knew bringing the children here would force me to be the bad guy."

I retort, "At least now you know how it feels."

Jabil wipes his forehead. Wood chips stick to his face. "What're you talking about?"

"When I first came here, you wouldn't let Leora anywhere near me. You wouldn't even let her ride along to town that night we went to the museum unless *you* rode along too."

"I didn't know you then."

"But you still don't want Leora around me."

Jabil continues sawing. Bark flies. The yellow wood releases a sweet odor, like vanilla beans curing in a bottle of rum. I slice the saw into the bark, anger fueling my strength so that—despite our size difference—I am cutting into the tree just as hard as he is.

Jabil finally says, "I think you're only attracted to Leora because she can't be yours."

"This is the modern world. We don't treat women like cattle, something we can own."

Jabil groans in disgust. "I don't *own* her. We're engaged."

My grip falters on the saw, the blade wobbling with the release of kinetic pressure. I don't look at Jabil, but quickly retake my stance, my entire body trembling with a different kind of fatigue. We work in silence, sweat dripping down our noses and chins. The afternoon light angled through the forest changes from gold to bronze to pewter. One by one, the other men stop working, the rhythm of their diligence gradually fading as they leave, going back to their families and homes. Seth and Luke Ebersole are among them, and Luke looks between Jabil and me. But then he leaves as well, and Jabil and I continue.

Our bodies become drenched with sweat, so that even my jeans are heavy with perspiration. And then, finally, we hear a crack. For an instant, Jabil and I just look at each other. Energy renewed, we continue sawing in earnest. Sawdust accumulates, darkness looms, a squirrel attempts to leap from one tree to another and falls, shaking himself off and scampering away. Another tremendous crack. The tree begins to go. I stare up at it. A strange exhaustion has condensed, like marrow, in my bones.

"Move!" Jabil commands, but I don't. The tree continues its descent. I remember the term *widow maker* from my maternal grandfather's early logging days, when he was working in Minnesota. I see my brother, dead after the explosion. I see my grandfather, dreamlessly sleeping in the bed he shared with my grandmother for so many years. I imagine my parents being dead as well. I imagine *all* of us slaving away when the entire "modern world" is teetering on the brink.

This is what roots me here. We are all dying, regardless of our inexhaustible efforts to stay alive. And then I am knocked off my feet with a force that wrenches the breath from my lungs. The black forest spins as the tree crashes, cones and old growth and the loamy smell of the woods whirling around me. But I am still alive. I look over and see Jabil lying on his back beside me, breathing hard, so that I am barely aware that I am breathing as hard as him.

"What were you thinking?" he rails. "Standing there? You could've killed yourself!"

I inhale in relief, eyes burning. "I know."

Jabil gets to his feet and searches beneath the fallen tree for the two-man saw, which he's too responsible to leave out in the elements, even for one night. "Take care of yourself," he says, before departing. And I hear something in his voice. Concern, perhaps. Maybe even pity.

I stay on my back there, surrounded by destruction the same as I was surrounded by destruction in the desert, and realize I've put too much weight on my relationship with

Leora, the same as Jabil has done. In my mind, if nothing else, I've begun to own her, believing she holds the power to heal my scars when no one holds that power but God himself. I have to be the one to walk that healing out by trusting there's a plan for my life, even if Leora's not in it.

Sitting up, I push off the ground and begin walking back toward the community. The ground wafts with the scent of damp earth before I feel the rain.

CHAPTER

13

Leora

BOTH IN THEIR PAJAMAS, Anna and the orphaned child, Elizabeth, are putting the rag baby to bed on the small porch outside our home. They've made a fuss of tucking it in with a tea towel, which they must've snatched from my kitchen, and taking turns rocking the rag baby and making shushing sounds: the most noise I've heard from them all day. Their age gap and my sister's silence don't inhibit their friendship. If anything, these factors have solidified their bond. Elizabeth is also mentally stunted, or at least she's refused to speak during the eight hours she's been here.

"Leora?"

I turn at the hesitant greeting and see Jabil standing on the other side of the clothesline. The rope is tugged down by the bulk of the rugs that got waterlogged during the storm. To his left, the blue moon renders the clouds visible; to his right, nothing but darkness and the sound of trees bending in the wind. His hair dampens the shoulders of his shirt. His face is smooth. The sight stirs the imprinted memory of his lips on mine. "Good evening," I reply.

Encouraged, he walks over and stands next to me, observing the girls too. "The children can stay for a few days," he says. "I see nothing wrong with that. But our community doesn't have the resources to sustain those kinds of numbers long-term." When I don't respond, he adds, "I know it's hard, but we'll have to find another place for them eventually."

I glance at his profile. He is pressing a shaving nick on his jaw with his thumb. I say, "Do you forget that, for years, I was practically an orphan? That, like Emmanuel raising his little sister, I was also responsible for raising my family on my own?"

He replies, "I don't like it any more than you."

"But you still won't change it."

"What do you want from me, Leora? Whatever I do, I feel . . . it's not enough."

I look up at the moon's scarred face, forcing back tears. "I want you to care."

He reaches for my hand. "I *do* care."

"Not just for me, or for our families." It's all I can do to keep my hand still. "What did your uncle quote, right after the EMP? 'If we have of this world's goods (no matter how much or how little) and see that our brother has a need, but do not share with him what we have freely received—how can we say that we would be ready to give our lives for him if necessary?'"

Jabil looks down. "I don't know where the balance is."

I glance over. That spot of blood has dried on his cheek. "That's just the thing," I reply, my heart softening to him again. "I don't think there is one."

"Charlie will leave," he says. "Taking the trapping gear.

The ammunition. And not only that, but all of his survival knowledge too."

"Let him," I declare, and squeeze his fingers. "We'll get through it, whatever comes."

Moses

Leora pulls open the door at my knock and places a finger to her lips. I peer around her, into the cabin, and can see the flames flickering across the face of Elizabeth, lying on the bed nearest the fire. "She sleeping?" I whisper.

Leora nods and steps outside, pulling the door closed. She's wearing the same shawl she was wearing the morning we went to the fire tower. But there's no use in bringing anything like that up now. "She just went down," she says. "It took a while for her to get settled."

"Yeah." I swallow. "She was like that at the airport."

"How are the boys doing in the loft?"

"Good. But it took them a while to get settled too."

Leora pauses, watching me. "How about you? You doing okay?"

"Not really." I take a breath. "We need to talk."

She looks away from me. "We do."

Together, we walk the path that winds around the cabins. Someone planted daffodils that sprout helter-skelter along the border, but the path itself is trafficked too heavily to let anything grow there, even weeds. We pass through the hidden door out into the garden. The earlier storm rinsed the sky clear, so that the Milky Way is scattered across the darkness like a glittering cloud. We don't talk, just as we didn't talk when we went to the tower. The only sound is the crunch of twigs snapping underfoot and the birds settling in their nighttime roosts.

Not able to stand it any longer, I ask, "What was the name of the man you killed?"

Leora glances over, as if surprised. "Alex Ramirez." She pauses. "Why?"

I dread being the bearer of bad news. "The ARC is still looking for him."

She says, "I feared as much."

"What are you going to do?"

"There's really nothing I *can* do, is there?" she asks. "It's not like I can run."

"No, I guess not." After a while, I say, "I heard about you and Jabil."

She nods. "Sorry I didn't get the chance to tell you myself."

"It's okay. You don't owe me anything." I hesitate. "Do you love him?"

"Yes," she says. "But nothing is the same as it was, even love."

It hurts me to hear her resignation. I want to reach out and take her solemn face in my hands. But I can't. A force field encloses her, formed by the knowledge that she's made her choice, and I'm not it. "When's the date?" I ask, trying not to sound like the question guts me.

"We haven't set one," she says. "It's not like I have a dress to make or a menu to plan."

"No," I reply. "I guess not."

She turns away from me, back toward the compound, and cups her elbows with her hands. "I waited and waited for you," she murmurs. "Why didn't you come?"

"But I *did* come." I move around to face her again and see that she is fighting tears. "I came back to you, but I knew you didn't need me. So . . . I left."

She begins to openly weep. "How are you allowed to tell me what I need?"

I can't keep myself from comforting her. Leora's body resists a moment before collapsing against mine. I pull back and look down at her, clearing the tears from her cheeks. "I'm sorry," I say. "I have no right to tell you what you need. But you are making the right choice, Leora. Choosing Jabil. I *wanted* you to choose him. That's why I stayed away."

Leora raises her head. "You manipulated me."

"That's not true," I insist. "Don't you know that I wanted to be with you as much as I wanted you to choose him? That I am *blind* with jealousy because you've actually fulfilled my wishes? But I know this is right. You and Jabil can take care of the community, together. You can live here, together. He needs you and you need him."

"And what about you?" she says, her voice raw. "Don't you need anybody?"

Jaw tight, I look away, trying to appear like I'm an island unto myself when all I can picture is my grandfather lying there, marooned in an empty bed, reaching for the portraits of his wife, his family. "I need to know you're going to be all right," I say. "If I know that—" I swallow again—"I'll be fine."

Leora straightens her shoulders before drying her face with the backs of her hands. "Good," she says. "Because I am."

We look at each other and then, by some unspoken agreement, begin walking back to the compound in the same shrouded stillness as when we walked out. My arm brushes against the skin of Leora's arm, the heat between us a force field as tangible as the one surrounding her. It takes willpower to honor her promise to Jabil and not reach for her hand, the dampness there, from her tears, contradicting her words—just as the dampness in my eyes contradicts mine.

Leora

I stand behind Jabil on the platform and can see the entire community fanned around the focal point of us. Moses and Josh are here, as are the Lost Children. From Emmanuel, their leader, to Marco, the toddler, each appears dirty and forlorn, though we've taken such care to bathe them and dress them in clean clothes; so it's almost as if the mien of poverty and deprivation has superimposed itself on the genetic material spiraling through their veins.

"As you are aware," Jabil begins, "the community has

recently expanded. After giving this prayerful consideration, we've agreed to let the children stay."

Charlie erupts, right on cue. "Who agreed? You? Leora? And what're we going to feed them this winter? Have you thought of *that*?"

Moses steps out of the crowd. "Actually, Josh and I—" he nods at the white-haired man, who's said almost nothing since his arrival—"we've offered to bring in food and supplies to compensate for the addition."

Charlie says, "And where're you going to get these so-called supplies?"

Josh informs him, "We're part of a bartering route that branches across the state."

Charlie rolls his eyes. "That sounds about as worthwhile as a Costco membership."

Jabil's attention moves back to Charlie. "At your suggestion, we offered no asylum to an orphan who then left the community; I will not make that same mistake twice."

"The only reason you won't make that mistake twice," Charlie sneers, "is because you know Leora wouldn't have you if you did."

Anxiety uncurls in my gut. Jabil says, "Leora's got nothing to do with this, and you would be wise to hold your tongue."

Charlie pauses, watching us, as if sizing up our weakest areas so he can calculate his best method of attack. "Unlike the majority of you people, I don't got my head in the trees, and I know that part of your reason for keeping these kids is because you know it'll force me out."

Somehow I experience sympathy for a man whom, most of the time, I'd rather not have around. "Charlie." I step forward. "Please listen. Nobody's forcing you—"

"Hogwash. Then my leaving's a fringe benefit. Whatever. But I think it's kinda ironic that you're forcing me out for not wanting to share food with every stranger that straggles in, when *you* yourself did far worse by your high-and-mighty standards by killing a man." Pointing a finger right at me, he says, "She shot and killed Alex Ramirez, the gang leader's son."

Jabil snaps, "Stop talking nonsense."

"It's not nonsense!" Charlie cries. "Go ahead. Ask her yourself." Heat rushes to my face, proof manifest. Jabil slowly turns. My insides flinching with shame, I hold his gaze steady. Charlie continues, "I overheard her talking to Luke after he came in."

My gaze tears away and shifts to my *vadder*. He looks physically ill, the black strands of his hair stark against his white face. This might be the first time we've truly looked at each other in weeks. "She didn't do it," he says. Even as the sentence leaves his mouth, I'm shaking my head, refusing to allow him to exonerate me. But he continues, sinking deeper with the weight of every word. "Leora was there, but I . . . I killed him—Alex Ramirez—to protect her."

The community's voices interweave before descending over everything like a blanket. Meanwhile, my *vadder* and

I continue looking at each other, and I realize he's giving me a gift, compensation for his absence during every critical part of my life. But I refuse it. This is neither just nor fair. Our relationship has barely mended, and I'm not sure debt is where I want to begin.

Jabil mumbles, "I don't know what to do."

I can't tell to whom he is speaking. I look over and see that he is staring out at the crowd, trying to come to grips with what just happened, and I understand he is caught between a rock and a hard place, a catch-22—any medium, really, that prevents you from being able to move. Should Jabil override the laws constructed in haste by his uncle, the honorable Bishop Lowell, who is even more honorable since he is dead? Yes, my Mennonite *vadder* apparently murdered a man, but at least he killed to defend his daughter, who will also be Jabil's future wife. What am I thinking? I know the truth. I won't allow my father to take the blame. "I did it, Jabil," I admit, so that—this time—my confession only reaches his ear. "Not him."

Jabil's face remains blank, his hands knotted at his sides. "Why didn't you tell me?" he asks. And then, more quietly, more gently, he adds, "We can't talk here."

Only now do I feel I am standing on a platform; only now do I feel the full gravity and unsteadiness of the stage. Jabil gives me a hand, but tension radiates from his skin. We step down together and walk away from the crowd. Once we pass through the gate, Jabil lets go.

❖

Jabil is standing on the edge of the compound, near where I used to wait for Moses's return. Even then, I sensed Jabil in the woods, waiting until he knew I was safe inside the gates before closing them behind me. I would see his torch sometimes, glimmering through the trees. But he never revealed himself, probably sensing I did not want found out. I have been cruel to him; I am aware of this, and yet I'm not sure I can convince him I will change. Or that, this time, I want to. "Jabil," I say, as I approach. "I'm sorry." But the space between us is so incalculable, the few words might as well be communicated across a void.

He doesn't turn but wipes a hand over his face. "It's not as much about what you did," he says. "It's about the fact you didn't tell me. That you didn't *trust* me enough to tell me."

"I was scared you wouldn't want me if you knew."

Jabil looks over, his expression pained. "I could never not want you, Leora. It's just—"

"What?" I interrupt.

"Marriage is hard enough without secrets."

"But that's it," I say, pulse pounding. "There's nothing else."

Jabil sets his jaw, as if trying to keep from speaking rather than preparing to. "My brother saw you last night, with Moses." He stops before adding, "Did you tell him what you did?"

"About the soldier?" Jabil nods, and I swallow hard.

"I—I told him weeks ago, back before you and I had an understanding."

"There clearly *is* no understanding, Leora," Jabil says. "You trusted Moses with the darkest part of your heart. You trusted him with something you weren't willing to entrust to me."

"I was scared, Jabil," I again reply, my tears falling unchecked.

"I understand." He turns. "But that's not the point. The point is, marriage is supposed to be built on honesty, on revealing our best and our worst and knowing we'll still be loved."

"But *am* I still loved?" I ask. "I can already feel you pulling away from me."

"Of course you're loved, Leora. That's not in question. What *is* in question is if you truly want to be with me. I think I need to take some time. To seek the Lord and see if we're truly meant to be together." He smiles sadly, touching my cheek. "Maybe you just need time too."

The sky is lapis, studded with clouds, but watching Jabil walk away, shock falls around me as palpably as a sheet of rain. I continue standing here while thinking of Elizabeth, crying out in her sleep: the fluency of her dreams so contradictory to the mute state she assumes when awake. I think of the other Lost Children, of my own family, of everyone who needs me to remain. But then, drawing upon my *vadder's* example, or upon my own genetic predilection to escape,

I forgo these responsibilities to pursue my own wants, and I want to get away from Jabil: another man who's promised to love me without condition, and yet finds that promise too hard to keep.

With my palms, I angrily smudge tears away and head down the mountain. My rapid stride soon accelerates into a sprint. I cover acres of forest in an adrenaline-fueled blur of motion—slapping at regrowth and ducking beneath trees. The ground, pillowed with pine needles, becomes aromatic as I crush the foliage beneath my feet. I hear someone call my name. I stop running long enough to see who is following. Expecting Jabil, I instead see my *vadder*, running just as hard as I despite his bad back. I don't want him to catch me because I don't want to explain. I especially don't want to explain to *him*: the man who left me first. But it's foolish, even juvenile, to run. I force myself to stop and slump against a trunk, breathing heavily. The strips of bark grate my spine; the branches around me have turned copper with disease or age.

My *vadder* gasps, hands on his knees. "Why—are—you—running?" His hair is hanging loose. It's grown a little longer since he's been here.

"Why did you tell them you did it?" The words fly out of my mouth, laced with venom.

He straightens slightly and looks at me, confused. "Our family needs you."

I laugh. "The community wouldn't cast me out."

"You have no idea what they might do."

"I have some idea." I stand from beneath the pine and face my *vadder*. "I'm engaged to the new bishop, Jabil." I pause, heart constricting. "Or at least I was."

His confusion deepens. "I didn't know you loved him."

I reply, "You haven't been around long enough to know."

He puts a hand on my shoulder. "I'm sorry. I realize a lot can change."

My entire body tenses. He lets go and steps back, and only then do I dare glance up. "For years," I say, "I wouldn't give in to a relationship with Jabil because he was who *Mamm* wanted for me. But the EMP forced me to grow up, *Daed*. To surrender such childish rebellion."

"Don't get me wrong," he says, "but is it right to have to 'give in' or 'surrender' to love?"

"Proverbs tells us he who trusts his heart is a fool."

"*Jah,*" my *vadder* says, his familiar inflection returning. "It also says God will give you the desires of your heart." He pauses, smiling sadly at me. "What does your heart desire?"

"More and more, I find it desires peace." I cradle my arms, holding myself together. "Besides, I love him—Jabil— in my own way."

My *vadder* lifts my chin to meet his eyes, a troubled version of my own. "If you really did, Leora, 'I love him' would've been enough."

❖

A treasure trove of sunlight tumbles down through the forest. The golden warmth reminds me of the months we have left to store up food for our families, and that the addition of ten hungry mouths shouldn't wreak havoc on our community like Charlie claims. Courage renewed, I pass through the entrance gate only to see Malachi standing behind it.

"Leora," he says.

I nod at him tersely. "How's your shoulder?"

He touches the place where he was shot. "Healing."

"Good." I pause to scan the space behind him. "Did Jabil come back?"

He shakes his head.

The awkwardness undergirding our mundane exchange confirms that he was the Snyder brother who told Jabil about me and Moses talking in the garden last night. I say nothing else, but go inside to find Moses with the men. They have begun dismantling a portion of the perimeter so they can expand it around the schoolhouse and church they are going to build, along with four other cabins. Seeing how little effort it takes to destroy the perimeter causes me to realize that, all this time, we've been using the gate and walls for our own sense of security, not because they actually protect. I walk over to the group and call for Moses.

He turns, the string of a plumb line trailing behind him. "How you doing?"

I can't give him an honest answer here, in front of all these men. "Fine."

"Well—" Moses falters, clearly wanting to say more. "I can't believe he did that."

I unthinkingly ask, "Jabil?"

He scans my face, concern saturating the blue of his eyes. "No, I was talking about Charlie. What did Jabil do to you?"

"Nothing," I quickly reply. "I just need to get away, and I thought of the fairgrounds."

He glances at Josh, who is watching us, like he always seems to be watching everything. Moses says, "Do you think that's a good idea, considering the ARC could be looking for you?"

I reply, "Probably not, but I have to warn Sal about what's coming."

"I told her," Moses reminds me. "She already knows."

"Yes," I say. "But for Colton's sake, I have to try again."

Moses

Leora and I arrive at the base of the mountain, where the blacktop begins, each twist and turn framed with precise yellow lines. I've walked this highway more often than I would like, but the sight still catches me off guard. Paved roads, airports, banks, post offices, and schools—even the smoke-stained, concrete facades of the small businesses parading down Liberty's Main Street—hark back to a first-world civilization that has become a figment from another time.

We pass another mile marker, leading us toward town. The soundtrack of our journey is the uneven slap of our rubber soles on pavement, since even the military boots I took from that soldier are beginning to fall apart. I say, "If only we would've stored up some shoes."

Leora glances over. "*Jah*, and socks."

I stop walking after a moment. I pull out my knife and untie one boot, sawing the black lace in half. I call to Leora, "Let me see your foot a minute."

Bewildered by my request, she doesn't move. I walk over and kneel in front of her, picking up the booted foot that was giving her trouble, resting the sole on my knee. I glance at her face, which is vivid red. I wrap my severed lace over the middle of the shoe and press my finger on the spot where the lace crosses, trying to double-knot it as tightly as I can. Finished, I hold my hand over that small, worn boot and look down at it, thinking of all those miles this strong woman has had to walk, and knowing she's soon going to be walking so many miles without me because I don't have the gall or the heartlessness to ask Leora to leave him.

"Thank you," she murmurs.

I don't reply, but just squeeze Leora's foot before setting it down. We continue walking, each of us taking our time. After a while, we come upon an older woman—or maybe she just *appears* old—wearing the ragged layers of a wanderer. She is gathering dandelion from the gullies alongside the road and putting the greens in a basket hanging over her arm, which is as sun-browned as a piece of old leather. The woman glances up as we pass. Her eyes beneath the brim of an oversize straw hat are chillingly blank. She says nothing, and we say nothing to her. I don't care to leave our backs exposed as we walk away, so I slow my step even more and walk directly behind Leora. She is still hobbling slightly because of the boot.

To our right, we come upon the old cast-iron tub, continually filled by a spring running out of the side of the mountain. Water spills out of the hole where the drain catch used to be. Like the highway, I've seen this spring numerous times—a watering hole that draws bipeds and quadrupeds alike—but Leora has not. She stops and leans over the rusty rim. She cups her hands in the tub and laughs, splashing her face and then splashing me with what's left.

"Running water!" she cries, as if we've uncovered the fountain of youth. Droplets cling to her eyelashes and highlight the wisps of hair twining out of her bun. I can't help but laugh with her as she cups more water and drinks.

She leans back and sighs. "Least the EMP's taught us not to take anything for granted."

I stand beside Leora, drinking her in. "Isn't that the truth."

We pass beneath the bridge supporting the railroad tracks, and a shadow moves above us. I step to the side, drawing my gun. Pigeons screech, beating their wings against the cages the city once set to contain them. Now I am sure those traps are set for entirely different reasons. I wish I had a flashlight. The screeching goes quiet, and the silence is more disturbing than the noise had been. A small person—perhaps a teenager?—jumps from the ledge of the bridge down onto the road. The tails of his khaki trench coat sweep the ground, and the cage with the dead pigeons clangs in his hand. He sees us then—this boy, wearing as much dirt as he is clothes—and then he sees my gun. I lower it, and he runs off with the soles of his sneakers flashing in the gathering dark. Leora and I are both too invulnerable to surprise to make a fuss about a teenager eating pigeons, but I notice she walks a little closer to me, in case. Above us, on the hillside to the right, is government housing, each of the slapdash, one-story buildings made from tan brick. Behind them are the factories: nothing but empty boxes punctured by smokestacks.

We walk past this sketchy section of Liberty, and then past the gas stations and pawn shops with bars bolted over the windows, old motels with marquees hawking everything from hot breakfasts to outdoor pools. The fairgrounds are across from Motel 6, and as soon as I see the grounds themselves, I know that everything in town looks deserted because it is. The tents are here; the families are here; but the fence and gates are locked down tight.

Leora asks, "This the right place?"

I look over, not sure what to say. "Yes."

Panic lurches through her voice. "How do we get in?"

Even from this distance, I can see the ominous shape of the guards standing in watchtowers overlooking the land, and more guards standing in front of the gates—which I entered and exited just two weeks ago—prepared to open fire with one wrong move.

I tell Leora, "The main trouble is that it looks like nobody can get out."

❖

We stand on Main Street, looking right and left, but everything looks abandoned. Leora points out Friendly's Garage, and I see it: the barrel of a rifle nosing through the broken front window. "I'll talk to him," I say. The owner, Snake, lunges forward as I approach, reminding me of the reptile for whom he's nicknamed, striking against the confines of his crate.

"I come in peace," I say, hands up.

"Hey." He lifts his chin. "I know you. You're from the warehouse."

"I *was*." I look around. "You know where everybody's at?"

"Depends," he says. "Who's asking?"

I glance at him. "Probably depends more on who's offering."

A smile moves across his face. "That too."

The currency of commerce has changed. Where before I would've offered cash, I now can offer just about anything but. I reach into my boot and pull out the hunting knife I've been carrying with me since I was a kid. I give it to Snake. He turns and tosses it on his desk, piled with items, maybe all confiscated from people like me, searching for someone.

"Got anything else?" he says.

"That's all I have."

He nods. Waits. When I don't budge, he says, "They rounded them up."

"Who did they round up? The people?"

"Who else?"

"They put them in the fairgrounds?"

"Yeah."

"Who moved them?"

He spreads his hands. "I don't know that either. All I know's they came in a line. At night. Army trucks, back to back."

"Like . . . a convoy?"

He nods. "I watched it all from here."

"Who were they?"

"I already told you. I don't know."

"Were they old trucks? New trucks?"

"They looked like regular, tan Army trucks. *Our* Army trucks."

I stare at Snake, trying to comprehend how a fleet of military vehicles could be running if the electromagnetic pulse affected our entire nation. "Sounds like martial law."

He shakes his head. "There didn't sound much lawful about it."

Leora

Moses and I wait on the warehouse's front stoop. The town of Liberty spreads before us like a black canvas, clouds erasing moon and stars, making it hard to gauge the depth of anything.

"Just think," I murmur. "Somewhere out there, a family could be eating supper. With a fruit salad and vegetables on the table. Tap water in clean glasses. The entire room lit by electricity." I pause, the fantasy fading. "But if life's good somewhere, why aren't we hearing anything?"

Moses says, "Maybe they don't want us to. Desperate people are easier to control."

Before I can reply, the dead bolts click. Moses and I turn. The door opens. Sal's grandmother, Papina, steps out carrying a prayer candle, earrings swaying in her stretched lobes. She looks between Moses and me, and then reaches out as if to touch his face. He flinches but holds steady until she withdraws her hand. "Papina," he begins, "I know you've taken a vow of silence. But can you *please* break it this once to tell us what's going on at the fairgrounds?"

For a full minute, Papina says nothing—just stares out at the dark—and I am certain she will refuse to answer, even though there is so much at stake.

Then she coughs dryly into her fist and surprises me by speaking. "All I know's the soldiers didn't want me and Colton 'cause we can't work."

"Who are they?" Moses asks.

Papina shrugs.

He continues, "Were they wearing any kind of uniform?"

"They were wearing a uniform like my grandson's," she replies. "Black."

Moses and I look at each other. He says, "The ARC."

Papina looks between us, her wrinkles deepening. "Who's that?"

I hold her gaze and catch a glimpse of the scared woman beneath the eccentric guise, meant to keep people at bay. "I wouldn't stay around here, Papina, or you're bound to find out."

CHAPTER

14

Leora

WE PREPARE TO LEAVE the warehouse before it is even light: Moses, to leave for the airport; I, for the compound. Papina won't let me take Colton. I won't fight her for him, though the separation makes me physically ache as if Colton were also mine. But, I remind myself, he's not. Therefore I pass the sleep-warm child to Papina. She nods at me, cradling his head against her. I ask, the same as I asked my *vadder* all those months ago, "You sure you won't come with us?"

Nodding curtly, she lays the child on the bed.

"What are you two going to eat?"

She whispers, "My son . . . he brings food."

"Mike?"

She nods.

"I thought nobody was allowed out?"

"He's not a prisoner," Papina replies, swallowing. "He's one of the guards."

It takes a moment for me to comprehend. "Then how come he won't get Sal out?"

"He doesn't want to lose his position."

"Yeah, well," I snap, "she could lose her life."

Papina's lips are wired tight, so I wonder if I've angered her enough to incite her vow of silence. But then she picks up a candle and crosses the room to the filing cabinet. Setting the candle on top, she inserts a key—connected to a chain looped around her waist—into the top drawer. She pulls open this drawer and runs her gnarled fingers over pieces of jewelry, whose real or synthetic gems reflect light on the warehouse ceiling.

She unlocks the second drawer, opens it, and leans in, glancing over her shoulder from time to time so I know she doesn't want me to see what she's doing. Eventually Papina comes back, bearing a tarnished cuff bracelet inset with a stone the size of an egg.

Holding it out to me, she rasps, "Tell Sal this is just in case she needs it."

I accept the proffered bracelet. "In case she needs it for what?"

Papina's eyes glitter like those gems. "She'll know."

Unsettled by this exchange, I place the bracelet in my rucksack because I don't feel comfortable putting it on, then begin retracing my steps. But I stop and gaze down again at Colton, still sleeping. The sheet hanging in front of the window swells and recedes with the cross breeze, the gentle motion nearly lulling my anxiety as well. Watching the boy-child dream so effortlessly, I cannot help comparing his sleep with my own these past few nights.

Confused and heartsick, I walk through the warehouse's front door and find Moses waiting for me at the base of the cement steps. "How you holding up?" he asks.

I explain what I just learned. "How could Mike imprison his own family?"

Moses puts a hand on my shoulder. "Don't lose heart," he says. "You go talk to the community. I'll talk to the militia. Between us, we should be able to come up with a plan."

At the crossroads, branching our paths, Moses stands on Main Street's centerline, looking back. I can't make out his features in the gloaming, but I understand what he feels. Just as my chest ached holding Colton, my chest aches seeing him. You can't help knowing what someone means to you when, each time your eyes meet, it seems you are one glance closer to good-bye.

❖

Jabil isn't waiting for me outside the gates. Instead, Malachi lets me through as he's always done. I don't know what I expected; maybe for someone to be worried—my *daed* or Seth, perhaps. But soon I see that life is continuing the same as before. The wind snaps laundry, the uniform dinginess fading to white by the sun. The small kitchen gardens, in between cabins, are redolent with the scent of compost. The rooster and hen peck a circle around Judith's toddler while he plays in the dirt. Hammers create a steady percussion as the men work on the schoolhouse, where the community expects me to teach until I have Jabil's children. I doubt anyone knows our wedding might be off. Jabil's not the type to tell; but then, neither am I.

I walk up to the Snyders' cabin. The door is open and

Jabil's *mudder* is inside, kneading bread on the table dusted with flour, though I'm sure none of the ingredients come from wheat. "Hello, Mrs. Snyder," I say.

She looks up, eyes guarded. "Good afternoon." She smudges flour on her temple as she pushes back her graying hair. "Jabil's in the garden."

"Thank you." I back out, aware that this is not my place. Maybe it's never been.

Jabil is working a new, rectangular patch of ground. Without horses, his only option is to turn each clod with a shovel. The process is taxing—that much is clear—but he is doing it with the single-minded intensity with which he approaches anything. His sweat-soaked back is to me, and I am relieved. I don't want to see if the uncertainty surrounding our engagement has worn on him, like it's worn on me. He turns at the sound of his name and holds up a hand to block the sun as he scans the field. I see the moment he registers my presence. His hands wrap more firmly around the shovel, so that I wonder if he's going to continue working, ignoring me. But then he sets the shovel down and crosses the field, taking large strides to navigate the ruts.

"Thought you ran off," he says.

This greeting is so carefully devoid of emotion, I don't know if I should laugh or cry. "I just needed time to think," I say. "Like you said. But I was away longer than I planned."

He raises his eyebrow, as if he hadn't noticed.

I continue. "Sal's locked up, as are Angel and the families that were staying at the fairgrounds in Liberty. It appears that the government came in—or some other organization that has overtaken the government—and forced the people into a detention camp." I pause, giving Jabil time to register the news. "They are separating the parents from the children. Leaving the grandparents behind too. Papina, Sal's grandmother, told us everything firsthand."

"'Us.'" Leaning back, Jabil closes his eyes. "Charlie told me you went with him."

"With who?"

"Moses. Don't play with me, Leora."

"I'm not. I just don't understand why Charlie has to make my personal life his business."

Jabil looks to the side. I can see the undertow of anger, glimmering just below the surface of his indifference. "Charlie was getting ready to leave for the militia when he told me you'd already left with Moses. He said it in front of everyone. It was like he was trying to retaliate."

"I'm sorry, Jabil. I wasn't thinking clearly. I just knew I had to get away."

"Yes. But you didn't have to go away with *him*."

"No," I murmur, looking down. "I guess I didn't." Jabil and I are silent, as if we are each aware anything said will only heighten the tension. And then a child begins to cry in the compound, causing me to remember why I came back. "But don't you think that what's happening at the fair-grounds is more important than what's happening here?"

Jabil looks at me. "Is that really what you think?"

I sense this is a trick question, but I answer honestly. "Yes. I want to help them get out."

The lines carved between his thick brows remind me so keenly of his uncle, I wonder if the expression came with the role. "How?" he asks.

"Our community. We could help them."

Jabil pinches the bridge of his nose. "You are talking about using force, aren't you?"

I nod. "My vision is to join our community with Moses's militia."

He shakes his head. "I'm sorry, Leora. I can't sanction that."

I speak in more of a whisper, forcing myself to measure my words. "So you want to let Angel get worked to death in a camp, when we're practically the ones who sent her there?"

"No. We will pray that God will release her."

"Don't hide behind your faith when you're really just scared to take a risk."

Jabil rears back, eyes wide. "You are on dangerous ground, Leora."

I look up at him. "Yes, perhaps, but I believe I'm not the only one."

❖

It's nearly dusk, and Jabil still hasn't called a meeting. I approach him in the barn, where he's forking chicken dung and old straw from the coop into a wheelbarrow for the raised beds. I lean against the doorjamb for a moment—just watching him work—and realize that, for as long as I've known him, he's almost always been in action. What is he trying to prove? That he is worthy of love and respect, the same as I am always trying to prove? The same as we *all* are?

I ask, "Aren't you going to tell them?"

His shoulders tense. He doesn't turn. "There's no life in it."

"Says the person who's not trapped inside the camps."

"Fine." He forks another scoop. "*You* tell them, if you want to so badly."

I stare at the back of his dark head, the strong neck tapering down to the broad line of his shoulders. It makes me nearly hurt to look at him—not with the desire of a lover, but with the proprietorship of a mother looking at her child. "How'd we ever get here, Jabil?" The words are spoken so softly, I'm not sure he's going to hear them. But he does.

Only now does he turn and meet my eyes. "You know that better than me."

❖

The hollow sound of the triangle, which I just struck, resonates throughout the compound. I stand in front of the well with the cast-iron piece in hand, waiting to see if anyone responds. They do, of course. They've been trained the same as Pavlov's dogs, and for the first time, I see the similarity between the families gathered in the fairgrounds and the families gathered here. We all harbor an innate need for community. Sometimes there is safety in numbers; sometimes those numbers make it easier to round us up.

Slowly, the community gathers and converges around the platform. They shift uneasily, scanning the space behind my head, as if expecting someone else to step forward to conduct this meeting. Most importantly, a man. Instead, I clear my throat, finding myself assaulted with stage fright, despite knowing the faces staring from the crowd. Perhaps that makes the fear even worse.

"Good evening," I begin. "I'm here to share some unsettling news with you."

I haltingly go on to tell them about the barbed-wire fence and guards surrounding the fairgrounds. Anxiety distorts the faces of the community as they understand how this information might one day affect them. For who says we are exempt from being placed inside those gates? "I am going to the airport in Kalispell," I conclude. "Moses and I are trying to come up with a plan to free the people. Anyone here is more than welcome to join us. I will be leaving directly after this. But please—" I hold up my hand—"before you make any decisions in haste, know that I have no idea what we will face, nor can I even say that we will make it back."

I step down from the platform. No one says anything. Jabil is not here, having decided—I guess—to remain in the barn while I gave my speech. And then *Daed* and Seth come up to me. Side by side they stand, their heredity in such lockstep, it takes my breath.

"We will go," my *vadder* says.

"Thank you. But who's going to stay with Anna?"

Judith Zimmerman, overhearing this, leaves the women's group to walk closer. "Let me watch her," she says. "Consider it my contribution, since I'm unable to do anything else."

"You're sure?"

She smiles.

"Well, I guess I'll go with Seth and *Daed* and then come back for Anna in a few days, if that's okay?"

"Take your time," she says. "What's one more when you've got five?"

Such generosity threatens to unravel my emotions, but I instead remain standing in front of the platform while *Daed* and Seth leave to pack a few items for the trip. But no one else approaches to say they will join. After a while, I wind my way toward the barn, staring at the ground so the members of the community won't see how disappointed I am.

Jabil is still working, the wheelbarrow now heaped. The dirt inside the coop is scraped clean and bears marks from the tines.

I tell him, "*Daed*, Seth, and I are going to be leaving soon."

Jabil turns and slants the pitchfork against the wall. "Well, I am glad they're at least going with you. Be careful."

"We will." Jabil and I are so cautious with each other. I look away from him. Dust motes twirl in the light slipping through the west side of the barn. "I'm sorry it's come to this."

"No one's forcing you to go."

"Then the situation is."

"Leora—" he sighs—"we live in a fallen world. There will always be 'situations.'"

"Yes, but I don't think our forefathers meant for pacifism to be passive."

"Well, I *know* they didn't believe in taking up arms. I will not be unequally yoked."

Waves of fear break against the wall of my chest as I understand that the security, the safety, which Jabil represents is about to be cut away. "You're calling it off?"

"If you leave—" he won't meet my eyes—"then, yes."

"Please don't make me choose."

Finally, he looks up. "Leora. Don't you see? You already have."

❖

Daed, Seth, and I arrive at the airport sometime during the night. A man is guarding the entrance. A leather gun strap pulls across his right shoulder. I can see the stock of the weapon poking around the other side of his back. "Can I help with something?" he asks.

I lift the cage of my ribs, drawing in breath. "Yes. We're here to see Moses Hughes."

"He expecting you?" The man's face is nondescript in the darkness; his caution is clear.

"No," I reply. "But we're from the community. Where he stayed after his crash."

The man pauses, looking at each of us in turn. He doesn't open the gate. "Wait here a minute," he says. We watch his outline grow fainter as he walks away.

Much longer than a minute passes before Moses materializes on the road. "Everything okay?" he asks as he fumbles a key into the padlock. His hair is matted on the back of his head.

"Yes. Sorry for waking you. We just wanted to help."

"Nothing to be sorry about. There's just not much to help with at this point."

I glance at him as the three of us pass through the gate. "You have no plan?"

He shakes his head. "Not yet."

Seth asks Moses, "You think you could take me up in a plane tomorrow?"

Daed says, "I think he would like to take your sister up first."

This embarrasses me, but Moses just grins. "Luke, you might be right."

My face flushes even more. Mumbling something incoherent, *Daed* cuts in front of us beneath the airport sign. Seth plods along until *Daed* turns and gestures for him to catch up. Moses laughs beneath his breath. "Looks like your dad's trying to give us some privacy."

I quickly change the subject. "I told the community about what happened, Moses. With Sal and the families. Seth and *Daed* were the only ones willing to come help."

"I guess I shouldn't be surprised."

"Well, *I* am." I pause. "And disappointed. Jabil said we could pray they'd be released."

"And what did *you* say?"

I glance over, and Moses seems genuinely interested. "I told him not to hide behind his faith when he's really just scared to take a risk."

He shakes his head. "You sure know how to cut to the chase."

"It was too harsh, I agree. But I'm fed up with it. This—" I gesture wide—"this whole religious apathy thing that's really just a cover-up for fear."

"Listen to you." A smile softens Moses's voice. "You sound so different from the timid girl you were when we first met. Like you could bust in there and break them out yourself."

"If only I could." I look down at the road's painted dividing lines passing beneath my feet.

Moses stops walking. "I'm glad you came, Leora." I stop walking as well. When I look toward him, his smile is gone. "I—" He hesitates. "We need you here."

❖

Josh doesn't have much to say when Moses and I encounter him in the hangar the next morning. He just looks at me and then smiles meaningfully at Moses, humming a tune I don't recognize, but which makes Moses give him a pointed look. Josh goes quiet and continues working on the Cessna, which doesn't make me particularly excited to go up in it.

I ask Moses, "You sure you remember how to fly?"

"Pretty sure." He winks. "I only crashed that once."

Before I can retort, Josh slams the hood on the nose of the plane and moves back to let me and Moses slip past him. Moses gives me a hand up into the passenger side. The interior is dusty, the dashboard a faux wood grain embedded with numerous gauges. A checked, blue-gray material covers the bucket seats. Stuffing sprouts along the ripped seams. The seat belts make no sense to me, since they can't protect a body if the plane smashes into the ground.

I ask Moses, as he climbs into the other side, "How'd you talk me into this again?"

"The same as I talk you into anything. I reminded you that you can only live once."

"Well—" I snap the seat belt across me—"I'd like that once to last a long time."

"It will. Or as long as the EMP will let it." He hands me a headset and smiles, tempering his words. "Would you feel better if I explained everything, or do you just want to ride?"

I pull the headset over my ears. "Just ride."

Pulling on his own headset, he says, "Relax. You can trust me."

I make a noncommittal sound and lean back against the seat, closing my eyes. I hear Moses pushing and pulling knobs and flipping switches. He rolls the window down and yells something to Josh about taxi clearance, though

I sense the comment's tongue-in-cheek. The engine sparks to life, and the plane begins rolling. I look out the window and see Josh watching from the tarmac, his face solemn behind his sunglasses. I shift my gaze to Moses, studying his profile, his hands gripping the yoke as the engine's whirring grows.

We gain momentum, and the plane lifts. It's as if we're not rising as much as the ground is tearing away. The force presses me back against the seat. I close my eyes as my stomach drops. Moses reaches over and touches my knee. I feel like I could die at any moment, and yet my entire body is electrified by his hand.

Moses lifts my headset and calls over the drone, "Open your eyes!"

I do and glance through the window. The light sears my vision, nearly blinding me with its potency. Distant, linen-colored clouds billow into the never-ending expanse of azure sky. I look down, out through the side window, and watch as the ground gets farther and farther away, making everything on it seem so much smaller and less significant. We fly over what must be a campsite, and I can see the bare ground where trees have been cut for buildings and firewood. Smoke rises from the middle, its wispy trail disappearing as it merges with air below us. The truth of what we are doing, and the reason for our flight, tries to slip its way into my thoughts, attempting to steal this moment of peace and surreal beauty. But I force myself to let these thoughts and worries fade. Here, no people are imprisoned or starving; here, no promises are made only to be broken. The only thing that matters is that Moses and I exist.

❖

Moses flies low over Glacier National Park so he can search for another camp set up by the ARC. I came here once, years ago, with my family. My *vadder* insisted we visit soon after we moved, so we hired Ronnie to drive us and went. I remember how *Daed* carved bear tracks in the mud to scare hikers, and then he took us out for burgers and shakes at the diner in the park. The whole day, he was tightly wound—frenzied, almost—and I feared he was on something until I realized he was merely exhausting himself in his efforts to make sure we had a good time.

The park looks much like I remember it, though I've never seen the aerial view. Lake McDonald is here, and so is Avalanche Lake, fed by the plunging mountain stream that this distance reduces to a fishing line dangled over a small, blue pool.

I can see roofs of the alpine cabins and the larger roof belonging to the main lodge. Moses looks over at me and shakes his head, communicating that this isn't it. He cuts the plane west—or I think it's west, though my inner compass is confused. Moses stares out the window, studying every geographical shift. And then he raps the glass with the knuckle of his left hand.

He glances over and yells, "I think I see something!"

Picking up a notebook and a pencil, he jots down the

reference points so he will be able to locate the spot again. This time when he circles, I peer out the window rather than at him. And I see it: the massive fence bracketing the grounds, along with the roof of the main building and the six smaller buildings, constructed in two lines of three. Watchtowers mark the corners of the square. But none of this captures my attention like the people, reduced to ants, milling aimlessly around inside the compound.

I look at Moses. He is looking at me as well, his eyes raw with emotion, and I understand that this celestial plane is not transcendent; earthly woes affect us, even here.

CHAPTER

15

Sal

THE ONLY THING WORSE than not knowing what's going to happen is having nothing to do to occupy your time. The guards haven't explained the purpose of this camp besides slinging around "the Harvest Project"—the name of the agricultural resurgence we're supposed to take part in, as if we have a choice. But word has it, we're going to be shipped somewhere and grow crops to feed this famine-riddled "Land of Plenty," and if we do as we're told, the family members the ARC separated us from will be allocated a portion of what we produce. This questionable promise is the reason no refugees have recently tried to escape—along with the trigger-happy guards.

Walking through the serving line, the same as we do twice daily, I glance across the glorified chicken run, set up in the old showgrounds, and watch my uncle talking to a guard. Unlike the other guards, who wear the same dingy gray sweatshirt and sweatpants combos as we do, this female guard is wearing all black. Her eyes sweep across the grounds, and while I'm watching, I see my uncle point me out. She nods and jots something on her clipboard.

"What's wrong?"

I glance behind me in line and see that Angel's standing stock-still while balancing her tin plate. The space appears oversize considering the portion of rice and beans, which I used to dole out and is now, ironically, being doled out to me in half the portion.

I muster a smile despite my sore tooth. "Nothing." I hope I'm right. There's no telling what my uncle would do if he thought I could help him climb the ranks.

That night, the same female guard is waiting for me outside the bathhouse. It is nothing more than a log room with a gravity-fed shower head that sprouts from the base of a massive galvanized tank supported by a steel frame. Angel looks between the woman and me, whose hair is in a bun, pulling her hatchet-sharp features tight. The girl pulls the hood of her sweatshirt over her dripping hair and nervously twines the strings around her fingers, chewing on the plastic ends.

"It's okay," I tell her. "Head back to camp. I'll be there in a minute."

I watch Angel walk away, completely dwarfed by the sweatshirt and pants that are purportedly one-size-fits-all. The woman says nothing. I convey my subservience by glancing down at my bare feet that are dirtier than before I showered, since the mud surrounding the bathhouse never fully dries. The new guards don't let us wear shoes, just like my uncle didn't let anybody wear shoes when people first started camping at the fairgrounds, which makes me realize the rule was—more than likely—not created by Uncle Mike, only reinforced.

Tired of waiting for orders, I look up at the woman. She is watching me with clinical detachment. Her own skin is still smooth, her lips not chapped from exposure. No one would call her beautiful, but she's arresting in a way that forces you to look twice. And one thing's clear: whatever life she's lived since the EMP has been a whole lot easier than mine.

"We are seeking information about the Mt. Hebron Mennonite Community," she says, her voice pitched low so it reaches only my ears. "Your uncle said that you lived with them at one time."

I ask, "Why do you need to know about them?"

"Someone on the Agricultural Resurgence Commission's board suggested the Mennonite community when we were discussing the most sustainable ways to grow crops."

The woman's explanation seems harmless, but I don't fully believe it. Wouldn't an agricultural committee be composed of those who already possess such knowledge?

"I only lived with the Mennonites for a few weeks," I say. "Then their property was invaded by a gang and almost burnt to the ground."

"Where did they go after that?"

I breathe, focusing on keeping my expression neutral. "I'm . . . not sure."

Her head tips in a curt nod. "And you've not been in contact since?"

I do not trust myself to speak, and so I only shake my head.

The woman's face shifts into an indiscernible expression. "Thank you—Sal, isn't it?—for your time. I'll let them know what you've told me."

As she pivots on her heel and walks off, I can't help wondering who "them" actually is.

Moses

Josh leans back against one of the concrete beams and folds his arms before conveying—in his terse, no-frills manner—the information about the ARC and the work camps in Liberty and Glacier National Park. "Right now," Josh concludes, "we're not even going to *think* about the camp in Glacier, but Liberty's camp's too close for comfort. I'm afraid if we don't do anything about it, that threat might very well end up here."

For a while, the parking garage beneath Concourse A is silent but for the sound of a bird making a nest in one of the fluorescent lights. And then our newest—and easily most opinionated—recruit, Charlie, addresses the gathering. "I really don't see why either camp's our problem." He folds his arms. "I say let the threat come and *then* fight."

Frustrated, Leora looks away, toward the morning light stretching across the threshold of the garage. I step forward and look at Josh. "What kind of militia are we," I begin, "if we're only concerned about our own protection and aren't willing to risk our lives and fight for others?"

Charlie says, "I'm willing to fight for something I believe in, but this is a lost cause."

"Families separated." Leora spreads her hands. "Children abandoned. Who says—" she looks from Nehemiah to Dean—"that your own family members aren't in there too?"

Luke comes to stand beside his daughter. "I'm with her," he says.

Seth comes to stand on her other side. "I am too."

I am standing near the exit sign, but Leora still catches my eye and nods her thanks when I step forward too. Looking at her, situated between her father and brother, I can't help thinking how strange it is that a mission to reunite families is also being used to reunite the Ebersoles.

❖

Leora's bare legs are resting next to the blank-faced computer. She is wearing a pair of my running shorts and one of the T-shirts I've had for years. I am wearing one of Josh's shirts and a pair of his pants, and Luke and Seth are wearing stuff scrounged from some of the other guys, so seeing her in my clothes shouldn't affect me. But it does. For the past two nights, we've met up here after everyone else has gone to bed, and it affects me just the same.

Leora flexes her toes, and I shift my gaze back to the arena of stars performing outside the traffic control center: a safer view. "When do you think we'll go?" she asks.

"We've got to come up with some kind of game plan first."

She breathes in her tea, steeped with chamomile she

found growing in wild yellow clumps next to the tarmac. "We can't just go in there and get them."

"No, I know," I say. "We can't."

A long pause. "What if *I* go in?"

I try to gauge if she's serious, but her profile is hidden by her hair. "If an entire militia, small as we are," I say, "can't overtake a camp, I don't think you can do it single-handedly."

"Then I could pack explosives, or poison."

I slowly release my breath.

"Stop it, Moses. I can't think of another way."

"I could go instead."

"They'd be more suspicious of a man. I'd tell them I was hungry and there to work for food."

My tone is calm, though I feel like I'm talking her down from a cliff. "And what are you planning to do if they actually let you in?"

"I don't know. Sal and I couldn't free the families by ourselves. But maybe—" setting her mug on the desk, she pulls her legs in and cradles them—"we could figure it out."

"Sorry, Leora." I shake my head. "But 'maybe' won't cut it. Not in a situation like this."

"There has to be something we can do!"

"We're not doing anything until we come up with a workable plan. It's not worth the risk otherwise."

"You sound like Charlie. That it's not 'our problem.'"

"And you sound like you've turned your back."

"On what?" She turns in the swivel chair.

"Everything you were raised to believe."

She levels her gaze. "I'd gladly lay my life down for someone I love. That, I still believe. But when it comes to protecting the lives of those I love, I am willing to fight. So in that, yes, I suppose I have."

I reach out and brush back that curtaining half of her long, dark hair. "Hey, I'm on your side here. I believe the same as you. I just don't want you to lose your faith in the process of . . . surviving."

She stands from the chair, the wheels rolling across the plastic square covering the floor. "I'm not giving up my faith," she says. "I've just decided sometimes it's easier to do things myself."

"Easier than what?" I ask. "Asking God to do them for you?"

Leora pivots away from me, arms cinched across her chest. "If he can see all of this—" she gestures to the darkness outside the tower—"why doesn't he do anything to change it?"

I stand and point to the row of computers. "We're not machines, Leora, with programs telling us what to do. God gave us a free will. It's as simple as what happened in the parking garage today. Men stepped forward. Others stayed back. We are given the ability to choose. To take wrong or right paths. To love or to hate." I stop, lowering my voice. "Each and every day."

Leora is quiet, staring out at the night. She faces me with a half smile, tears spilling from her eyes, and steps away from the chair over to where I'm standing. She presses her forehead against my chest, and I feel her sob shudder through me. My body aches with the need to wrap her in my arms, but I force myself to respect her space, and her hard-won independence, so I don't move—or breathe— until I feel her arms come up around me. She leans forward and whispers in my ear, "I choose love." She then touches her salted mouth to mine, sealing her declaration with a kiss.

Leora

High noon and the militia is once again gathered in the parking garage beneath Concourse A, cleaning their guns on a rudimentary sawhorse covered with a sheet of tin, no doubt culled from somewhere in the rubble above. The shade provides a respite from the sun, blazing across the terminal and through the windows of the traffic control center, creating a greenhouse effect that sends condensation streaming down the glass, puttying the window ledges with mold.

Moses is among these men, and sees me as I approach, but then he drops his eyes back to his gun, darkening the barrel with an oil-soaked cloth. He and I have barely talked since I kissed him in the tower three days ago. I am not sure if he's avoiding me, or merely required to work every guard shift that comes available: meaning that he spends his time either pacing back and forth in front of the gate—as if his racing thoughts will catch up to him if he sits still—or sleeping off his exhaustion. I understand he is afraid and cannot discuss the details of our relationship without evoking more fear, and yet our relationship is not what I am here to discuss.

"Moses," I say, "I need to speak with you."

Some of the militants catcall and make tactless remarks. If the apocalypse can't make them grow up, there's not a whole lot that can.

"Knock it off, guys," Moses says and sets down his gun.

He strides over to me, and we walk out of the parking garage without talking. The concourse's mosaic of broken glass catches the light, causing me to squint against the glare.

"I need to return to the community," I say. "Judith Zimmerman is watching Anna, and I told her I'd come back in a few days."

He looks to the side and breathes shallowly through his mouth—a habit whenever he's agitated. "Are you also going back to *him*?"

"Don't be like that," I say.

"Like what?"

I sigh, exasperated. "You know I never cared for Jabil like I cared for you."

He doesn't turn toward me, just asks, "Is that past or present tense?"

"What?"

Moses looks over, blue eyes gleaming. "Do you care for me now . . . or only back then?"

I force my mouth to form the syllable holding the power to change everything. "Now."

His hands shoot out. "Then stay!"

"I can't just abandon my sister!" Our voices rebound against the tomb of debris.

"The entire community loves Anna, Leora. She would never be abandoned."

I close my eyes as tears threaten to form. How can I choose between saving other people's families and saving my own? And yet, isn't this what brave men and women throughout history faced when they opened their homes—or basements or attics—to the ones being oppressed? Heroism requires sacrifice, even if that means sacrificing my family, along with the man I love. I step closer, holding the warm fold of his arms. "How bad is it going to be, Moses?"

He won't meet my eyes as he says, "Your father and brother are going to hole up at Motel 6 with Josh while I go into the camp by myself. Hopefully I'll have enough time to learn the guards' schedules, ferret out the weakest slot, and notify Josh, your dad, and Seth to attack accordingly. Once they overthrow those guards, I will direct the refugees to the gates, so—in the chaos—they won't think the ARC is being overthrown by a group as volatile as their captors."

I say, "I would go along too, if Anna didn't need me."

He clenches my fingers. "It'd *kill* me if something happened. Do you realize that?" He holds them tighter. "Do you?"

"We could die every day," I murmur. "But I at least want to know I've made a difference while I've lived."

"You *are* making a difference," he says. "You're making a

difference just by staying alive." He releases me to cup my face so that his calluses abrade my skin. "I love you," he says. "More than anything. I want to marry you. Build a life with you. I know we should wait for a better time, or until this world makes more sense. But none of this is going to change, Leora, and I can't stand the thought of going inside that camp without first knowing you as my wife."

I look up at him—this maddening, beautiful man full of perplexity and truth—and know, more than I've ever known, what path I am supposed to take, what path I've *always* been supposed to take. "I will," I say, conviction vibrating through the conduit of words. "I'll marry you. I *would* marry you, and be your wife, Moses Hughes, even if we have only this day."

CHAPTER

16

Moses

MY HANDS SHAKE as I hold Josh's scissors—blades open—next to my beard. He sits on a chair beside me, the wedding officiant and my best man, using a rag to polish the toe of his boot.

"You think she wants me to cut it?" I ask.

He doesn't even look up. "Believe me, she wants you to cut it."

I begin sawing through the coarse facial hair, trying not to worry about her somewhere in the center, trying to prepare herself for a wedding with the shortest engagement period known to man. "You think she regrets saying yes?"

Josh grunts.

I look down at him. "What's *that* supposed to mean?"

"I think she's going to regret saying yes if you show up with half your beard."

I chop some more, making a pile on the tarp Josh made me spread out before I began. "But it's all so fast," I continue. "She's had no time to think."

"Ah." He sets his boot on the floor. "Sounds like you've got cold feet."

I groan and keep hacking. "It's just that . . . I'm not sure how to *be* a husband."

Josh looks over. "Sorry, but, uh . . . you need some fatherly advice?"

I roll my eyes and splash water on my face. "I think I've got that part figured out."

"Then what part's the problem?"

"I don't know, Josh. *Every* part. Leora's different. Beautiful. Good in a way I can never be." I swallow and look at myself hard in the mirror. "I don't want to wreck her life."

Josh stands and passes me a bar of soap that feels like a brick. "You love her?" he asks.

I sigh. "So much sometimes it almost physically hurts."

He claps my back. "Don't forget that, and you'll do fine."

Leora

I call, "You can come in."

My *vadder* opens the door and steps inside, holding a butcher-wrapped package and a bouquet of Indian paint-brush, which flares bright against the gray-on-gray walls. He glances around at the break room Moses turned into my bedroom: my cot in the corner next to the defrosted mini fridge I use for a cupboard. He turns to me. "You look beautiful," he says.

I touch my cape dress. "It'll have to do. I didn't pack for a wedding."

After a moment, he passes the package to me. "You didn't

take it with you that morning after you and Seth spent the night."

Mamm's wedding dress. Again I unwrap the brown paper, and the waterfall of white silk cascades into my hands. "You brought it?"

He shrugs, lightly. "It's been in my backpack since I left the valley."

"You don't mind if I wear it today?"

"Of course not. I'd be honored." *Daed* passes the bouquet. "They're *Mamm*'s favorite."

Present tense. Once we've loved, a part of us never stops caring. "I remember." I stare down at the flowers, forcing myself not to cry. "Are you shocked I'm marrying him?"

"Shocked?" He shakes his head. "No. Not shocked. I guess, though . . ." My *vadder* hesitates, tracing the rickety card table with the flat of his hand.

"What?"

"I guess I just never expected you to marry a guy like me."

"Daed." My tone is both affection and admonishment. I cross the small room to where he's standing, his shoulders hunched like he's become accustomed to warding off blows. *"Mamm* married you," I say, "not because she was rebellious, but because she could see the worth in you that some other people were too blind to see."

He looks up, his eyes red. "I didn't deserve her."

"Maybe not," I murmur. "But that never stopped her from loving you."

He extends his arms. "I don't deserve you either."

"Maybe not," I reply, welcoming his hug. "But the same goes for me."

❖

My wedding day is not like I imagined, but it is better than anything I could have planned. Moses and I get married in the flat airport field tucked against the wall of trees. Birds wheel across the cloudless Montana sky, and I raise my gaze to watch them, the warmth bathing my face and the wind tangling my unbound hair. It is ethereal, this moment—Moses's hand holding mine, reminding me of all the other moments that he and I have spent together, each a granule of sand in the hourglass of my life, culminating in this point.

Josh, obviously coerced into officiating the ceremony, holds a worn Bible in his hands and reads the love chapter from 1 Corinthians, asking us to repeat the vows after him. Our vows are simple and yet profound—*'Til death do us part* takes on new significance when you are going to be parted soon. There are no rings exchanged, and because of my Mennonite heritage, I am not sure I would exchange them even if they could simply be purchased and slipped from a velvet bag.

However, Moses surprises me by bringing out a folding chair he must've leaned against the tree beforehand. I see the towel over his shoulder, the basin in his hands, and I know.

Blanching, I cover my mouth. "Are you serious?"

His eyes hold mine. "I've wanted to wash your feet since you limped beside me to town."

I glance beyond my *vadder* and brother toward the traffic control center, but all the other men are working on their individual projects, as if this is just another ordinary day. I look back at Moses and nod my compliance. He dusts a piece of grass off the chair, and I take my seat.

The soles of my feet are thick and hard, the nails ragged and bloodstained from where they've been daily bludgeoned by so many miles of walking without proper shoes. I want to weep with embarrassment, and yet Moses takes my feet and places them in the water, warmed by the sun, and bathes them. Gently, as if I'm a child, he bathes my wounds until the water darkens and my emotions run clear down my face, dampening the neckline of my *mudder's* dress.

"I love you," he says, squeezing the rag so that droplets fall. "I will care for you, lay my life down for you, and esteem you better than myself, until my dying day."

I lean forward on the chair and clasp my arms around his neck. I feel the rag against my back, and he holds me there—against him—and overhead the birds sing against the blue.

❖

Moses and I fly off right after the ceremony. As the Cessna rises, he lifts up my headset and plants a kiss on my ear, and then forges a trail of them down my neck. The thrill of desire runs through me, and yet I find myself nearly jittery with the details surrounding our wedding night, which we've had no chance to discuss. I gather from what he hasn't said that I will not be his first, but Moses will not only be my first, he is also the first man I ever kissed.

It is difficult to talk over the noise of the engine, and this only heightens my nerves as the plane continues slicing diagonally through low-hanging clouds. What does he expect from me? I have no nightgown—no fancy *Englisch* peignoir—my *vadder* even lent the clothing covering my back. Moses reaches over and rests his hand on my thigh. "You okay?" he asks.

My whole body trembles, but I nod, for how can I explain?

The topography of the earth resembles a roll of crinkled cardboard paper, parts slathered with green overlaid with threads of road. And then we begin descending as quickly, it seems, as we ascended. Interspersed among the pines are the roofs of the buildings we saw only a few days ago. Glacier Park. Lake McDonald. Avalanche Lake.

I look at Moses's smooth profile, the bottom portion of his face paler from where he shaved off his beard, and I embrace the peace that comes from the awareness that this man has been part of my life for a year, and yet he knows how to meet my needs better than anyone.

Leaning over, I kiss his cheek, and then I kiss his neck just like he kissed mine. He glances over, smiling with surprise. "Wife," he says, "you're going to make me wreck."

Moses

Leora and I walk away from the plane, parked in an open field, just as the sun is beginning to sink behind the Rocky Mountains. I take my wife's hand and can feel the rhythm of her pulse against mine. I adjust the backpack I'm carrying. Two blankets and a pop-up tent are tucked inside. I see, with relief, that nobody is around.

"Where would you like to camp?" I ask.

Leora's grip tightens. "Avalanche Lake."

I look over, heart thudding, both of us cognizant of what's going to take place. And so we begin: finding our way over rocks and decaying stumps as dusk blends the trees into an indeterminable smudge of forest. Miles pass before we arrive at the shore of the lake—the Big Dipper perfectly aligned above the point of the ridge. I hold my pinesap torch aloft and search the perimeter, but there are no signs of shoeprints, just as there were no signs all the way here.

I say to Leora, propping the torch in an old fire pit, "I wonder where everybody went."

She looks down at the sand. "Maybe they're at the camp too."

I touch her back, and she turns to me, waltz-stepping into my arms. I kiss the top of her hair, feel the warmth of her body through her white silk dress. "Should I set up the tent?"

Leora shakes her head.

"It's all right," I whisper. "We've got time." It's an adage from the old world—something you say to calm someone down. But in this world, it is a lie, and we both know it.

"I've never been here before, Moses," she says.

"To Glacier Park?" I look out at the water so perfectly tranquil, the surface reflects the blemishes on the moon's tired face.

"No," she says. "I've never been . . . with someone."

Lining my fingers up with the nodules of her spine, I press her closer to me still. My whole body trembles with the responsibility. *Oh, God,* I pray, kissing her hair again, *let me do right by her.* For the first time, I notice that she is trembling too.

"I would be content all night, Leora, just holding you in my arms."

She pulls back and looks up. The torchlight glimmers on her skin. "I wouldn't be," she says, and steps farther back until she's centered between the lake and me. Leora begins unfastening her cape dress. She watches my burning face as I look at her, and I have to fight the inclination to turn away, to protect her from men like me. But that was before, I remind myself: before I realized there's no shame when I've already asked for forgiveness.

Leora, my Leora, turns and walks down to the water— her hair drinking up Avalanche Lake before it closes over her hips. She enters and hugs herself against the cold, and then she calls to me. "Come on," she says. "It's great. Aren't you going to come in?"

An echo of what I once said to her. My throat tightens

with gratitude for such a gift. And so I do follow my wife down the shore, until there is nothing between us but water.

Leora

I awaken to the long shadows of trees sweeping back and forth across the top of our tent. Dewdrops cling to the edges of the material, which is as vibrantly colored as flags. I look over. The sunlight filtered through the screen gilds the stubble on Moses's jaw.

"Good morning," I say, kissing him.

Half-asleep, he links arms behind my back, pulling me closer. "Morning, Mrs. Hughes." He cracks one eye. "Or is it Ebersole-Hughes?"

I laugh, brushing back his tousled hair, but that's when the cruelty of our timeline crests over me like a wave. I lie on my side and press my body against his.

Moses leans toward me, eyes cleared of jest. "Are you crying?"

I lift my hand to my face, as if I can't tell. He takes that hand and kisses the tears from my palm. I tell him, "I want to putter around in our kitchen on Saturday mornings, making pancakes and coffee. I want to get annoyed that you keep three water glasses next to the sink. I want to find your socks balled up at the bottom of our bed when I make it in the morning." I pause. "I want to get so wrapped up in 'normal' that I forget what a gift normal really is."

"I want normal too," he says. "But just think—" he traces my collarbone with his thumb—"if we got normal, each moment wouldn't be priceless."

"That's where the heartbreak lies," I whisper. "Normal *would* be priceless, after this."

❖

I glance at my husband, who's sitting on a log, eating his lunch. His jeans are pushed up to his knees and his feet are in the water. I tentatively spoon a bite from the pouch and grimace. Moses says, "Now don't get too excited. We still haven't tried the—" he digs into his backpack to read the label of another MRE—"vegetarian taco pasta from 2009."

"Vintage entrees," I quip. "Give my compliments to the supplier."

"Pretty sure this was just Charlie's way of apologizing for harping about the mission."

"He doesn't need to apologize," I say. "I never expected him to go to Liberty. He doesn't have a personal reason for wanting the families out like I do."

Moses says, "And what *is* your reason?"

"I care about Colton and Sal."

"Do you think she would care about you if the tables were turned?"

I pause a moment, watching him. "Probably not, but that's because Sal doesn't know *how* to care. Even with

Colton . . ." I pause, trying to think before I speak. "I can tell she's scared to love him because she doesn't want to get hurt."

Moses asks, "Does she remind you of yourself, before you let yourself love?"

His revelation hits hard. "Yes," I admit. "I guess I want to save her so she can have a second chance to love and be loved the way she deserves. Isn't that what we *all* deserve?"

Reaching into his backpack, Moses pulls out a smaller package. "Here's to second chances." He tears the thick brown wrapper and extracts a saucer-sized chocolate chip cookie that he breaks in two. I choose the smaller piece. He grins. "You can tell we're newlyweds."

"Just wait 'til next year." My laughter is shaky. "I'll be eating both."

We go quiet again. For who knows if we'll have next year? After he enters the camp, we might not even have tomorrow. He rests his hand on my thigh. I look over, his features blurred.

"Leora? If something happens, I just want you to know that—"

I rest my finger against his lips. "Don't. Nothing will."

Moses

I approach the fairgrounds at dusk and force myself not to look over my shoulder at Motel 6, where Josh, Luke, and Seth are watching from the second-floor balcony to see if I make it in. A large-boned man I've never seen before steps out onto the road as I draw closer. He's holding a gun and dressed in the black uniform of the ARC. "What do you want?" he says.

I look down, wanting to appear desperate but not deranged. "Work."

The soldier doesn't say anything at first; then he about-faces and marches back to the barbed-wire gates, checking with a higher command of authority before deciding if he should let me in. He returns, the gravel crunching beneath his boots. With one hand, he pats me down like he's done this a hundred times before. I left my gun and holster with Josh at the motel, knowing the ARC would confiscate it, but I forgot they'd also take my boots. He sets them to the side and shakes out my backpack. The bracelet Leora wants me to give to Sal falls onto the gravel, along with a ratty T-shirt and jeans. I hold my breath as the soldier studies the tarnished silver. I'm not willing to sacrifice my life to make sure Sal gets her gift.

But then the soldier says, "You're clear," and gestures for me to pick up my stuff. "You can stay in the camp tonight," he adds. "You'll be assigned your number in the morning."

"Thanks," I reply. As the metal gates open and then close behind me, I pray, *Oh, God, be with Leora,* because I don't want to make her my widow so soon after I made her my bride.

CHAPTER

17

Sal

OSES IS EASY to spot the next morning since he's the only one on the grounds wearing civilian clothes. I'm not sure if I should approach him because I'm not sure who is a spy, reporting back to the guards anything they overhear in exchange for a few extra hundred calories of food. But after I check to make sure Angel's safe and asleep, I still find myself striding down the dirt path worn between the rows of tents where, at the end, Moses is sitting on a plank of wood.

I call his name, and his head snaps up, sun-blanched hair hanging over his forehead. I subconsciously reach to touch my own botched layers, which are even shorter than his. I miss the weight of the locks the ARC stripped off of me, like they've stripped just about everything.

"Hi, Sal," he says.

Moses's face is startlingly handsome without his beard, making it difficult to look him in the eye. But I can tell he's not as surprised to see me here as I am to see him. I take two steps to the right, blocking his view, along with the view of anyone who might be watching in an effort to read our lips. The refugees use gossip not only to barter for food, but also to distract themselves from fear.

"How did the ARC find you?" I ask.

He gives me a rueful look. "They didn't."

"What do you mean, they didn't? Then why are you here?"

"I turned myself in."

I repeat, "You turned yourself in."

He nods and stands up, smoothing his sleep-wrinkled shirt, and I'm suddenly filled with such fury, I want to smack his crooked smile straight. "You've *no* idea what you've done!"

"I have some idea," he says, displaying a nonchalance that causes me to understand this was a very purposeful move.

"What are you going to do?" I ask, fear in my voice, but he doesn't respond to my question. Instead, he turns and unzips his backpack. I see that he's holding something up. I step closer and see my grandmother's poison bracelet. I say, "Did she put anything inside it?"

Moses says, "I have no clue. Papina gave it to Leora and said it was for 'just in case.'"

I put the bracelet on my wrist and bend it tighter, my eyes burning with the contradiction of such a strange gift. My grandmother made an effort to smuggle in poison, but she has made no effort to talk Uncle Mike into freeing me and Angel from the camp. And what is she suggesting I do with the poison? Kill myself? The guards? Surely not the latter, since her son is among them.

Moses says, "Leora and I found out the ARC locked you

and the families inside, and we couldn't stand the thought of you being trapped in here alone."

"So you decided to trap yourself with me." I roll my eyes to cover how touched I am.

Moses cocks his head, trying to look cheerful. "Isn't that what friends are for?"

My heart pounds with hope. "We're not friends."

"Yes, we are," he responds. "Or you wouldn't be so upset that I'm in here too."

❖

After the day's first meal, I go with Moses to the camp's registration office, where a pudgy woman is sitting inside the old ticket booth. She slides open the plastic door and hands Moses pages of handwritten forms held in place with a paper clip. Moses takes them and clicks the pen. He holds it over the small, square writing. I notice his hands are shaking, in spite of his tireless good humor. He steps away from the booth and sits at one of the weathered picnic tables near the concession stands. I sit across from him.

He asks, holding up the paper, "Did you have to do this?"

"Nope," I say. "There are too many of us to go through such formalities. They must do this for the ones who straggle in."

Moses nods and clicks the pen twice. Sighing heavily, he flips through the pages, writing *N/A* in every ruler-straight line but for the last one. Leaning closer, I see that he wrote

Married. On the blank line beside *Spouse,* he carefully printed, in all caps, *LEORA EBERSOLE-HUGHES.*

It feels like someone's kicked me in the chest. "You're kidding me."

Moses shakes his head. "We got married," he says. "Yesterday."

My mouth goes dry. I make an effort to swallow before asking, "What?"

"Yesterday."

"I heard you. I just can't believe it."

He says softly, "You're not the only one."

"And you chose to come here. On your—your honeymoon."

Moses looks up, his expression brimming with happiness, so I know he's telling the truth. "That's why it was so quick," he says. "I didn't want to come here unless we were married."

"That's irony if I ever heard it."

"What?" He frowns. "Why?"

But I say nothing because nothing can change.

❖

My uncle files through the serving line the day Angel and I are randomly selected for kitchen duty. Giving me a wolfish smile, he leans across the picnic table. A silver whistle swings like a pendulum in between the tabletop and his chest. "Like your new job?" he asks.

I keep my eyes focused on the pot, scraping out one

last greasy scoop. Four prisoners move around him, preferring to eat later rather than disturb a guard. "What do you mean?"

He says, "Yvonne told me you acted like you didn't know where the community was."

"Who's Yvonne?"

"The head guard."

"So you're saying kitchen duty's some kind of punishment?"

That smile again. "I bet you'll be a little more talkative next time, won't ya?"

The night the ARC came marching in and, within hours, transformed the fairgrounds into a detention camp, I believed my uncle and I were in the same perilous position, and I was shocked to feel a twinge of warmth for my dead dad's brother. Now, though, I realize he's never been in the same position as me and was possibly one of the very people who allowed those guards to quietly dispose of the few refugees who were willing to ask questions or fight back.

"What does Yvonne want with the Mennonites anyway?" I ask.

He doesn't look at me. "They know how to work the land better than we do."

"So, what?" I ask. "You're going to turn them into slaves?"

"It doesn't matter what we're going to do. You need to tell me where they are."

I hold his gaze steady, a challenge in my own. "I don't know."

Spider veins on Uncle Mike's nose and cheeks disappear as his face grows red. "You're lying through your teeth. Where was Colton the whole time you were staying at the warehouse?"

"Everything okay, Sal?" I automatically turn at the question and see Moses staring my uncle down. My uncle lifts his chin, padded with fat, since he's consuming more than the minimal daily calories the ARC distributes to keep us tired but alive.

"Be careful," he warns. "Blood ties might not be as thick as you think."

I grip the ladle tighter. "I already know that, Uncle. Or I wouldn't still be in here."

Moses

I could swear I haven't slept, but I can see the fairgrounds swirling with the pale-gray mist that always seems to rise with the dawn. A few refugees are already sitting up in their tents, their dark shadows drawn across the white canvas like old-fashioned daguerreotypes. The fairgrounds, even at night, never grow quiet. Someone is always crying or fighting or making up the fight. So I don't sleep as much as I doze in between these nocturnal interruptions. This is why I see the ARC guards cross the campground over to me. I'm lying on my side next to the fire, which has burned down to nothing but a round bed of hot coals. The grass is my sleeping bag; my backpack, my pillow. I get up before the guards reach me and face them head-on. The guards, each

carrying a gun, stop walking. But they are mannerly enough
not to point the weapons right at me.

The guard on the left asks, "Are you Moses Hughes?"

I nod.

"You've been called in for questioning."

I smile in an effort to keep the mood light. "Don't tell
me I've already broken the rules."

The guard on the right I recognize as the one who was
all business when I came here to see Sal before the camp
was locked down. He says, "You've not broken any rules.
There's just some information in your profile we need you
to clarify."

"Before sunrise?"

The guard on the left says, "It'll be easier on you if you
come along."

"Fine," I say. "I'll go." But the compliance is subterfuge.
They know I have no choice.

❖

The guards don't touch me until we reach the cement path
leading up to the white tin building. Then they each seize
an arm and force me toward the entrance. I have made no
effort to resist them, so I'm not sure if they think I'm suddenly going to run for it (and where could I run with the
gates locked?), or if the manhandling's for the benefit of
someone watching from inside the building. Perhaps the
same someone who had them bring me in.

The tin door slides open, and we walk into the square of

darkness. The cement floor is cold against my feet. A kerosene lamp hangs from the rafters, which cross overhead, but it's not enough illumination to see the warehouse clearly. The building is almost empty, but as my eyes adjust, a long white table becomes visible toward the back.

The guards lead me toward this, their fingernails in my arms communicating nonverbal warnings. Three guards, dressed in black, materialize and take seats at the table. A pale woman—dark hair and severe features—sits between two men. The man on the left is Sal's uncle. The sight of him causes my stomach to tip with fear. The guards on either side of me step back. I turn and see they're standing with their guns bracketed over their chests.

The female guard says, "Do you know where the Mt. Hebron Community is located?"

I look at her, trying to gauge her motivations and, therefore, my approach. "No."

The woman sits up. The folding chair supporting her creaks. "Is that true?"

"Yes." I hold her gaze. Mike slides a page across the table, and the woman picks it up. One of the guards behind me turns on another kerosene lamp, and the room flares bright. I blink against the shift.

The guard resumes her interrogation. "It says here that Leora Ebersole-Hughes is your wife."

I grimace at my stupidity. I wrote Leora down as my spouse partly because seeing it printed helped me believe my luck, and partly because I knew Sal was reading my answers, and I sensed the importance of letting her know where things stood. But now I understand that I have inadvertently risked my wife by wanting to protect her, and us.

Mike says, "I know Leora's dad, Luke Ebersole. He used to work for me."

A Doppler of my heartbeat roars in my ears, causing me to wonder if it's audible to the five gathered here. "Leora left the community," I say. "Before we were married."

The woman just watches me, her dark eyes as brittle as a beetle's husk. "So you're still insisting that you have no idea where the community is."

"Yes." I clear my throat. "I have no idea."

The woman's lips press together, blending the twin slashes into her skin's colorless hue. She flicks out a hand. I turn to see what she means when the guard gives me the courtesy of showing me by driving his fist into my stomach. Breath drains from my gasping mouth. I hunker over in an effort to protect myself, but the other guard takes hold of my shoulders and forces me up. The first guard pummels me again. This dual assault is so perfectly coordinated, it's clear they've performed it many times. The frame of my vision is edged in black. I blink hard, wheezing, and the woman repeats, "Are you sure you don't know where the community is?"

I spit out, "No." I brace my abs, so the punch to my face takes me by surprise. Pain explodes across the bridge of my nose. Warmth trickles through my tented fingers, and then my teeth are coated in the nauseating, salty wash of blood.

A chair pushes back. Boots march across the floor. Someone stops in front of me, but my eyes are streaming too much to look up.

"You get one more chance." It's the woman. Her breath is redolent of the kind of dental hygiene only available in the old world.

I force my eyes up to hers. "I already told you the truth."

The woman nods. A force comes down on top of my head, as if intent to cleave my skull. Before the lights go out, the screen of my mind defaults to my last image of Leora.

CHAPTER

18

Leora

I WAKE INSIDE my family's cabin with the taste of dread thick on my tongue. Fifteen miles away, my husband is trapped inside a detention camp.

With so few men and so little firepower, the mission is unrealistic at best and hopeless at worst. But it is our only option. Moses and I were in complete agreement before he left, but only now do I realize what I've done—and what I've risked—by letting him go. I'm not sure I would make the same decision again, and this is what haunts me. It is too late to change my mind.

I sit up in bed and look toward my sister, Anna. She was overjoyed by my reappearance two days ago and hasn't left my side since. Even now, in her sleep, she remains close to me, and my heart aches at the thought that, when Moses returns, she and I will no longer share a bed. But if my husband does *not* return, I will be so gutted by his loss, I fear I will be unable to continue without him. The truth is, life is changing. I just don't know to what extent.

Finding no water in the kettle for tea, I leave the cabin. The worn cape dress and *kapp* I'm wearing feel like pieces to an outdated uniform whose symbolism I'm beginning to forget. But in my cowardice, I want to adhere to the community's standard, so my outward appearance doesn't notify them of the inward change. Though impetuous, I am glad I married Moses Hughes. However, I worry the level of grace that has been bestowed upon my family and me might be retracted if Bishop Jabil learned the truth. But I also cannot avoid him forever.

Providence lends a hand in the confrontation. On my way to the spring, I see two men working on the schoolhouse roof, but their straw hats and raggedy clothing make it impossible to tell who they are. Seconds later, Jabil crosses through the opening in the wall, still holding his hammer, which he tosses from hand to hand. He dully says, "Sorry I haven't been over."

"You've been busy," I reply. "I'm sure."

"I have." As he looks at me, intimacy adds depth to his eyes. I pivot on my heel when I really want to run. Jabil calls, "Hold on a minute, please." He returns to the schoolhouse to give instructions to Malachi, who offhandedly waves a greeting. I wave back, knowing he will regret the gesture after his brother informs him of what I've done. Jabil comes closer before he speaks so he won't unintentionally inform Malachi. "I'm sorry we had that disagreement."

I look around. Anxiety stiffens my lungs. "That was far more than a disagreement."

Jabil draws me away from the schoolhouse as Myron and Benuel pass through the wall gap into the community. "More like a crossroads, I guess," he says. "But you chose correctly." He swallows. Pulling off his leather work glove, he takes my hand. "By coming back."

I step away from him, and he lets go. "I came back for Anna."

"What?" His forehead creases, deepening the rare smile lines imprinted around his eyes and mouth. "Did they treat you well?" he asks. "At the militia?"

I expel a shaky breath. He's misinterpreting my behavior, imagining something dreadful happened to make me be this reserved. "Everything was fine."

"Then what is it?" he asks. "Are you still mad that I didn't go with you?"

"Of course I'm not mad, Jabil. I never really was. It's just . . ." I don't know how to say it. How do you tell your former fiancé you got married in the few days you've been gone? Pulling back from him, I determine that the guileless approach is best. "We got married, Jabil."

"You got—" He stumbles around the word, unable to repeat it. "To Moses?"

I nod. "It all happened so fast. He asked me, and he was about to leave to enter the work camp, and we both knew he might never make it back."

But Jabil is no longer listening. "I didn't mean it, you know," he says. "When I told you you had to make a choice. I was just angry. I—I didn't think you'd leave."

I hurt for him; I really do, and yet I am Moses's wife, and therefore it's no longer my place to bring Jabil comfort. "I'm sorry," I murmur. "You will heal. It just takes time."

He laughs, bitterly. His gaze is unfocused as he peers into the middle distance over my shoulder. "Time," he says. "We still talk like that, you know? Using time like a barometer. A way to measure out what we have left. But we have *nothing* left." He pauses. "And I'm glad."

My teeth ache from being set on edge. "I'm sorry," I repeat. "I never meant to hurt you."

He looks back at me, his dark eyes like cut jet. "You didn't."

Sal

Angel's cracking eggs against the rim of a large, stainless-steel bowl. She taps each egg twice—*tap, tap, crack; tap, tap, crack*—and sets the four-dozen fragmented shells into a mountain on the wooden countertop, where they will be glued fast within the hour. I'm hoping that, by the end of that hour, I will know if Moses left last night on his own or was forced to disappear.

"Do you have to do it like that?" I snap.

Angel says, "I don't know any other way to crack 'em."

Striding over, I take an egg, tap it once against the counter, and crack the shell with one hand, smoothly releasing the egg white and yolk. "Like *that*."

Angel bows her head. "Are you really mad at me about eggs?" Only those who are used to being a catchall for anger know how to so expertly divine its source.

Ashamed, I stay quiet for a long time. "I'm scared that a friend of mine's hurt."

Angel blinks hard, but I can see the tears rising. "That's no excuse to be mean."

I walk around the table and see her small fingers are gripping another egg. "I'm sorry," I say. "I shouldn't have gotten onto you like that."

Her head comes up. She looks at me with wariness but whispers, "Thanks."

I put my arm around her shoulders. She stiffens, but I keep it there until I can feel her body relaxing. Only then do I ease the egg from her hand. "Here," I say. "Let me teach you."

❖

I pull my uncle aside the instant he moves to the end of the serving line. He glances down at me, his plate pillowed high with scrambled eggs, and jerks his sweaty arm from my grip. "I'm a guard now," he seethes, glancing back at the others. "You'd be smart to remember that."

Ignoring this, I peer up at him with my hackles raised. "Where's Moses?"

There is not a spark of compassion or conscience in my uncle's eyes. This, more than anything, frightens me. "Solitary confinement," he says.

"Solitary confinement?" I rear back, but Uncle Mike crosses the distance. Putting his hand on my shoulder, he pinches the strip of muscle between it and my neck, an old trick to make me behave in public without bringing any backlash on him. Steering me past the serving table into the rudimentary kitchen, he nods at Angel, who's washing pots and pans in the stainless-steel, gravity-fed sink. He takes me past this, also, into the old concession stand, which now serves as our supply closet. The darkness cocoons us. No one can hear anything. Uncle Mike lets go of my shoulder. I stare up at his large, shadowed figure. My chest heaves and tears of rage spill from my eyes at being mistreated like I am still a child.

"He's in there," he hisses, "because he wouldn't tell us where the community's located."

I say, "This is *still* about the community?"

"It's only a matter of time until the ARC finds them. You might as well cooperate during the process to keep your friend from getting killed."

Behind us, we can hear the refugees talking while dishing up the food the guards didn't take. No doubt they're thrilled I am not around to ensure they are getting the correct portions. My uncle watches me. "No," I say, bluffing. "Keeping him alive's not enough reason to tell."

He pauses, no longer my protector (did he ever truly protect me?) but a predator sizing up his prey. "I'll get Moses out if you tell me what happened to Alex."

Bile, conjured by his request, scales up my throat. "What?"

He repeats, "Tell me what happened to Alex."

"How would I know anything about that?"

"He was looking for your community when he disappeared."

"That doesn't prove anything." But my voice cracks, my discomfort sliding through.

My uncle shrugs, lightly. "Have it your way, then. Moses is in pretty bad shape."

I stand as still as a statue, trying to decide which sacrifice I should offer before trying to save both. "You promise you'll keep your word if I tell?"

My uncle looks at me, and the vengeful hunger in his eyes promises nothing.

❖

Warm afternoon light bakes the pie-slats of board, striping the dark hole with light, but I still can't see Moses's face. "Leora," he says. "That you?"

"No," I reply, swallowing against the sting. "It's me. Sal."

"Can you get me out of here?" he says.

"I—I'm trying." I lift the boards off one at a time and glance over my shoulder toward the tin building, but no guards are visible from here. Lying on my stomach, I unspool the thick rope Uncle Mike gave me and feed it down through the hole. "You see it?" I ask.

Moses calls, after a moment, "Yeah!" Hope adds strength to his voice.

"Can you pull yourself up?"

"I'll pull you right in. Can you tie the rope to a tree or something?"

I look around. Nubby stumps are all that are left, since the few trees have been used for either construction or firewood. I cautiously approach the twelve-foot-high barbedwire fence, fearing it's hot, but then I almost laugh at my foolishness. Of course it's not hot. There's no electricity. I tie the rope to a metal post and pull it taut, using my body weight for leverage.

Approaching the hole again, I call down to Moses, "It's ready!"

The serpentine rope straightens and tightens as he grips the other end. I grip it as well, just in case. His climb to the top is slow, and I constantly glance over at the building. But there are still no guards milling about, making me think Moses either must not be a very important prisoner, or the ARC is so accustomed to tossing dissenters down into this hole to die that they don't think about them again.

When Moses finally does reach the top, I gasp at the gruesome sight of his face. His left eye is swollen shut, blood cakes his nostrils, and the front of his T-shirt appears starched with more blood. He winces as he pulls himself out of the hole. Getting my bearings, I walk over and grasp him by the armpits, pulling him out. "We need to book it," I say, gesturing to the gate.

He glances up at me. "I don't think I can."

"You have to." I pause. "Leora's waiting for you to come back."

He sucks in such a deep, unsteady breath, I can tell he's fighting to keep it together. Wrapping his left arm around his ribs, he begins to run at an off-kilter pace. I run beside him.

Moses

It's difficult to transition from resigning yourself to death to hitting the ground at a dead run. But that's what I do, because that's what I *have* to do. I don't let myself think about the guards, or that my life rests entirely in Sal's hands. Instead, I dream about my life with Leora, once she and I can be together on the mountain. I picture coming home at the end of a long day spent hunting in the woods, and seeing my lovely wife in front of the fire, our young children gathered around her slippered feet as she reads a story to them that they already know by heart.

This daydream abruptly ends as Mike walks out of the old FFA/4-H building and approaches the gate. It is not the main one I entered when I came into the fairgrounds, but a gate that I never noticed before Sal pointed it out. Mike doesn't look behind or around as he places a key in the padlock. Sal and I slow our pace, trying to make our movements as nonchalant as his. Mike turns and walks away. He nods at Sal but doesn't acknowledge me.

Glancing over, I say, "Sure you don't want to come along?"

She shakes her head but her eyes are tearing. "I can't leave Angel."

I pull up on the padlock's rusty silver hook, and the gate creaks wide. The phenomenon seems ridiculously effortless now that it's unlocked. I am preparing to walk through it when Sal calls to me. I turn and see she's looking down at her tan, dirty feet, but then she glances up. Shame is as visible as the hunger-whittled points of her face. "I told him," she says.

I hesitate. "Told who what?"

"I told Mike where the community's located, and that Leora killed my cousin."

I just stare at her, my cracked lips parted in shock. "Why would you do that?"

"It was payment," she says. "For your freedom."

"I would've preferred to stay locked up than to risk the lives of my wife and community."

"I know that," she says. "It was selfish of me. I was scared you were going to die."

I'm at a loss. A complete and utter loss. My head pounds, the blood a steady concussion, which exacerbates the concussion blooming darkly inside my skull. "Good-bye," I say, nodding at Sal, and walk through the gate.

"Wait!" she calls. I turn to see a chain and ring glinting through the air. I catch it in one hand. "It's yours," she says. "It's always been."

Sal

I switch off the sink and carry the glass carboy over to the cart. Slipping off my grandmother's bracelet, I open the clasp and use a teaspoon to measure out the poison, having calculated everything beforehand, like life and death was as simple as math: *100 milligrams of strychnine is a lethal dose.*

100 milligrams is 1/50 of a teaspoon. There are fifty guards in the conference room; therefore, we need one teaspoon of poison to take fifty lives.

I watch the powder float through the water, appearing as innocuous as corn starch or salt. I run over to the sink, where I painfully dry heave. There is nothing left in my stomach. I haven't been able to keep anything down since I watched Moses walk through the gate this morning and decided to commit mass murder to atone for the fact I betrayed his wife.

"You okay?" Angel passes me a rag.

Taking it, I wipe my mouth. "Yes," I say. It's safer if she knows nothing.

Angel and I stand outside the building, watching as—one by one—the guards file in through the double doors and find seats in the folding chairs crowded around the tables. Most of the guards passing by acknowledge us as they would acknowledge two flies buzzing against a window: a nuisance, but not worth the energy to hit. And then my uncle appears, finger-combing his gray hair in the reflection of the narrow window inside the door. I look away from him toward the cart. The poisoned water glimmers inside the glass jug. The guard Yvonne—her boa constrictor bun pinned into place—is sitting at the head of the table. Her features appear even sharper, illuminated by the new skylights checkerboarding the roof.

Angel whispers, "Should I help you?"

"No," I snap. My uncle stops preening. He's watching my mirrored image in the glass.

"I don't mind," Angel insists. "You can't serve them by yourself." Before I can reply, she walks into the building, squats beside the cart, and picks up two towers of glasses. I march in behind her—feeling real or imaginary eyes, like arrows, piercing my back—and watch Angel place a glass under the spigot and turn it to the right. The water streams soothingly into the cup.

Breathe, I tell myself. *She's just filling them.*

But then I see her bring the cup up to her mouth. A dimple flashes as she purses her lips, preparing to drink. I dart over—a scream straining to escape my throat—and jerk the cup out of her hand. Water sloshes, darkening the sleeve of my sweatshirt. I try not to think about the fact that strychnine can be absorbed through the skin.

Angel looks at me in shock. "What's the matter?" she asks.

I say, "Be quiet."

Color blanches from the smooth planes of her cheeks, and then she glances from me to someone behind me. I never noticed that her left eye is unhinged, floating slightly.

"What are you doing?" My uncle's voice. I turn and see him, standing now at the head of the table beside Yvonne. His proximity proves his loyalty has never been in doubt.

"Nothing," I reply.

But Yvonne pushes back the folding chair, the metal scraping against the cement floor. "Then why all the commotion?" She walks toward us, gun glinting, carriage imposing and erect.

I clench the cup with both hands. "I thought it wasn't clean."

Yvonne's smile is the worst kind of sincere. "Really."

I nod, not trusting myself to speak.

She glances at the cup. "Looks clean to me."

I don't look down at it. Instead, I force myself to clutch her eyes with my own, make her believe I am telling the truth. But she doesn't. I can see that, like I can see the pulse leaping at the base of her throat. "Why don't you drink it?" she continues. "Just to make sure it's all right."

Except for rubbernecking guards turning in their chairs, the entire room is silent. Dread drops like a weight in my gut. I glance at the tray, where I reserved one cup of pure water for my uncle: the man who appears to have raised the head guard's suspicions in order to preserve himself. I reach toward this cup, but Yvonne says sharply, "No. Drink the one in your hand."

Still, I stand motionless, desperately trying to think of a way out.

Yvonne says, "Either you drink it, or this girl's going to." She nods at Angel.

That's all the incentive I need to make my decision. I glance from the guard, to my traitorous uncle, to Angel. The young girl's eyes glow green. Her freckles are pronounced on her unnaturally pale skin. She knows something's wrong, but she doesn't know what. Well, she will soon. *You are loved,* I think, but am silent as I drink from the cup in my hands.

❖

Fifteen minutes. That's all I have until my symptoms become visible. Yvonne and my uncle watch me with slitted eyes, waiting for who knows what. Apparently satisfied that I really was just concerned about the cleanliness of a cup, Yvonne strides across the room to the table where the food's spread out, steam rising from the platters of grilled chicken thighs and potatoes. "Well—" she claps lightly—"let's eat."

The guards get up from the folding chairs and form a line behind Yvonne, who's scooping a generous helping onto her plate. Angel, seeing this, pushes the drink cart to the end of the table. Yvonne pauses in front of the cart, and then reaches for the cup that's already poured: the one without poison. She stares down at it. I watch her, helpless, my mind racing, but I'm not sure if it's racing because of the uncertainty of my circumstances, or because of the drug.

Yvonne turns to survey the snaking line of guards and holds up the cup. She says, "Guys, let's hold off on the water today, all right? I want it dumped outside, just to be safe." With this, she places the cup back on the cart and looks at me as she takes her seat. The guards soon follow, maneuvering around the table while balancing their plates. No cups are in sight.

My heart thuds and jaw tightens—carbon dioxide and

oxygen warring in my bloodstream as my body begins to shut down, switch by switch. I wish I had a clock, but there is no clock. No way to tell the time, but I know it's not enough. I walk over to Angel, who's putting the lid back on the chafing dishes now that everyone's been through. The girl's eyes grow round as my fingers press into her spine like a volley of ellipses. She leaves the covered food on the table and walks out. I can hear Yvonne's lounge-singer voice as she begins conducting the meeting.

I try to kick out the wooden stopper, but my foot won't respond to the rapid-fire signals shooting from my brain. Angel glances over and kicks out the stopper. The door swings shut.

"You okay?" she asks.

"I need you to do me a favor." I say this quietly, as if controlling my volume can preserve my capacity for speech.

"Anything," she says.

"I need you to warn the community that the guards are coming for them."

"The guards—"

"Shhh." I put a finger to my lips. We walk through the kitchen. I point to the supply closet on the right. Angel, moving in front, opens the door. The room is dark, so we feel our way inside. All the while, my arms and legs jitter as if I've ingested my body weight in caffeine.

The door opens again. Turning carefully, I see Uncle Mike. I try to speak, but it requires too much effort—as if I've had a stroke. My uncle stands and reaches into his pocket. Sulfur wafts as a match sparks in the darkness, high-lighting the bulbous composite of his face.

He winces at my appearance. "You sick or something?"

I attempt to speak, but everything's garbled. Tears flow down my cheeks.

"You're scaring me, Sal," Angel whispers, taking my hand.

My uncle asks, "Is this because of what you drank?"

I nod.

"You were trying to poison the guards?"

I have no other choice. I nod once more.

He curses and snuffs out the match. "What were you thinking?"

"Help Angel." Those two words are miraculously clear.

Letting go of my hand, the girl wraps warm arms around me. Her stomach shudders against mine as she sobs. I push her back, filled with anger, but my senses are so distorted, this might also be the drug. Her beautiful face winks out until another match is struck.

"I—I'm sorry," she says. "I didn't know what was in the cup."

I reach out and grab my uncle. "Help 'er."

He wrenches himself away. "You could've killed me too."

"Help 'er," I say again.

He says nothing.

My breathing grows ragged. I sit on a sack of rice and rake fingers through my hair, only to tangle them inside the food prep net. I pull it off. The muscles of my lower body tremble.

Angel massages my back and my arms. I hear a jingling sound.

My uncle says, "This'll let you out of the gate. Use the south entrance, not the main one."

Angel removes one hand from my back. "There's no way they'll let me out." Her voice is thick from crying.

"You stayed with the Mennonites, right?" he says. "The ones on the mountain?"

A pause. "Yes."

"Then pray," he sneers. "Maybe their faith will save you."

❖

Even if I'd never heard the sounds of someone dying, my soul would recognize them just the same: it's a hard-fought battle between flesh and spirit, temporal and eternal, the earth and the unseen realm. The only difference is that, this time, the sounds are being made by me.

"You're my best friend," Angel murmurs, tears falling on my face.

My body rigid with pain, I groan my response. Angel's weeping morphs into a wail.

"Stop it," Uncle Mike hisses. "Right now." He is standing at the door, a blade of light cutting through the gap. "I mean it," he continues when Angel doesn't. "I won't cover for you."

Angel moves closer and slides a small sack of beans beneath my head, but I feel beyond comfort; I feel just about beyond everything. Kissing my forehead, she hugs me good-bye. Mike moves back to let Angel pass. "Don't you leave her," she, not even a teenager, demands.

The shadow of his profile tips in a nod. I have to believe him. It's the only way. Minutes have passed since we entered the closet, and yet my emotions are wrung dry as Angel leaves.

Tears drip down my face, but I can't wipe them. A coarse hand grips my paralyzed one, refusing to let go. "You've been like a daughter." That graveled voice. Those soft words. The smell of sulfur as another match is struck. My uncle, saying what he feels he needs to say to his dying niece. When the pain comes, all thought and awareness yield to the heat of the laser, beaming through every organ of my body. *Oh, God*, I think. *Oh, God.*

I've been saying this all my life, but it's never been a prayer.

This time is different; the litany spills off my lips. I just want it to end. And then the warmth changes to the sun-soaked feel of relaxing next to water. The hand in mine changes, the false words replaced with a welcome. The match replaced with a brighter light.

CHAPTER

19

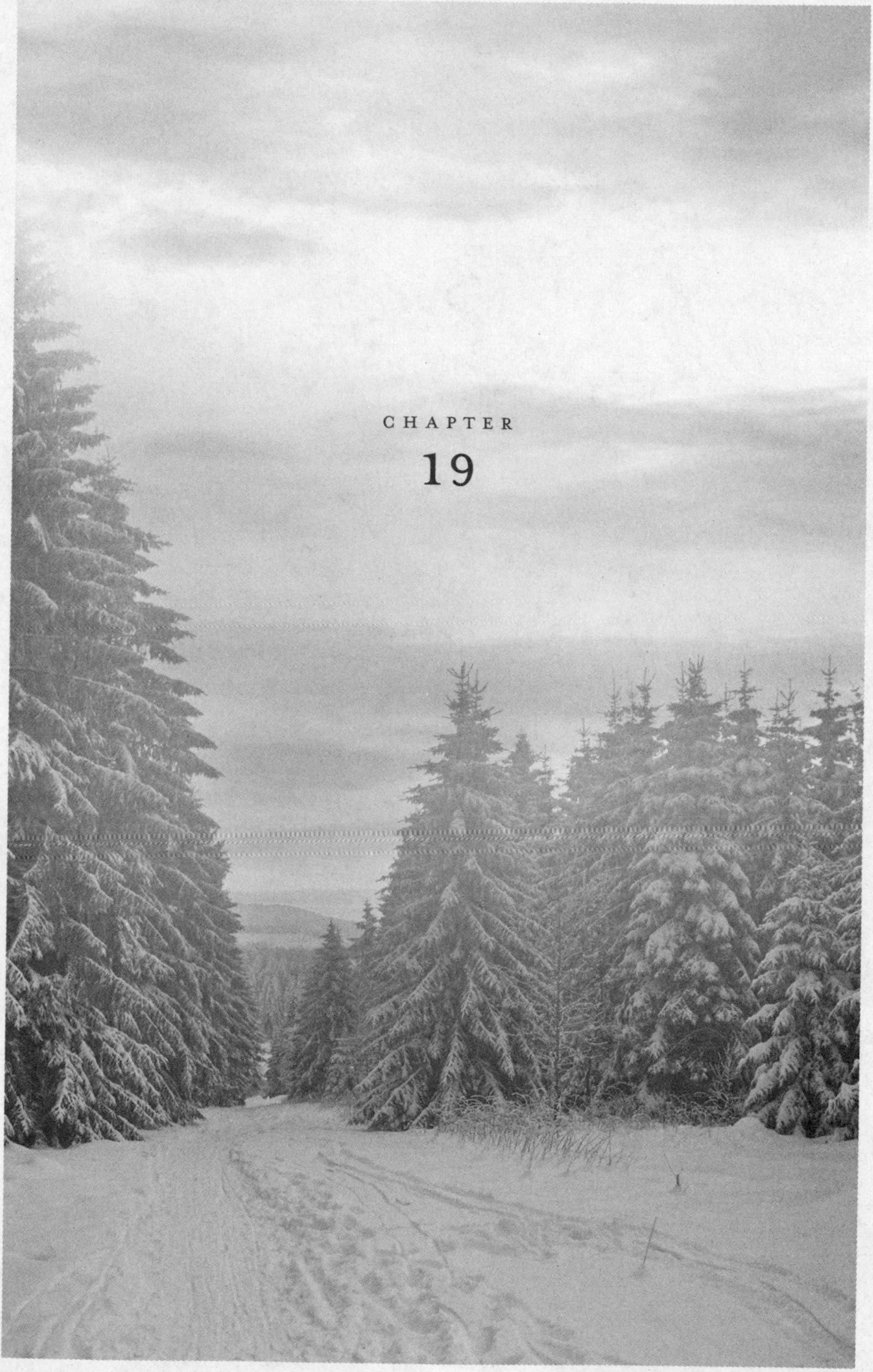

Moses

I EXIT THE MOTEL 6 LOBBY and find Josh standing next to the parched fountain with his arms crossed and aviators in place. Wind blows across the central courtyard, rocking the empty flower baskets and ruffling his comb-straight part. "Honestly didn't expect to see you again," he says.

My black eye burns with emotion and fatigue. "I didn't expect to see you either."

"You look a little worse for the wear."

"The guards beat me and put me in solitary confinement."

Josh says, "Told you not to go mouthing off again."

I smile. Even that movement hurts. "They wanted to know where the community was."

"Is the ARC suddenly preoccupied with tourism?"

"No. They said the Mennonites know how to plant crops without modern equipment."

Josh pulls a face. "Sounds fishy to me."

"I thought so too. That's why I wouldn't tell them."

"Good for you."

"Good for nothing. They got it out of Sal."

He sits on the edge of the crumbling fountain. A wishing penny winks on the second tier. "So you think they're going to go after the community?"

"Yes. But I don't think they want them for their knowledge. I think they want them because the camp's actively seeking more workers for this—this Harvest Project they're trying to hammer out, which is why they let me in so easily."

A door opens on an upper floor. I look up and see Seth Ebersole watching us from the balcony. With my one good eye, he looks like a man. I lower my voice, fearing what he might've overheard already. "A hundred people are congregated on that mountain," I murmur. "Including my wife." My voice cracks, and I sense that I'm cracking right along with it. "I'd rather die, Josh, than let them capture her."

Standing from the fountain, Josh puts a hand on my shoulder. "I know you would," he says, "and that's also how I know they won't win."

Bullet holes acne-pock the motel's stucco face. *ARC* is spray-painted on doors 201, 205, and 211. Something ripe and decaying is concealed behind one of them, which makes me wonder if the ominous acronym is how the soldiers checked off when they'd either killed or captured the refugees who were holed up inside. I call to Seth, who's still watching me from the balcony, "I know one thing: I'm not giving this place five stars on TripAdvisor."

He doesn't crack a smile. I explain, "TripAdvisor was this—"

Seth interrupts, "What happened to your face?"

"Ran into a door."

His ears turn red. He glances away, jaw throbbing, but not before I see the gleam of tears in his eyes. I finish hobbling up the steps and stand beside him. I touch his shoulder and say, "It looks worse than it is. Really. Nothing a little R & R won't mend."

Reeling toward me, he snaps, "You need to be more responsible."

"Hey, man," I casually reply, "it's not like I was out there skateboarding."

Seth looks down at the railing. He's gripping the twisted black metal, his fingerprints matching up with the burnished fingerprints of the thousands of other people who have held it before. "My sister's already lost so much," he says. "I don't want her losing you too."

"Seth," I say. "I'll do my best by her. I swear, buddy, I will. But she knows the risks. That's one of the reasons she didn't wait to marry me."

Nodding, he wipes his eyes and looks over. "It's not just Leora I'm worried about," he admits, "if something should happen. You're my brother now. I don't want to lose you either."

❖

I bite my tongue throughout the meeting at the Kalispell Airport, but my anger rises with the militia's every lame excuse: *It's not our problem; you should have listened to us in the first place; we have nothing to gain; the ARC is larger than us; if we defend the community against them, we could very well have no militia left.* I have to fight the inclination to close my hands around Charlie's neck, seeing if a little oxygen deprivation might help change his mind.

"Men, I am beseeching your humanity," Luke, my father-in-law, says with an eloquence that confounds me. "Your soul. Not your will to survive, but your ability to do the right thing."

It's so quiet, I can hear Josh flipping the stems of his sunglasses in and out. I glance over at him, standing at the entrance of the parking garage, a black silhouette against the backdrop of light. The other men turn toward our leader. He looks coolly back at them and says, "I've lost sight of what we're doing here, guys. There's no purpose to this if we're not willing to help. So take this as my resignation if something doesn't change."

Seth clears his throat before asking, "So . . . how do we do that? Help."

Josh smiles. "Good question." He turns to me. "Any ideas?"

I shrug. "Not really. But I think the most important thing is to guard the highway leading to the community. If we could ambush the ARC, it would at least give them a fighting chance."

Seth says, "But the community won't fight."

Charlie groans. "Like filling a bucket full of holes."

"I'd sure appreciate you keeping your comments to yourself."

Charlie spits and looks over at me. "Leora's already changed you, Moses."

I think of her, my beautiful wife, and the night the two

of us swam in a reflection of stars. "Yes, no doubt," I reply. "She's made me a better man."

Leora

I walk around the rudimentary schoolhouse, with its scabs of bark clinging to uneven planes of wood, and stand on the back porch. The gap in the perimeter allows me to see down the mountain. The forest, like everything else, is visibly altered, but its stark beauty is accentuated by our community's logging, allowing natural light to polish where there once stood trees.

My vision latches onto the slightest quiver of movement. Large and small game have become equally scarce. Therefore, I nearly bolt to ask if any of the community members still have bullets for their guns. And then I see that it's not an animal. A small boy, dressed in gray, with light-brown skin and closely cropped hair, is walking this direction. I step off the porch and walk toward him. It's imprudent, but I am beyond conventional wisdom. The boy sees me, standing here, for he stands stock-still, as if he can blend with the few trees ringing the clearing, and then he begins to run toward me. I hold my ground, for death is not as terrifying when so often brushed. But the boy stretches out his arms, and that gesture transforms my perception, allowing me to see that this boy is no boy, but Angel, the orphaned child we found in the cave.

I cross the distance in no time. "Angel!" I call as we meet, and I see that she is crying. Her narrow face is chapped with long-standing tears. "What is it?" I push her back by the shoulders. The child is gasping now in a desperate effort to swallow her sobs. "It's all right," I soothe. "It's all right." I press her thin frame against me. I can feel her small bones protruding through the dense sweatshirt. The child reeks of night soil and sweat.

"Sal," she chokes out, and her sobs—sensing their opening—escape.

I grasp her shoulders again. It takes all my self-restraint not to shake the syllables out of her. "What is it, Angel?" I ask, trying to keep my voice calm.

"Sal's dead."

My body flinches with the news, as if somehow apart from me. "No," I whisper. Looking down, I see silver lice tracing the black whorls of Angel's hair. "When did it happen?"

She looks up. "Yesterday," she says. "I was there, with her. She drank poison."

I close my eyes, remembering the bracelet her grandmother, Papina, insisted I take. Why didn't I understand what was inside? "Why did she do it?" I ask.

Angel shrugs her impossibly small shoulders, which carried the weight of this news the whole way up here. "I don't know. She made me come tell you that the guards are coming."

"The—the guards? From the camp? They're coming for us?"

She nods against my chest. Neither of us having strength for words, I hold her tighter.

❖

Heads turn as we pass the cabins. For months, we have seen only each other, and the novelty of another face makes it difficult not to stare. I understand, as does Angel, that the loss of weight and hair causes nobody to recognize her from before. This must be a small mercy, considering her father is the one who shot and killed Bishop Lowell. But Angel keeps glancing behind her as we approach the Snyders' cabin. I'm confused as to why until I realize she is searching the perimeter for a gate. "It's all right," I say. "You can come and go here as you please." She nods but stares at the ground, as if ashamed of her instinctual search for an exit.

The Snyders' front door is open. The children are gathered around the table, eating a stir fry that smells heavily of garlic. Mrs. Snyder is sitting in between the table and the hearth, stuffing chunks of purple cabbage in a crock, which she will salt and allow to ferment for weeks.

Jabil looks in my direction without looking directly at me. His sister Priscilla, whose extroversion is a genetic anomaly, says, "What's your name?"

Angel runs a self-conscious hand across her scalp. "Elyse." Confused, I look over. She shrugs one shoulder and whispers, "That's my real name."

I smile at her and address Mrs. Snyder. "Could Elyse stay with you while I talk to Jabil?"

Her eyes lift to mine and then drop back to her task. The intensity of her movements takes my breath. She is angry, I realize, with me. "Don't be long," she warns.

Jabil pushes back from the table and thanks his *mamm* for the meal. Even when we leave the cabin, he continues to stare straight ahead. "Did Angel escape the camp?" he asks.

"Yes. Sal told her to warn us that the ARC is coming." I proceed to quickly sketch out the details, including Sal's death. Jabil's face grows whiter with every fact.

"Who told them we are here?" he asks.

"I don't know. But we are only fifteen miles from Liberty. It's not like we can hide."

Turning, Jabil studies the breach in the wall. "We cannot abandon everything again, and yet we have no time to rebuild."

I step forward, beseeching him like a brother. "We will trust God to protect us."

"We have to." He looks at me. His voice shakes as he adds, "We have no other choice."

Moses

"Here," Charlie says. "Some makeup to help you look pretty."

I turn in time to catch what he's throwing at my cot. The outside resembles a tin of shoe polish, and when I crack the lid, the inside resembles it too. "You want me to shine my face?"

"Greasepaint," Charlie explains. "I made it myself."

I take a whiff. My nasal cavity will be clear for weeks. "Scared to ask with what."

"Hey," he says. "Your skin might feel like sandpaper in a few days, but at least it'll blend in with the trees while you're fighting." He points to a little square in the circle that looks more virulent than the rest. "See? I even put some green in there to bring out your eyes."

"I'm surprised CoverGirl hasn't contacted you for the patent."

"I've already applied for a patent."

"I'm sure my wife will appreciate your thoughtfulness."

"Well," Charlie drawls, "it was sure a hit with your mom."

Working to keep a straight face, I snap the lid on the tin and toss it into my backpack. Brian and Nehemiah are sleeping on cots a few rows over from mine. I know better than to wake a man who's sleeping off a night shift. I gesture. "Tell the guys good-bye for me, will ya?"

Charlie says, "Sure thing, old man. You want me to throw in a kiss as well as a hug?"

"A handshake will do just fine."

Shouldering my backpack, I move toward the door. Charlie shuffles up behind me. As always, his footsteps are as graceful as a gamboling bear's. He says, "Don't I get a hug?"

I turn with a smile, thinking he's jeering at me like he always does, but his bearded face is completely somber. "'Course you do," I say, recovering myself.

I reach out to clap him on the back, and Charlie scoops

me up with both furry arms. I hear my spine crack and realign as he squeezes me tight. My boots are all but swinging off the floor. Forget greasepaint and ammunition, his body odor alone could keep the entire ARC at bay.

"You take care of yourself," he says. "I wanna visit you and your wifey sometime on the mountain and see a whole bunch of little four-eyed towheads runnin' underfoot."

He sets me down, and I look up at him—this cantankerous behemoth with a heart as soft as canned bread. "I'd love that, Charlie," I say, and for once, I too am completely somber.

❖

Seth asks, "What's taking them so long?"

I shrug. "Who knows? Maybe they're waiting for dark. Or maybe they're not even coming this way, and we're all just overreacting." A fly buzzes near my ear, its sea-green casing shimmering in the afternoon sun. I bat it away, and it goes over to Josh.

"Thanks for that," he says dryly and claps the fly between his hands, smearing the remains on his pants. "This is ridiculous. We're just wasting time."

The four of us—Josh, Luke, Seth, and I—are sitting against a large rock above a place where the road narrows and a coarse escarpment rises on both sides. We chose this spot because it's a natural choke point that doesn't leave much room for the convoy to get away when, or if, it all goes down. The highway is visible for a mile or so, appearing to grow wider with every couple hundred yards before it reaches this location—giving us a heads-up if the ARC is nearing our ambush. The plan is to take positions apart from each other. The man who is farthest in will open fire when the lead vehicle reaches him. Then the rest of us will follow suit, hopefully taking out the front and back vehicles, and as many personnel as we can, before retreating over the ridge, out of their sight and range. It is textbook guerrilla warfare, but the odds of our success are not that good. But then, odds like this have become the norm since the EMP.

Sweat drips down our faces, smearing the greasepaint Charlie insisted we wear if we were going to be foolish enough to go through with the mission. It's seeming more foolish by the minute. I ask Josh, "What do you think we should do?"

Clambering away from the rock, he slides down the escarpment and looks up and down the road. He comes back and stares first at me, and then at Seth and Luke. For once, he's not wearing aviators, and his pale eyes are startling against the contrast of paint. "We need to go back to the airport and take the Cessna up for a flyover," he says. "To see if they're coming."

I ask, "Do we have enough fuel?"

He shrugs. "All your joyriding burned most of what we had in storage, but I reckon we still have enough to go up a few times."

"So you probably shouldn't be up there longer than you need to."

He grins. "Who says it's gonna be me?"

Leora

I grip Anna's soft hand and Elyse's calloused one tighter, as if the mere presence of them—positioned on either side—can tie me to the earth. In front of us, on the platform, Jabil's preparing to speak. I cannot look away from him, but it's terrible to see how unsettled he is.

"We—we are all refugees," he haltingly begins. "This is something I want you to remember, regardless of what happens today. The guards of this work camp, though they may not have been forced out of their homes or taken from their families, they are spiritual refugees, who are hungry for truth. And we, my people, we have the bread."

He takes a moment to gather himself by pinching the bridge of his nose. "I will not fight the guards, but neither will I judge anyone who does. Each man do what is right according to his convictions." He catches my eye. "And each woman do what is right according to hers."

Benuel Martin calls out, "Should we at least hide the women and children in the woods?"

Esther, stepping closer to her husband, wraps her hand around his arm and pulls him in. "If they take you," she says, "I want to go with."

One by one, the other women—Olga Beiler, Elizabeth Risser, Judith Zimmerman . . . the names are endless—nod that they feel the same way. My palms go damp as, in the field next to the garden, we can hear the symphonic squeals of the children playing kick the can.

Sensing this anxiety, Anna squeezes my hand three times: *I. Love. You.* My eyes burn as I squeeze her hand in reply: *I. Love. You. Too.*

Taking a breath, I call out, "You *do* understand that this work camp seems to be, like, a holding pen, right? That husbands and wives and children could all be separated in the end?"

Esther says in a clear voice, "Yes. But I still want to go wherever my husband goes."

Again, one by one, the other women nod. Jabil's smile is countered with sadness. "Well." He steps down from the platform and addresses his brother. "Can you lead us in a song?"

Malachi nods and walks toward the Snyders' cabin. He soon returns with Bishop Lowell's tattered *Ausbund*. He flips the book open and carefully turns the stained pages, and then he begins to lead us in song 31:4-5, written by Leonhard Schiemer during the persecution and execution of thousands of German, Swiss, Austrian, and other European Anabaptists. Schiemer himself died as a martyr—beheaded after extensive torture in the winter of 1528—but the executioners could not touch his last testament of faith, which is very applicable to us here:

We are counted like sheep for slaughter. They call us
heretics and deceivers.
O Lord, no tribulation is so great that it can draw us
away from you.

*Glory, triumph and honor are yours from now into
    eternity.*
*Your righteousness is always blessed by the people who
    gather in your name.*

Many of the community members begin to weep as we
sing, but their countenances are joyous, and I know they
are experiencing the supernatural peace that comes when all
you have left is him. The same peace, no doubt, our ances-
tors felt when they walked toward the stakes.

I close my eyes, willing myself to trust my future and
that of my family to a God whose existence I sometimes
questioned—or at least questioned if he would intervene
on our behalf. But in this moment, he is all I have left.
Meet us here. You must meet us here. Over and over, I pray
this until I am flooded with a divine awareness that God
has led me through every trial pervading my twenty years so
that I would eventually have the strength to stand when the
time came. Around me, the community stops singing. Even
the birds have grown quiet, their subdued nature foretelling
a storm. My eyes fling open. I glance through the breach
in the wall, toward the forest, and can see the approaching
group of people, all dressed in black.

Jabil lifts a hand. "Everyone stay calm," he says. "I'll go talk
to them."

Letting go of my sister and Elyse, I follow Jabil toward the gap in the wall.

"Jabil," I cry. "Please. Wait."

He turns to face me. His eyes are dark, his shoulders slumped with resignation, and I realize he does not need my warning. "I have to do this, Leora."

"I understand. I do, but—" I stop and swallow hard, quelling my emotion—"I want you to know I think you're an incredibly honorable man. You have led our community in the ways of *Gott*, just as your uncle did before you." Looking at the ground, I see grass pushing up through the soil where the perimeter used to be. "He would be proud. He *is* proud."

Jabil's smile is a default, an expression I sense he is putting in place to keep from breaking down. "I guess I'll find out soon enough."

My tears spill. I wipe them away and say through gritted teeth, "Don't say that."

"Leora . . ." He glances out through the gap. The incoming guards have passed the place where I always stood, peering down through the forest for Moses. "I wouldn't change anything."

❖

Standing next to the schoolhouse, I watch Jabil close the distance between himself and the guards. He meets them in the small glade that has been cleared by the men harvesting the forest trees over the past few months. They are still too far away for me to recognize if any of them are Liberty citizens turned rogue. A man toward the back is built like Sal's uncle, whom I met that night his gang intercepted our wagon in town. Surely he couldn't be so cruel as to lead them here when I did everything I could to help his niece. But he did. I already know.

A smaller guard, a woman, steps forward to talk to Jabil. He extends his hands toward her as he begins to speak. She gestures toward the community. He turns, looks over his shoulder, and shakes his head. Her gestures become more emphatic. Behind her, the guards stand like soulless automatons, awaiting their orders. Jabil again shakes his head. I watch her level a pistol right above his ear. Anna suddenly runs up to me, flushed and breathless. Her eyes are animal-wild when she sees the woman and the gun, and I understand that watching Charlie shoot her tomcat last summer has caused her damaged mind to correlate weapons with death. Together, we watch Jabil shake his head one last time. Anna cries out one of the few words in her lexicon, *"No!"*

I cover her eyes. The sound of *"No!"* ricochets through the forest, echoed by a greater one. The songbirds that have been so silent rise from the pines and wheel through the air. I wrap my arms around my sister, crying and fighting her surprising strength. "Shhh," I soothe. "Shhh."

She sobs against me. I hold her tight, still shielding her face. Over her shoulder, I watch Jabil sink to his knees and then fall back. Having stood firm until the end.

CHAPTER

20

Leora

THE RESOUNDING ECHOES from the shot that killed Jabil have barely made their way out of the mountains when the forest is unexpectedly ripped apart. The wings of the Cessna shear the smaller saplings as it dives into the clearing, splintering the wood like matchsticks. I drop to my stomach, pulling my sister down with me. There is a cacophony of noise—of metal being twisted and more trees being snapped—as the full force of the inbound plane smashes into the ground where the group of guards once stood, followed by an explosion that sends pieces of the aircraft all throughout the clearing. After it's over, I force myself to lift my head, squinting against the livid core of yellow flames. The bodies of the guards are sprawled around it.

Nothing moves except for the fire.

I rise from the earth as I stare up at the tops of the pines. The plane clipped them, as the pilot purposely glided through the sky, aiming for the guards. How could he? Tears run down my face, dripping off my chin, melding with the soot that has tainted me. That always will. My heart aches. Panicking, I leave Anna, my shell-shocked sister, and run through the forest. The broken branches cut my arms. Patches of ground are on fire. Acrid smoke clots my nostrils, the scent calling to mind the day Moses crash-landed in the meadow next to our house in Mt. Hebron. Ashes to ashes. Dust to dust. Did he believe the beginning was also how it was supposed to end?

"Leora?"

I glance up and see a man, turned ethereal by smoke. I stare at the image, not sure if it's real or just a figment of my longing. "Leora," he says, "it's me."

Still crying, I try to walk toward him but find that I can't. "Moses?"

He comes around the wreckage of the plane with one arm extended. "Come here," he says. "Are you okay?" His face is smeared with paint, and he holds his other arm at an odd angle. He presses me against his chest, and I sob in relief against the warm, reassuring solidity of him. "Josh," he says. "Josh was in the plane. We thought the convoy would come by the main road that goes by the airport. We never even thought of the other way." I feel him shake his head. "The guys and I found their trucks parked on the highway by the trailhead. We tried to catch up with them before they were too far ahead of us. But Josh, he must've cut the engine and . . ." His words die away as their meaning registers. Tears trickle down his dirtied face.

I take my husband's hand. "Josh barely even knew us, and he sacrificed himself."

Moses kisses my forehead and waves to two other men, my *vadder* and . . . Seth. My brother's right eyebrow is sliced open. Blood trickles down into his eyes. Somewhere in the woods, and in some way he might not want to recollect, my little brother transitioned from boy to man. "Thank you," I say. "For protecting us."

Nodding at me, he wipes the blood and says, "Thanks, Leora, for protecting us too." Our *vadder* puts an arm around his son's back. I look up at Moses and then over at the men.

"Come," I call. "Let's all go home."

EPILOGUE

Moses

MY WIFE PLACES the heirloom butternut and spaghetti squash in the basket and stands, resting the bounty against her hip. But I can't stop staring at her belly, which is just beginning to show our baby, growing inside it. Leora glances over at me, pieces of shiny, dark hair falling in her face. "Stop it," she says. "You're staring again." But then she smiles. Like she always does.

Stepping across the patch, I try to take the basket; she keeps holding on to the other end.

"Moses," she chides, "you've *got* to let me work."

"Not as long as I'm here to do it."

Something changes in her eyes. She lets go. "And I'm glad you are."

I curl my arm around her waist, and together we cross the field to the stand of trees where we buried Josh and Jabil four months ago. Leora gathers a clutch of fallen pine boughs—since the wildflowers she used to gather are long gone—and places one on each grave.

She stands, dusts off her hands, and says, "Someone could still come for us, you know."

Setting the basket down, I step up behind her and rub the sides of her arms. "I know."

"But life's almost better this way, I think. If I had to choose between going back to the way things were, before the EMP, and going through what we have, I would choose this. Every time. The uncertainty is what makes every moment beautiful."

I place my palms on Leora's belly, envisioning my daughter or son stretching and turning in her womb, unaware of this strange new world outside it. I want to protect this child with every fiber of my being, and I will, but I also know this child will be born into a generation fraught with more danger than any generation before. This would evoke more fear if I didn't know the One who loved this child before me, and whom I can trust with everything.

"One thing *is* certain, though," I say, resting my head on top of Leora's. "I love my wife and my baby, and I always will."

She reaches up to touch my face. "That makes it beautiful too."

Hand in hand, we walk back to the community, and she lets me carry the basket. There is no wall anymore, so the Technicolor beauty of everyday life greets us like it's staged: the new horse whinnying in the pasture; Colton laughing as Elyse and Anna chase him around the spring; laundry snapping in the cool, autumnal breeze; Papina drinking dandelion coffee on the porch with Judith Zimmerman as they talk soap-making and herbs. The easy rhythm of their rockers keeps time better than any electronic clock that is no longer ticking. Weaving around all of this—all of us—is the tapestry of Lost Children: Emmanuel, Elizabeth, and the others, whose parents, we've since learned, got sent to the camps. These ten orphans have found a home here, on the mountain, where my wife is determined no child will ever be turned away.

"Hey," Leora says, pointing. "Look who's here."

My heart pounds and body stiffens involuntarily, since even small surprises awaken my fight-or-flight response, but then I relax when I look toward the spring. Charlie is standing beside a haggard brown mule, whose swayback is packed down with dry goods. Squeezing Leora's hand, I let go and walk toward him. "You peddling now?" I ask with a grin.

But Charlie won't meet my eyes. "No," he says. "I'm holding up our end of the bargain."

"What bargain's that?" I ask.

"The militia brings food since the community takes care of the orphans."

I step closer until Charlie's afternoon shadow falls across mine. "You don't have to do that, Charlie. We're getting by."

Our gazes meet, and then he abruptly looks away. "Winter's coming." Charlie pulls on his nose and sniffs. "I'll keep bringing supplies as long as it doesn't take away from my men."

"Well," I say, "we're much obliged."

"There's no obligation." Charlie begins to turn, then stops and looks over at Leora. "That belly suits you," he says. "I know you two are gonna have a beautiful baby."

My wife blushes. "That's kind of you to say."

Feeling awkward, he quickly passes the donkey's reins to me.

I ask, "Don't you want to unload it?"

"Nope," he says. "This here's a package deal."

"Thank you."

"Don't thank me yet," he says. "This donkey's a real pain in the—" He stops and looks at Leora, but my wife just smiles indulgently. "I reckon," he says, "I'll be taking my leave."

Charlie is walking past the schoolhouse when Leora calls, "Charlie!" He looks back. "Tell my *vadder* and brother hello for me, and—" her voice catches—"to be safe."

"Will do," he says, nodding while mimicking tipping a hat.

Still holding the donkey's reins, I retake my wife's hand. We silently watch Charlie walk through the scarred heart of the forest, which will take years to heal, even though we long ago removed the wreckage of the plane. Maybe Charlie came today because he regrets not participating in the fight against the ARC. And though his presence probably couldn't have changed the outcome, upholding Josh's promise to provide for the orphans appears to be Charlie's penance for not stepping forward that morning in the garage when everything came down to a decision between survival and humanity. But there really is no decision: you must keep your humanity, your respect for life, if you are to truly live.

"Our beautiful normal," Leora says beside me, turning from the scarred view to take in our life. "I can't get over it."

Yes, I think, looking at her. *Neither can I.*

Also by

JOLINA PETERSHEIM

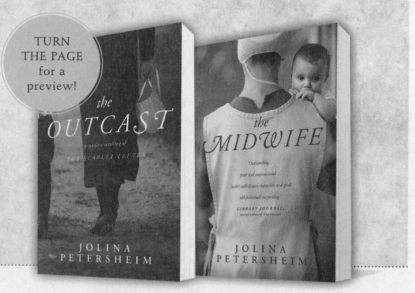

TURN
THE PAGE
for a
preview!

1

❧ Rachel ❧

My face burns with the heat of a hundred stares. No one is looking down at Amos King's handmade casket because they are all too busy looking at me. Even Tobias cannot hide his disgust when he reaches out a hand, and then realizes he has not extended it to his angelic wife, who was too weak to come, but to her fallen twin. Drawing the proffered hand back, Tobias buffs the knuckles against his jacket as if to clean them and slips his hand beneath the Bible. All the while his black eyes remain fixed on me until Eli emits a whimper that awakens the new bishop to consciousness. Clearing his throat, Tobias resumes reading from the German Bible: "'Yea, though I walk through the valley of the shadow of death . . .'"

I cannot help but listen to such a well-chosen verse, despite the person reading it. I feel I am walking through the valley of death even as this new life, my child, yawns against my ribs. Slipping a hand beneath Eli's diapered bottom, I jiggle him so that his ribbon mouth slackens into a smile. I then glance across the earthen hole and up into Judah King's staring, honey-colored eyes. His are softer than his elder brother Tobias's: there is no judgment in them, only the slightest veiling of confusion not thick enough to hide the pain of his unrequited love, a love I have been denying since childhood.

Dropping my gaze, I recall how my braided pigtails would fly out behind me as I sprinted barefoot down the grassy hill toward ten-year-old Judah. I remember how he would scream, *"Springa! Springa!"* and instead of being caught by Leah or Eugene or whoever was doing the chasing, I would run right toward the safety of base and the safety of him. Afterward, the two of us would slink away from our unfinished chores and go sit in the milking barn with our sweat-soaked backs against the coolness of the storage tanks. Judah would pass milk to me from a jelly jar and I would take a sip, read a page of the Hardy Boys or the Boxcar Children, and then pass his contraband book and jelly jar back.

Because of those afternoons, Judah taught me how to speak, write, and read English far better and far earlier than our Old Order Mennonite teachers ever could have. As our playmates were busy speaking Pennsylvania Dutch, Judah and I had our own secret language, and sheathed in its safety, he would often confide how desperately he wanted to leave this world for the larger one beyond it. A world he had explored only through the books he would purchase at Root's Market when his father wasn't looking and read until the pages were sticky with the sweat of a thousand secret turnings.

Summer was slipping into fall by the time my *mamm*, Helen, discovered our hiding spot. Judah and I had just returned from making mud pies along the banks of the Kings' cow pond when she stepped out of the fierce sun into the barn's shaded doorway and found us sitting, once again, beside the milking tanks with the fifth book in the Boxcar Children series draped over our laps. Each of us was so covered in grime that the jelly jar from which we drank our milk was marred with a lipstick kiss of mud. But we were pristine up to the elbows, because Judah feared we would damage his book's precious pages if we did not redd up before reading them.

That afternoon, all my *mamm* had to do was stand in the doorway of the barn with one hand on her hip and wag the nubby index finger of her other hand (nubby since it had gotten caught in the corn grinder when she was a child), and I leaped to my feet with my face aflame.

For hours and hours afterward, my stomach churned. I thought that when *Dawdy* got home from the New Holland horse sales he would take me out to the barn and whip me. But he didn't.

To this day, I'm not even sure *Mamm* told him she'd caught Judah and me sitting very close together as we read from our *Englischer* books. I think she kept our meeting spot a secret because she did not want to root out the basis of our newly sprouted friendship, which she hoped would one day turn into fully grown love. Since my *mamm* was as private as a woman in such a small community could be, I never knew these were her thoughts until nine years later when I wrote to tell her I was with child.

She arrived, haggard and alone, two days after receiving my letter. When she disembarked from the van that had brought her on the twelve-hour journey from Pennsylvania to Tennessee, she walked with me into Leah and Tobias's white farmhouse, up the stairs into my bedroom, and asked in hurried Pennsylvania Dutch, "Is Judah the *vadder*?"

Shocked, I just looked at her a moment, then shook my head.

She took me by the shoulders and squeezed them until they ached. "If not him, who?"

"I cannot say."

"What do you mean, you cannot say? Rachel, I am your *mudder*. You can trust me, *jah*?"

"Some things go beyond trust," I whispered.

My *mamm*'s blue eyes narrowed as they bored into mine. I wanted to look away, but I couldn't. Although I was nineteen, I felt like I was a child all over again, like she still held the power to know when I had done something wrong and who I had done it with.

At last, she released me and dabbed her tears with the index nub of her left hand. "You're going to have a long row to hoe," she whispered.

"I know."

"You'll have to do it alone. Your *dawdy* won't let you come back . . . not like this."

"I know that, too."

"Did you tell Leah?"

Again, I shook my head.

My *mamm* pressed her hand against the melon of my stomach as if checking its ripeness. "She'll find out soon enough." She sighed. "What are you? Three months, four?"

"Three months." I couldn't meet her eyes.

"Hide it for two more. 'Til Leah and the baby are stronger. In the meantime, you'll have to find a place of your own. Tobias won't let you stay here."

"But where will I go? Who will take me in?" Even in my despondent state, I hated the panic that had crept into my voice.

My *mamm* must have hated it as well. Her nostrils flared as she snapped, "You should've thought of this before, Rachel! You have sinned in haste. Now you must repent at leisure!"

This exchange between my *mamm* and me took place eight months ago, but I still haven't found a place to stay. Although the Mennonites do not practice the shunning enforced by the Amish *Ordnung*, anyone who has joined the Old Order Mennonite church as I had and then falls outside its moral guidelines without repentance is still treated with the abhorrence of a leper. Therefore, once the swelling in my belly was obvious to all, the Copper Creek Community, who'd welcomed me with such open arms when I moved down to care for my bedridden sister, began to retreat until I knew my child and I would be facing our uncertain future alone. Tobias, more easily swayed by the community than he lets on, surely would have cast me and my bastard child out onto the street if it weren't for his wife. Night after night I would overhear my sister in their bedroom next to mine, begging Tobias, like Esther beseeching the king, to forgive my sins and allow me to remain sheltered beneath their roof—at least until after my baby was born.

"Tobias, please," Leah would entreat in her soft, high-pitched voice, "if you don't want to do it for Rachel, then do it for *me*!"

Twisting in the quilts, I would burrow my head beneath the pillow and imagine my sister's face as she begged her husband: it would be as white as the cotton sheet on which I lay, her cheeks and temples hollowed at first by chronic morning sickness, then later—after Jonathan's excruciating birth—by the emergency C-section that forced her back into the prison bed from which she'd just been released.

Although I knew everything external about my twin, for in that way she and I were one and the same, lying there as Tobias and Leah argued, I could not understand the internal differences between us. She was selfless to her core—a trait I once took merciless advantage of. She would always take the drumstick of the chicken and give me the breast; she would always sleep on the outside of the bed despite feeling more secure against the wall; she would always let me wear her new dresses until a majority of the straight pins tacking them together had gone missing and they had frayed at the seams.

Then, the ultimate test: at eighteen Leah married Tobias King. Not out of love, as I would have required of a potential marriage, but out of duty. His wife had passed away five months after the birth of their daughter Sarah, and Tobias needed a *mudder* to care for the newborn along with her three siblings. Years ago, my family's home had neighbored the Kings'. I suppose when Tobias realized he needed a wife to replace the one he'd lost, he recalled my docile, sweet-spoken twin and wrote, asking if she would be willing to marry a man twelve years her senior and move away to a place that might as well have been a foreign land.

I often wonder if Leah said yes to widower Tobias King because her selfless nature would not allow her to say no. Whenever she imagined saying no and instead waiting for a union with someone she might actually love, she would probably envision those four motherless children down in Tennessee with the Kings' dark complexion and angular build, and her tender heart would swell with compassion and the determination to marry a complete stranger. I think, at least in the back of her mind, Leah also knew that an opportunity to escape our yellow house on Hilltop Road might not present itself again. I had never wanted for admirers, so I did not fear this fate, but then I had never trembled at the sight of a man other than my father, either. As far back as I can recall, Leah surely did, and I remember how I had to peel her hands from my forearms as the wedding day's festivities drew to a close, and *Mamm* and I finished preparing her for her and Tobias's final unifying ceremony.

"*Ach*, Rachel," she stammered, dark-blue eyes flooded with tears. "I—I can't."

"You goose," I replied, "*sure* you can! No one's died from their wedding night so far, and if all these children are a sign, I'd say most even like it!"

It was a joy to watch my sister's wan cheeks burn with embarrassment, and that night I suppose they burned with something entirely new. Two months later she wrote to say that she was with child—Tobias King's child—but there were some complications, and would I mind terribly much to move down until the baby's birth?

Now Tobias finishes reading from the Psalms, closes the heavy Bible, and bows his head. The community follows suit. For five whole minutes not a word is spoken, but each of us is supposed to remain in a state of silent prayer. I want to pray, but I find even the combined vocabulary of the English and Pennsylvania Dutch languages insufficient for the turbulent emotions I feel. Instead, I just close my eyes and listen to the wind brushing its fingertips through the autumnal tresses of the trees, to the trilling melody of snow geese migrating south, to the horses stomping in the churchyard, eager to be freed from their cumbersome buggies and returned to the comfort of the stall.

Although Tobias gives us no sign, the community becomes aware that the prayer time is over, and everyone lifts his or her head. The men then harness ropes around Amos's casket, slide out the boards that were bracing it over the hole, and begin to lower him into his grave.

I cannot account for the tears that form in my eyes as that pine box begins its jerky descent into darkness. I did not know Amos well enough to mourn him, but I did know that he was a good man, a righteous man, who had extended his hand of mercy to me without asking questions. Now that his son has taken over as bishop of Copper Creek, I fear that hand will be retracted, and perhaps the tears are more for myself and my child than they are for the man who has just left this life behind.

A NOTE FROM THE AUTHOR

Thank you, precious readers, for taking the time to read this series. Each story I have had the privilege to craft becomes so personal to me by its completion, and this is certainly the case with *The Alliance* and *The Divide*. Leora, Moses, and Jabil feel as real to me as family, as do their struggles and triumphs, and I have learned so much from them over these past three years. I pray that you have learned as well, and that the themes presented will provide you with some food for thought. If you would ever like to discuss, please let me know. You can contact me through my website, www.jolinapetersheim.com. I love hearing from my readers!

ABOUT THE AUTHOR

Jolina Petersheim is the bestselling author of *The Alliance*, *The Midwife*, and *The Outcast*, which *Library Journal* called "outstanding . . . fresh and inspirational" in a starred review and named one of the best books of 2013. That book also became an ECPA, CBA, and Amazon bestseller and was featured in *Huffington Post*'s Fall Picks, *USA Today*, *Publishers Weekly*, and the *Tennessean*. *CBA Retailers + Resources* called her second book, *The Midwife*, "an excellent read [that] will be hard to put down," and *Romantic Times* declared, "Petersheim is an amazing new author." Her third book, *The Alliance*, was selected as one of *Booklist*'s Top 10 Inspirational Fiction titles of 2016. Jolina's nonfiction writing has been featured in *Reader's Digest*, *Writer's Digest*, and *Today's Christian Woman*.

Jolina and her husband share the same unique Amish and Mennonite heritage that originated in Lancaster County, Pennsylvania, but they now live in the mountains of Tennessee with their daughters. Follow Jolina's blog at www.jolinapetersheim.com.

DISCUSSION QUESTIONS

1. In both *The Alliance* and *The Divide*, Leora struggles with her pacifist ideals in light of her current reality. Did you find her struggle realistic? Were you surprised at where she ended up on this issue, or was it what you anticipated?

2. When faced with the likelihood of being killed, Leora shoots—and kills—a man in self-defense. Did this surprise you? Was there another option you would have liked or expected Leora to pursue? How do you think you would respond in a similar situation?

3. During the funeral service in chapter 7, Bishop Lowell quotes John 1:5, "The light shines in the darkness, and the darkness can never extinguish it." In what ways do we see light shining in the darkness throughout this story? In what ways have you seen light shine in the darkness during your own life?

4. As Moses reflects on his grandfather's life and death, he realizes, "Yes, if I pursue Leora, she will no doubt experience more pain than if she were alone, or with Jabil. But the joy of companionship—of daily love—far exceeds the pain." When have you been tempted to withdraw from others to protect yourself from pain? In what ways have you found Moses's conclusions to be true?

5. At one point Leora laments that living in crisis has robbed her of a "normal" life and expresses her hope that one day life will return to some semblance of normalcy: "I want to get so wrapped up in 'normal' that I forget what a gift normal really is." Has there been a time in your life—illness, the death of a loved one, a job loss—when you wondered if life would ever be normal again? How do such experiences change us?

6. Leora wrestles with the age-old problem of pain: If God can see everything that's wrong in the world, why doesn't he change it? Do you agree with Moses's answer, that it's because God gave us free will—that people have the ability to choose right or wrong, love or hate? If this is something you have thought about, what conclusions have you reached?

7. Josh is a minor character who fills an important role in Moses's life. How would you describe the

friendship between these two men? Do you have a mentor in your life like Josh was to Moses, or do you fill that role for someone else? In what ways can this be an important relationship, in both directions?

8. What were your reactions to Jabil's character? Do you think Leora should have married him? Why or why not? Was Jabil's fate realistic? Appropriate? Do you see it as a positive or negative thing?

9. Are there aspects of your family's or church's teachings that you have reexamined as an adult? How significant are the differences between what you believe now and what you were taught as a child? How will you feel if your children grow up to reject some of what you are teaching them?

10. Is there a place for pacifism in today's world? Do you personally know anyone who takes this stance? What are its pros and cons?